No P

From S

Tony Richings

Captain Charlie Armstrong

Royal Northumberland Fusiliers

France 1918

Copyright

Published 2017

Dedication

This book is dedicated to my wife Sandy Hudd with acknowledgements to the many people who encouraged me during the four years it took me to write and then completely re-write a final version. In alphabetical order these people are Bernie Tarr (who also produced the image of Captain Armstrong), Michelle Garland, Cheryl Kerr-Dennis, Ken Mackenzie, Lee Ping Yiing, Emily Rudling, June Schott and Phillip Young. My sincere thanks to you all.

Outline

During World War One, 140,000 Chinese labourers were contracted to perform logistical support tasks on the Western Front, 100,000 with the British and a further 40,000 with the French. They weren't armed, they were civilians, although prior to going to France, they underwent a form of military training, short of being trained with weapons, and they were exposed to much of the horror that was to be the War to End All Wars. This is the story of Captain Charlie Armstrong and his life-changing experiences with the Chinese Labour Corps, the CLC as it became known. It is a tale of a Geordie coal miner who enlisted in the Royal Northumberland Fusiliers in 1910 to escape life 'down the pit'. He is sent to the Western Front at the outbreak of hostilities in 1914. Wounded in early 1916, he is recruited while recuperating from his injuries to serve with the CLC towards the end of that year. Travelling to Shandong province in China, he becomes involved in the recruitment and training of hundreds of Chinese 'coolies' contracted to carry out logistical roles, thus freeing up British and French nationals to shed their blood for their respected Empires. Later, Armstrong sails to France with a CLC contingent he helped to train, arriving back at the Front in early 1918.

We follow the actions of the Captain and his men as they deploy to support Allied fighting troops and the bigoted response to their efforts from so many of those they were assisting. Underlying the story of Charlie Armstrong's struggle with the effects of the injuries he sustained in the early part of the war is the struggle the men of the fledgling Chinese Republic need to face in order to gain recognition for both themselves and their new nation.

Cast of Main Characters

Captain Charlie Armstrong.   Principal British character. A Geordie coal-miner from Kibblesworth in the North East of England who enlists in the Royal Northumberland Fusiliers to escape a life down the mines.

Malcolm Wilberforce, also known as 'The Padre'.   A Presbyterian missionary who has spent many years in China spreading the gospel. A fluent speaker of Mandarin and a lay preacher.

Major Roberts.   Company Commander (CO), CLC Company number 21, who formerly served in France with the Seaforth Highlanders.

Doctor Hammond.   A country GP from a small village in Norfolk who is suffering with major psychological problems having been deployed to cope with the battlefield slaughter in France.

Count Asmiroff.   A Cossack officer, driven out of Russia and into China by the Bolsheviks, who joined the CLC as a means to return to Russia via the Western Front.

Lieutenant Hastings. Born and bred in Shanghai. A staunch supporter of the fledgling Chinese Republic and a fluent speaker of Mandarin.

Lieutenant Bertram. A seventeen-year-old, brought out to China to avoid conscription in the UK, he is shamed into joining the CLC by members of the British community in Shandong province.

CSM Peters. Company Sergeant Major and senior non-commissioned officer (NCO) in CLC Company number 21.

Sergeant Fredricks. Senior Trainer in CLC Company number 21.

Corporal Anderson. Highly regarded by Captain Armstrong.

Corporal Higgins. Held in low esteem by the Chinese trainees and regarded by Captain Armstrong as being a weak NCO.

Corporal Thompson. Good value junior NCO.

Sergeant Jenkins. After his leg is amputated due to combat in France, he is posted to China to serve as the Camp Quartermaster.

Sergeant Ford. Also wounded in France and posted to China as the Camp Caterer.

Zhao Da-hai. Interpreter with Company number 21. Unpleasant, superior attitude. Suspected of failing to interpret accurately to suit his own ends.

Ma Long. Replacement interpreter with Company number 21 in France.

Foremen (also known as *p'aitous*).

Number 1 Section.

Li Cheng-fang. Principal Chinese character in the story. A gentle giant with an aristocratic background from a family that has fallen on hard times, he joins the CLC as a means of assisting the family fortunes. A natural leader, well respected by other trainees.

Li Zhang. Li Cheng-fang's cousin. A deserter from the Chinese National Army, he has joined the CLC as a means of escaping detection.

Sun Jun. Recruited in Qingdao at the same time as Li Cheng-fang

Number 2 Section.

Zhou Xiao-bing. A member of the Honourable Qing Bang Society, also known as the Green Gang, a Shanghai based Secret Society. A gangster and homosexual psychopath.

Wang Lei. Recruited in Shandong province.

Yang Fa. Recruited in Shandong Province.

Other Chinese Characters.

Su Ting-fu. Renowned for acting the clown. Li Cheng-fang's chum.

John (aka Gong Lei). Secretary, YMCA Qingdao.

Zhou Xiao-jin. Zhou Xiao-bing's brother, also a member of the Green Gang.

Hu Chu-xing. A mechanic recruited in Qingdao, former merchant marine who speaks excellent English.

Chapter One
The nightmare

Billy Bissel is grinning at me as he passes me on his way down the tunnel. Stripped to the waist, his body is soaked in sweat; rivers channel down through the coal dust he is covered in.

Coal dust?

But we're in France digging in clay.

Aa can hear me heart pounding.

This is not right.

Aa'm in France with Billy and lots of other Geordies.

Aye, we're coal miners, but we're digging tunnels in clay under German trenches so that we can blow the bastards to Hell where they belong.

Billy comes back up the tunnel towards me with that stupid grin of his still on his face.

"Aa've set the fuses for five minutes, Sir. Bags o' time."

There's a huge gust of wind coming out of the tunnel behind Billy.

Wind that lifts me off my legs and sends me flying.

Wind that comes with lumps of clay and gravel and splintered wood and bits of Billy Bissel who shreds before my eyes.

Aa'm flying backwards when the noise hits me.

It's a huge, horrible noise that deafens.

A second or two more and then comes the heat from the flames of the blast that is far too soon.

"Five minutes", Billy said.

My face and hands are on fire but all aa register is the pain in my left eye.

As aa hit the ground me lungs tear apart and aa scream soundlessly into the silence.

Blackness.

"Ni hao, Captain Armstrong. So sorry. More recruits here, Captain, Sir. Please you come now."

The singsong, grovelling voice of interpreter Zhao Da-hai wakes me back into reality.

Aa'm not on Tyneside or in France.

Aa'm in bloody China.

It's been nearly a year since a solid piece of Billy Bissel's webbed belt demolished my left eye. Close to twelve months of pain as I worked through the never-ending Army medical process. That blast in the late spring of 1916 was followed by evacuation to a field hospital. Was I dreaming, semi-conscious or rambling or all of the above? I was with crowds of overworked stretcher-bearers and doctors and nurses and orderlies and orderly-room clerks all processing us in a world of madness. Men were lying and dying all around me. More men, mangled but mendable like me, crying, moaning or screaming all in a nightmare that has stayed with me ever since, asleep or awake, or in the private, sheltered world I slip into to find sanctuary.

And now I'm here in China where my job is part of my 'rehabilitation'. My name is Captain Charlie Armstrong, Fifth Battalion, Royal Northumberland Fusiliers. Born and bred a proud Geordie lad in Kibblesworth, near Gateshead on the banks of the River Tyne and orphaned at the age of nine, I grew up with my Grandad Norman as my guide in life and I could not have asked for one better. Senior Foreman in the Kibblesworth Colliery, he raised my three brothers and me in a hard but fair manner after our dad was killed in massive cave-in down the pit back in 1898. Our mam was into her seventh month with her fifth child when the news broke and the shock killed her and our stillborn sister. My early life in that small coalmining community was harsh but softened by the love of our Nanna who raised my brothers and I with words of encouragement to look beyond an inevitable life down the pit. When I won a place at Gateshead Grammar School, Nanna filled my head with thoughts of a life in the wider world and at the age of seventeen, after spending a year at the coalface wasting a good education, I joined the Fusiliers at Fenham Barracks in Newcastle as an officer cadet. By the time I was nineteen I wore the exalted rank of Second Lieutenant. Four years later the War to end all Wars broke out and the slaughter that followed saw eighty per cent of our Battalion officers killed in the first three months of fighting. It was in France and Belgium that the best trained army that England had ever had marched into the machine guns of the Kaiser's army.

I'm a professional soldier. Fighting in a war is my job but when the bulk of our professional army was destroyed, two of my brothers answered the call in the flood of patriotism that swept over the whole of England and her vast and glorious Empire so that they too could go to war to defend England's honour. Within weeks they became two of the Durham Light Infantry's finest who were slaughtered in the pointless madness that has engulfed the whole of the civilised world. With so many of the professional officers killed in the early part of the war, my brothers joined an army that one newspaper described as 'lions led by donkeys'. At least young Norman is safe. Our eldest brother works in the pit with our Grandad, the man he's proud to be named after. He's a pit foreman as well now and a member of the pit rescue squad for North Durham, which means that he has a reserved occupation and will be kept at home.

At the beginning of 1916, our High Command was looking for more and better ways for us to kill each other and I found myself promoted to Captain and posted into a special unit, one that was made up of men well-versed in underground mining. Our role was to tunnel under the enemy lines. The Germans used this technique first, then the French and then us. We dug tunnels under the lines of trenches to our front and then packed them with explosives. The first thing the enemy would know would be massive explosions from beneath, killing hundreds instantly or burying hundreds more alive. The Generals were slow in adopting this form of fighting, if we can call it that, but Sir John Norton-Griffiths persuaded them to go ahead.

Empire Jack, we called him. He established an engineering company prior to the war, Griffiths & Co., which specialised in the construction of tunnels through clay, using methods known as clay-kicking. You lie on an angled board and kick out with both feet, digging out the spoil with a special kind of spade. It was perfect for the kind of mining we needed to do at the Front. It's a quiet process that's used in limited working spaces, and progress is hard for the enemy to detect. Empire Jack persuaded the War Office to take up his offer of help and they appointed him liaison officer to the Engineer-in-Chief. The units he formed to do the job were made up of experienced miners, coalminers from South Wales and Yorkshire and, of course, my lads from Tyneside. We also had Londoners who had worked building the London Underground, good lads with bags of experience working in clay that was just like the clay in Ypres where I was posted.

It was terrible work. The air was always foul and there was water seeping everywhere. We were worried about poisonous gas like methane too. The lads took white mice and canaries down to test the air regularly. If they died, then the men got out sharpish. Flooding often caused drowning or whole tunnels would collapse, trapping or burying miners where they worked. At first we went down about twenty feet or so but then we started going lower down, to as low as ninety feet. The problem both for us and for the enemy coming the other way was noise. Sometimes we could hear each other and sometimes our efforts met and we fought with pistol, knife, bayonet or even picks and shovels, tin hats, bare knuckles and teeth, all the time underground in tightly spaced hellholes. It was a shocking way to go.

The men wore felt slippers and used small trolleys with rubber wheels that ran on wooden rails. There were no machines used, of course, everything done by hand. The London Water Board gave us things called acoustic listening rods that were made to detect leaking pipes, but we used them just as well to detect any noise of enemy activity nearby.

Waste was another problem. Our men, those doing the digging, were paid six times the pay of an ordinary soldier - six shillings a day against the one shilling a day for infantrymen, and they earned it. But in a unit of three hundred miners, we'd have three hundred other men whose job was to get rid of the 'spoil', clay and what have you, that was removed. It was put in sacks and taken out of the trenches and then shipped miles away, to hide the fact that we were active in any particular area.

Once the surveyors we had with us told us we were under what they knew to be the enemy lines, we stacked in explosives. At first we used gun cotton but that was unstable and got damp easily, giving us all sorts of problems. Then we started using Amatol, an explosive that is much more effective in wet conditions. Up to twenty tonnes of explosives at a time would be packed in to target areas and then yards of padding, using sacks of spoil that we put in place to drive the force of the explosion upwards.

At a given time, the charges would be detonated and the enemy lines breached. Hundreds of souls sent heavenward without warning. That was the idea and the tactic was used heaps of times. The main problem though was to coordinate things on the surface. Once a tunnel was blown and the enemy lines breached, our boys would then have to charge forward and take advantage of the situation. We mainly targeted enemy strongpoints like machine gun nests and those concrete affairs we call pillboxes, but this coordination didn't always happen and an exploding tunnel would alert the enemy to an impending attack. If the order to advance wasn't given to our lads in the trenches to link in with the timing of the explosion, then men could be charging into enemy fire that was ready and waiting for them. Either way, we became experts in the art of industrialised slaughter. There's nowt glorious about this war.

After Billy Bissel's blunder, my recovery was slow and by the start of 1917 I found myself back in England billeted in a country mansion in Kent performing tedious staff duties. I was surrounded by other officers, equally bored, mainly snotty-nosed Southerners who took great pleasure in mocking my Geordie accent and my background as a coal miner. I sported a black leather patch to cover the gaping hole that once was an eye and a scarred cheek that gave me the look of a comic book pirate. When they saw this, those who made my life a misery gleefully grabbed more ammunition for their taunts.

It was during a particularly unpleasant lunch in the officer's mess one rainy Tuesday that my saviour arrived. Major Tom Mackenzie of the Seaforth Highlanders had been staying in the mess all week on 'special' assignment. There was much speculation about his intent, however, as he too spoke with a strong northern accent, he was also regarded with disdain by my fellow subalterns.

"Captain. Armstrong. A word in private when you have finished your dessert, if you please. I'll be taking coffee on the balcony."

I stopped eating at once and followed the Major, filled with curiosity. What could he want of me?

"What do you know about the Chinese Labour Corps?" he asked and my spirits fell.

"Aa've nivva heard o' them, Sor", I replied lapsing into Geordie brogue.

"Not many people have, lad. Grab yourself a coffee and sit down. I'll tell you a story about pigtails, boxers and eating rice with every meal."

Chapter Two

Another truckload of recruits

"Afternoon, Sir. Another truckload of Chinks has just arrived."

My head is pounding and the empty socket of where my left eye used to be aches horribly. This is not a good day for Corporal Higgins to be his usual miserable self. He stands rigid to attention in his smart, civvie clothing, his face expressionless, with his bulbous, red nose as prominent as ever but his insolence hangs like a cloud between us.

Damn and blast the man! He reacts to the Chinese mockery of his snout by treating them like cattle, and I will not have it. I know how much the Chinamen laugh at him - but it is not two hours since I took him to task for abusing one of the labourers with his cane. Despite the orders that we are all to wear civilian clothing to play down the fact that this is essentially a military operation, he's a junior NCO in the British Army. He may have a little bit of power but he's not a leader of men, he's a bully and he simply cannot grasp the bigger picture and his place in it! I've seen the carnage in Europe and I'm more than aware of how desperately we need these men, foreign or not. So many of our boys are being slaughtered and we need every bit of help that we can get to end the madness that our so-called betters have sunk us into. These Chinamen need to be trained but they also need to be motivated to get the best out of them. I'll have Higgins for dumb insubordination one day soon if he continues like this. He's bloody well running out of rope!

"Right! Follow me."

I've been in China just over a month now, billeted in an old silk factory in Qingzhou, ten miles from Qingdao in the East of the country. It's a run down, ramshackle place like so many training areas the Army uses nowadays. I've been here ever since Major Mackenzie handed me a lifeline back in Blighty and had me posted out here. I like the Chinese though. They have a hard life but they seem to accept their lot in life much as our Geordie miners do back home. My role is to help train Chinese coolies, as the Scottish Major called them. Labourers who will be sent into France and Belgium to do basic logistical tasks that need to be done to free up British and Frenchmen to do the fighting. We'll use them to move ammunition and stores, to dig the trenches and repair rail links, and to clear the Front of dead animals and other unwanted hazards. We'll use them in any non-combat task that our lads can be spared from, freeing them up to die in glory for King and Country.

"Steady, bonnie lad, steady," I tell myself. My disgust at the war is something I need to hide. I've heard of men being shot for such defeatism.

"The War's a long way off so keep your head down and bite your tongue".

When he was briefing me on the background to the CLC, Major Mackenzie touched on some of the politics involved. The Chinese government declared war on Germany in the hope that any peace settlement after the war, in the event that Germany was defeated of course, would result in German concessions in China being handed back to them. The British were keen to get the help that 100,000 Chinamen could bring, but were concerned that using the men as troops, rather than as hired labourers, would harm relations with Japan and risk damaging England's prestige. It could also indicate Western weakness and damage Britain's position in the colonies. From my perspective, the Chinese seem to be getting a raw deal. I'm learning quite a bit of China's recent history from the Padre but for now I need to stop dreaming and focus. There's work to be done.

Outside in the main assembly area, I watch as the latest delivery dismounts from the back of a truck. They look like the usual rabble of humanity as do military recruits the world over, but I'm confident we can soon whip them into shape, those who pass the medicals of course. So many of these people suffer from trachoma, tuberculosis and venereal diseases but the chance to earn more money than they would ever get tending the land draws a never-ending stream of hopefuls to us. I've been told that they accept and cope with all of these health problems in their daily lives, but France is no place for people with any weakness. The medical staff will sort them out.

I follow the recruits into the Assembly hut and wait as they are lined up. Zhao Da-hai, the interpreter, is already there. He's an unpleasant man who displays a superior attitude towards the recruits. Obviously sees himself as a cut above but, like Corporal Higgins, he's an unpleasantness I have to live with. When I get there, he tells the new arrivals to strip naked. As usual they are reluctant to do so.

"Coy lot of beggars," I mutter to myself and then, in case Higgins hears me I add, "Just like any other bunch of recruits."

Higgins begins yelling as the new arrivals undress as slowly as they can, but soon they all stand as nature intended them to be, many covering their private parts like young maidens. That'll soon change as Army discipline knocks the edges off their sensibilities. In the back row, there's a huge man. He's standing expressionless, well over six feet three inches tall, one of the tallest Chinamen I've yet seen. Early twenties perhaps? I think I'll keep an eye on him.

Doc Hammond comes into the hut ten minutes later and moves down the lines of men, examining each in turn. He's another member of our staff who shows the Chinese little respect. I try to hide my disgust as he examines the recruits as if they were in a sale-yard, thinking to myself, "He's seen the carnage of the trenches and is out here recuperating just like me, and yet he inspects these men as if they're animals. The poor bastard has lost his humanity."

For many of the hopeful Chinamen, the process ends with this examination. Those with rotten teeth, weak chests, eye problems, the 'pox' and so on, are weeded out. Thirteen men, out of the forty men who arrived, are told to get dressed again and are moved to one side. Higgins roughly herds them back outside where they will get on the truck that's returning to Qingdao. For them the adventure is over before it begins. "Thirteen of them!" It makes me wonder what the people in Qingdao are thinking in sending such men to us.

Time to move on to the next phase of the process.

The interpreter is smirking as he tells the remaining bunch that they are to have their heads shaved, and there's a loud grumbling sound from some of the Chinamen. The Padre's told me about the problem some of the locals have with their hair. Apparently, there's an old Manchu tradition that male children do not have their hair cut … ever. They wear it in what they call a queue, twisted in into a lock that hangs down their back. It's what we call a pigtail. The Padre also told me that during the time of the Chinese Emperor, it was a criminal offence to cut the queue. "Lose your hair and you lose your head" was a threat lodged into the minds of small boys from the time of their birth. The Padre's been a missionary here in China for years and knows about these things. He told me that since China became a Republic a few years back, many modern Chinese have shed the queue, but most of these men in front of me are from the countryside and they are slow to change. The old barber comes in and the interpreter barks orders. No one comes forward until the giant steps up. The others watch as the big man sits and allows his head to be shaved. He sits expressionless and, when he is done, re-joins the lines stoically. Others follow his lead. Some are reluctant until the last and some even shed tears and hold their shorn locks in their hands in despair. No one refuses however and I think to myself that the need for the employment we offer must be strong.

The camp boasts a terrific modern facility. A Canadian engineer posted here with an earlier contingent constructed a series of hot showers in one of the rooms. Men can stand under a continuous flow of hot water and get themselves clean. I have taken photographs and made drawings and have sent them back to my brother, Norman. What a boon it would be to have something like this built at the pit for the miners to use as they come off their shifts below ground. While I dream of this happening, Higgins moves the recruits into the shower room with the help of Zhao Da-hai. I'm not sure who is the worst of the two. Neither treats the recruits with any semblance of respect or humanity. I'm amused though when I see the reaction of these young country lads when they see the showers. It's invariably a new experience for them and they hesitate before ducking under the flowing water. The giant is someone I follow carefully. He has the look of a leader about him and we need to identify potential junior leaders, *p'aitous* they call them, as soon as we can. Men who, with extra training, can assume the roles of corporal or even sergeant and help us muster and train the other men into an effective unit. There's more money in it for them, if that is their only incentive, but we need an effective unit and not a loose mob if this program is to be of any use.

The giant goes under the shower and grins with pleasure. Eventually they are all in there taking turns and splashing around like schoolboys. Higgins wants this cut short but I hold him back and let the fun continue. They'll be facing the negative side of training soon enough. After a while I tell Zhao Da-hai to get them dried and dressed in the clothes they came in and to march them off to the Q store. Time to get them kitted out in what will pass as their uniforms. The clothing store is an Aladdin's cave to the new recruits and again it amuses me to see the looks of wonder on their faces when they first enter.

Sergeant Jenkins is well versed in dealing with recruits. A regular soldier who lost a leg on the Somme he is happy in his new role, far from the fighting, working as Quartermaster. He has a pile of kit bags ready by the door and as the recruits enter, Zhao Da-hai tells each man to take one and to put all the clothing they are wearing into it. Once more we have a crowd of naked men nervously fooling around until both the interpreter and Higgins begin shouting and forming them up in a line. The men are directed in turn to approach Sergeant Jenkins and his three helpers behind the Q store counter. The Sergeant's expert eye is brought to bear as he assesses each man and barks out orders. Each man is issued with two pairs of underpants, one to put on and the other to go into their kit bags. Two vests follow and then they get one pair of sturdy trousers to wear and another pair for the kit bag. The men become excited and those in line begin to push forward until Higgins starts his yelling again. Thick shirts follow, again one to wear and one to pack away. Jenkins has an eye for size and each recruit is given clothing that fits his frame well until the giant steps up. He's told to stand to one side and the staff continue issuing stuff to the others. Each man is given three pairs of socks but they have no idea what they are for. One of Jenkins' staff vaults the store counter and demonstrates how the socks are to be worn. The recruits view this with interest and eventually all are wearing this new apparel. The British Army Issue boots they are given are greeted with huge smiles and happy chatter although I can see that some of the men begin exchanging with each other boots that are too small or too large. Most of the men find the boots to be comfortable and they walk and stamp their feet in appreciation. All that is except for the giant who is told to put back on the clothes he arrived in. Jenkins tells me that he will have shirts, trousers and boots made to measure for this man and have them here in a couple of days. I get Zhao Da-hai to interpret and once again take note of his superior attitude. I learn from the interpreter that the giant is called Li Cheng-fang, a name I'll make sure to remember. Finally, each man is issued with a quilted bum-length jacket, a towel, a bar of soap, a tin bowl, eating irons, mess tins and a hat. They are moved outside and once again put into a semblance of lines.

Higgins and the interpreter march them back to the Assembly hut and they're told to grab a chair and to sit down quietly. Zhao Da-hai hands each man a copy of our employment contract and he calls for silence as he reads out the conditions they will work under. Each contract is in English on one side and in Chinese characters on the other. I'm slowly learning how to speak in Chinese, Mandarin that is, but the written characters have me stumped. There must be an easier way surely?

The contract I'm now very familiar with begins with the words: 'By the terms of this contract dated this 21st day of October in the year 1917, I, the undersigned coolie, recruited by the Qingzhou Labour Bureau, declare myself to be a willing labourer under the following conditions, which conditions have been explained and made clear to me by the Qingzhou Labour Bureau, namely …'. It goes on to state that each recruit is to agree to work on railways and roads, as well as in factories, mines, dockyards, fields, forests and so on. It is specifically noted that, as employees, they are not to be employed in military operations. The interpreter continues to read the terms of the contract, now focussing on what each recruit will get in return for their labour. Pay for a labourer is to be one franc per day paid in France and ten silver dollars a month paid to their families here in China. Rates for a *p'aitou* who supervises up to 60 men are one and a half francs in France and fifteen silver dollars a month paid here in China to his family. These rates are generous when compared to the sort of wages that can be earned in a village or even, I suspect, in the town of Qingdao, and I've been told that the money is a huge incentive to many of the locals who live impoverished lives. In addition, there is to be a bonus of twenty silver dollars paid over and above basic pay rates when they leave here for the journey to Europe. I notice the Chinamen are smiling and nodding with pleasure. So far, so good.

Next, the document details the sort of compensation that will be payable in the event that any of the men die or are rendered totally disabled during service. This is set at one hundred and fifty silver dollars, payable to the family. An amount of up to seventy-five silver dollars is payable in the event of partial disablement. Previous recruits have accepted this as fair and this lot nod happily as Zhao Da-hai continues. The recruits are offered free passage to and from China under all circumstances and are guaranteed free food, clothing, housing, fuel, light and medical attendance while they are employed. In return, they agree to employment for a period of three years, with a note that the employer, that's us, can terminate the contract at any time after one year by giving six months' notice, or at any time for misconduct or inefficiency on the part of the labourer. Free passage home to Qingdao is assured. It's a contract my lads back in the pit would find acceptable, if a bit long winded.

The recruits now hear the list of deductions that will be made. There will be no daily pay in France during periods of sickness, but the men will be fed and cared for. After six weeks' sickness, the payments to families in China will cease. There will be no daily pay when abroad in cases of misconduct. In cases of offences involving loss of pay for twenty-eight days or more, deductions of monthly pay in China will cease. The interpreter continues to drone on but most of the men are listening. The giant, Li Cheng-fang, is paying particular attention. He seems to be an educated lad, more so than the others alongside him, and I mark him down again as a potential leader. The contract ends with details of the hours to be worked. There's an obligation to work ten hours daily, with times varied if circumstances warrant it, but with ten hours as a mean average. The final clause in the contract reads: 'Liability to seven days' work a week, but due consideration will be given to Chinese Festivals, as to which the Labour Control will decide'. The contract covers every aspect we can think of and the men 'sign' their copies with a thumb print quite happily.

Now for the part I truly hate. We are to allocate each man a 'regimental' number. All of us in the Army have a regimental number that is embossed onto the tags we wear on a chain around our necks. These tags identify who we are in the event that we are killed, but for some reason I don't understand the Chinese are to have a bracelet riveted onto their wrists with each man's number inscribed. To my mind this just emphasises that we regard them as animals. It will be interesting to see how they react. We line them up and move them to another room.

Our senior NCO, Company Sergeant Major Peters, is seated at a table with a sheaf of papers in front of him. It's the unit roll and the names of these new recruits have been added alongside what will be each man's 'regimental' number. As each man enters the room, Zhao Da-hai calls out his name and helps Peters locate it on the roll. Peters then calls out a number, which Sergeant Jenkins enters into a small machine. He presses buttons and then opens a flap and exposes a brass ring, duly numbered, with a hinge set in it. Corporal Anderson steps forward, takes the ring and places it around the wrist of each unfortunate Chinaman clamping it shut with a strong pair of pliers. This bracelet will be the man's identifier at all times, but the resentment to this process from the recruits is almost universal.

When the giant walks in, I pay particular attention. The interpreter calls out 'Li Cheng-fang' and points to his name on the list. Peters calls out '35754' and Jenkins produces the ring and hands it to young Corporal Anderson. As he clamps it on the Chinaman's wrist I wonder for a fleeting moment if 35754 Li Cheng-fang is going to strike the Englishman as a wave of anger passes over his face but he controls himself. Anderson looks as if he is about to fill his pants, but the giant's anger fades as quickly as it rose. His self-control is admirable and I think that I will enjoy working with this man. He works the bracelet a few times to make sure it is loose enough not to bite into his skin and then follows Zhao Da-hai's instruction to leave and send in the next man. He does as he is told, giving the interpreter a look that makes him shrink back in fear. Another mark in his favour.

When the last man is done and the recruits are lined up outside, I decide that it's getting late and I'm ready for my evening chat with the Padre. I tell Higgins and Zhao Da-hai to get the men settled in the barracks-style huts that await them, and I head off to the mess. As far as my role here is concerned, tomorrow is another day.

Chapter Three
Drinks with the Padre

The Officer's Mess is located in what used to be the residence of the old silk factory manager. It's an uninspiring, functional place but it does the job. There is no sign of any of the thirty or so other officers we have posted here at the moment, which I'm quite happy about. I'm more relaxed in the company of these people than I was in the snotty messes back in England, but I still keep my own company to a large extent. I order a whiskey and the steward knows to pour me a double. Dinner is not for a while so I go and sit on the veranda. Young Bertram comes in but he orders lemonade and avoids coming near me. He's the son on of a local English businessman who operates in nearby Qingdao and he sailed out here with me from Portsmouth. During the voyage, I learned that he was travelling to China in order to avoid the call-up in England, and I've ignored him whenever possible ever since. His cowardice did not go down well with the British community in Shandong province either and he has been shamed into enlisting in the Chinese Labour Corps as a penance. He's been given the rank of Lieutenant due to his daddy's pull but he's worse than useless and we are stuck with him. God help us if he is to deploy back to France with the next contingent of labourers. A couple of other junior officers come in and then the steward comes to tell me that dinner is now being served. I grab another whiskey and dine in my own world to the muted chatter of the others. We're having fish for a pleasant change. The fare is basic and a bit dull but, after tinned beef and whatever came along in the trenches, I'm forever grateful. As I'm finishing my meal, the Padre arrives with the Russian chap, Count Asmiroff. I indicate the veranda to the Padre who nods with a smile and I get the usual unfriendly glare from the Count. To Hell with him. I finish my meal and head back outside, away from the others, waiting patiently for the Padre to finish his meal and join me.

He's an interesting man, the Padre. Referred to universally by the military title accorded to his calling, he made sure to tell me when we first met that he's a Presbyterian missionary, not priest, as if I cared. My grandad brought us up without any contact to religion at all. He believed in the 'dignity of labour' as he called it. We had no need for belief in a loving God, especially after our mam died. The Padre's been out here in China for some years spreading his Christian beliefs and he speaks fluent Mandarin, putting my pathetic attempts to learn this alien tongue to shame. I'm told that he survived the so-called Boxer rebellion twenty years ago or so when thousands of

Chinese took up arms against the foreigners intruding into their country, slaughtering thousands of Christians, both foreign and local, in a mad fury. I'd assumed that he was dedicated to a life in China but his whole attitude changed a couple of weeks ago and he now seems keen to join the next lot who will go to France. He hasn't said why and I don't feel I should probe. He'll tell me in good time what I need to know and when, I'm sure. In the meantime, he runs English classes for the men we have identified as *p'aitous*, the men we'd call charge hands or foremen down the pit.

"So how are the latest batch looking, Charlie me boy?"

As usual the Padre is cheerful as he breaks into my thinking and my spirits lift a bit as he joins me in 'our' usual secluded spot.

"Same old, same old, Malcolm. Far too many rejects, plus Higgins and that interpreter bloke, Zhao Da-hai were in fine form. I'm not sure who I detest the most".

The Padre looks at me in a kindly way but does not admonish me. He sees the good in everyone and often takes me to task telling me to do likewise. But he does not have my memories or my nightmares and I'll judge as I see fit. Even so he's a good and needed friend.

The steward brings him his usual end of day glass of gin and I order another whiskey.

"How many is that, Charlie? The CO's in the mess talking to Captain Asmiroff and I know that he is concerned about your drinking. You can only expect a limited amount of sympathy for your injury, old chap".

The Padre's right, of course, but I order the drink anyway.

"I'll cut back tomorrow," I reply with a grin. "I need this".

We begin talking about the latest batch of recruits and we laugh when I describe their reaction to getting kitted out.

"This lot were no different. They were like children at Christmas when stuff was handed to them. They remind me so much of the lads I grew up with back home. They too have a hard life but they are always making light of things, always ready for a laugh. There's a giant among them. Good-looking bloke who I have earmarked as a potential *p'aitou*. Name's Li Cheng-fang. He looks every bit the type I need. Jenkins had to take his measurements and order a special delivery of clothing for him, including socks and boots. His feet are gigantic. Have a look at him for me, would you? We also had the usual bewilderment when they were given socks. They had no idea what they were."

The Padre chuckles.

"Jenkins will get your man fixed. He has remarkable contacts in town. Mark my words, the kit for your giant will be here in no time. As to the socks, I told the men in my English class that they are being dressed like the Emperor! I said that he wore *zu dai*, 'pockets for the feet', just like the ones we have issued. They were impressed"

"We gave them each a copy of the contract too, which they accepted without a quibble".

"That's just another difference between them and us. A Chinese employer in the village would tell any men he hired what he wanted and they would shake hands to make it binding. We have them each put their thumb-print onto a paper that is just that ... a piece of paper. Still, it keeps our top brass happy, does it not? It also keeps the trade unions in England happy; as the agreement is that after three years the Chinese will all be returned to China. No cheap labour left in Britain, eh?"

I look forward to these evening chats with the Padre. He's got a wealth of local knowledge which he loves sharing. Story after story, no matter what subject comes up in conversation, the Padre has a tale to tell that's relevant. After a while the whiskey begins to work its magic and I say goodnight to my friend and head for my bed. Hopefully I can get a good night's sleep for a change. I want to be in good form for tomorrow when the latest batch begins their training.

0600 hrs. and I wake as usual to the sound of the bugle. We are supposed to play down the fact that we in the Army for political reasons I haven't quite grasped yet. We dress in civilian clothes yet we run the camp along military lines. It is surrounded by high walls with high fences erected to close in the gaps. We have armed soldiers guarding the gates to the camp but what message this sends to the Chinamen we are 'employing' is anybody's guess. We train them with drill lessons each morning followed by strength building exercises and sports activities after lunch to get them as fit as we can. They will need to be fit to cope with conditions over in Europe. With that in mind we feed them well too and they react in a positive way. It is rare to have any discipline problems. Our main concern is to counter the danger of boredom as it is taking some time to assemble a large enough force to ship over to Europe.

The current Commanding Officer of CLC Company Number 21, Major Roberts is another Seaforth Highlander. He conducts an Orders Group, or 'O' group, each morning at 0700 hrs. The 'O' Group is the forum for key members of his staff to exchange progress reports and to receive any pertinent orders that he may wish to hand down or any directives from further up the line. They are usually short, dull affairs as the training is very basic and routine but it is a useful way to start the day. We are the third company in the current contingent. The other two have reached their quota of around five hundred men while we continue to take the newcomers until we reach our target. Three companies totalling between fifteen to sixteen hundred men is the aim before we contract a ship to take us all to France. This is a journey I am not looking forward to, but, as I take my place at the table in the CO's office, I feel relaxed. Billy Bissel gave me a miss last night and I slept a reasonable, if whiskey-induced, sleep for a nice change.

Lieutenant Bertram is already seated to the left of the CO's chair, his note pad before him, ready to take the minutes of the meeting. At least he can perform this function without any difficulty. He's a miserable lad who's just turned seventeen. I feel angry when I look at him and think of my two brothers who answered the call and died as a result, but perhaps I am being harsh. The horror that's the Western Front is not something I should wish on anyone, especially one so young, but my compassion is hard to maintain. Others arrive, taking my mind off Bertram, and we greet each other gruffly.

Lieutenant Hastings is a couple of years older than Bertram. He too is the son of a British businessman operating here in Shandong province, but, unlike the younger lad, he has grown up in China, speaks fluent Mandarin and is keen to see the new Chinese Republic benefit from its participation in the war effort. I need to have a longer chat with him than I have managed so far. Like the Padre, he can give me a better understanding of China's position and the aspirations of the Chinese. I want this so that I can relate better to the men and get the most out of them during their training and preparation to go overseas.

Captain Asmiroff takes his place, arrogantly ignoring my greeting as usual. He's a weird one. A Russian count who has been stranded in China following the Bolshevik upheaval in his homeland, he has joined us with the expressed intent of returning to Europe and fighting his way back through the German lines to engage Lenin's revolutionaries once again. In a rare moment when he opened up a bit, he related how he had been a Cossack officer in the Tsar's Imperial Army, how he had fought with the White Russians in the East of Russia and how he had been forced to retire into China due to lack of support. I'm sure that his arrogance in part is a cover for the fact that they were routed. He no doubt carries a certain amount of shame and his new role is a way to cope with that. However bizarre his reasons, he regards me as working class and a potential revolutionary. We have a mutual disregard for each other. Doc Hammond is the only other officer present. As usual he sits quietly, lost in his memories of mass casualties, an overloaded world of medical despair that saw him too shipped out from France to a quieter posting.

The senior NCOs arrive together. Sergeant Major Peters is the Company Sergeant Major, the CSM, and as such is the senior member of the Other Ranks, those not holding the King's Commission. He's an excellent professional soldier, wounded in the knee during one of the carnages on the Somme. He's been posted out here in a much-needed training role. He's accompanied by Sergeant Jenkins, the Quartermaster, Sergeant Fredricks, one of the senior training staff and Sergeant Ford, the Caterer. Each man carries wounds they suffered in combat, which took them out of the line but wounds not serious enough to warrant discharge. We desperately need all the expertise we can hang on to.

Sitting to one side as always is the interpreter Zhao Da-hai, his face set with his usual grovelling smirk. I make no secret of my distaste for the man and feel sure that the feeling is mutual. As we wait for the CO to arrive, I can hear Corporal Anderson begin drilling some of the men on the parade ground we have established in the forecourt of the former mill and my mind drifts off to the parade ground back home in Fenham Barracks. Major Roberts enters the room and we stiffen to attention. After initial pleasantries, the CO asks for reports and he is briefed on the medical rejects from the latest arrivals, figures he is not at all happy with. He's then briefed on the successful kit issues, the feeding and bedding down of the recruits who survived the medicals and in no time at all we are dismissed to our duties. Another day begins.

Chapter Four
Basic Training

The latest recruits are standing in a bunch watching Corporal Anderson put a squad of fifty-odd men through basic drill movements. He's an effective junior NCO who handles the inherent boredom of the drill quite well. The men being drilled are conscious of being watched by the newcomers and they perform the movements with a hint of pride. As Anderson finishes, I'm joined by Peters, the CSM.

"Look how the 'old hands' are being questioned by yesterday's arrivals," he says with a quiet smile. "They're like children in many ways, don't you think, Sir?"

Once again the men are all chattering and laughing. I'm pleased to see that morale is not a problem. At this rate they still have a long wait ahead until we have recruited and trained sufficient to fill a ship to take them to Europe so morale is a major concern. If they were British troops we were training, the program would include weapons handling, navigation, living in the field and so on and then we'd be shipping them off to the trenches. All these men need is to undergo very basic training and then to wait for the numbers to grow. Time is our enemy.

"That fellow Zhou Xiao-bing's up next. He's giving them PT today. He's shaping up well as a *p'aitou* but the men seem to fear him rather than respect him. There's a nasty steak to his character that I can't put my finger on, but he gets results. He has a brother in the same squad, not as bright as he is but even nastier. The men are wary when they are around".

I learned early in my military career to listen carefully to our Senior NCOs so I make a note of Peter's observations and will talk to the Padre later. As a *p'aitou*, Zhou Xiao-bing is in the Padre's English class. He can give me a different idea of the man.

"Right CSM. I'm going to do the rounds of the huts and the canteen so, if you have nothing better to do, come with me".

We march off together towards the accommodation blocks and it gives me the chance to raise another issue with this experienced man.

"CSM, I notice that your sergeants refer to the men as 'Chinks'. I'm not so sure I like that. We're not going to gain respect if we don't show it first and 'Chinks' to me is a big put-down. What do you think?"

Peters is quiet for a moment and then says, "Sir, it depends how the word is used. You've been around long enough to know when a name is being used in a friendly way or not. We call the Irish 'Paddies' and the Welsh 'Taffies' and we English do this to show that we are the best, but more often than not the Irish and the Welsh just roll with it. No offence meant so none taken. And look, Sir, we call the Germans 'Huns' and the French call them 'Boche' but that is usually to make them sound like animals so that killing them is much easier". His logic is quite startling but I listen with interest. He then makes me chortle out loud as he goes on, "Now we call the French 'Frogs' and there is no love lost there. My father and his before him used to tell me when I first joined up that, whoever we get into a war with, always remember that it's the French who are the real enemy".

I'm still chuckling as we arrive at the hut that was allocated to yesterday's recruits. The double bunk beds are neat, as are the tin chests each man has to store his kit in. These are secure at the foot of each bed, with one exception. Two trunks are stacked one on top of the other at the foot of one bed with the bedding extended to provide extra length for the man sleeping there. "Li Cheng-fang, the young giant", Peters says with a grin. "Good initiative that. Have you given any thought to him being trialled as a *p'aitou*, Sir?" The big Chinaman is obviously standing out quite early, and not just because of his size.

The other huts are all neat and tidy and we head for the canteen. Sergeant Ford is there to meet us and we carry out our inspection in a routine manner. Not much goes wrong, as the men are being well fed and, according to the Padre, at a better level than anything they could expect in their home villages. It's no wonder we have a steady stream of men wanting to join us.

Back at the parade ground, Zhou Xiao-bing has the men running laps and I'm pleased to see that the new recruits are joining in, even the giant who runs in his own clothing and bare feet despite the chill. A whistle is blown and the men congregate to rest. The fitter old hands are teasing the newcomers but it's done with much light-hearted laughter. Corporal Higgins arrives to run the second drill lesson and I note that the light heartedness evaporates. The old hands form up while the newcomers sit back to watch. Peters avoids eye contact so I make another mental note on Higgins and head back to my office. There may be something there that needs my attention, other than the bottle of whiskey I keep in a drawer to help counter the pain and the boredom. Lunch comes and goes and I wander back to the parade ground where Sergeant Fredericks has organised a football match. None of the men would make the English First Division but the laughter and enthusiasm is infectious. Full time is called and the men are dismissed to their huts. Time for my evening snifter.

Young Bertram is standing at the bar with his lemonade as I wait for the steward to pour my drink.

"How are the latest lot of Chinks settling in, Sir", he asks timidly.

It's one thing for experienced NCOs to use the term but not this young dodger. Like so many foreigners in this land he may see himself as being superior to the Chinamen but I don't share that view and certainly not in his case.

"Don't use that term when referring to my men, Lieutenant". Bertram face turns the colour of beetroot with the tone of my voice and I pick up my drink and leave him with tears welling up in his eyes. Damn the man.

I'm still angry with myself for my response to Bertram when the Padre joins me.

"I thought that I would take an early mark just like you Charlie. How are you today?"

The Padre has clearly heard of my earlier run in, the steward being anything but discreet and I confess to my treatment of the lad.

"I've been the butt of many and various nasty name-calling during my time away from my regiment and I get angry when I hear derogatory names being used about people. I do not approve of the word 'Chink' to describe my men."

It's a weak response and I make a vow to control my dislike of the boy in future, but the Padre just grins.

"You should hear how the Chinese refer to us. They call us *yangguizi*, which means 'foreign devil' or '*dabizi*', which means 'big nose'. As you can imagine. poor Corporal Higgins gets called that all the time and worse".

I'm much more interested in discussing the CSM's comments about Zhou Xiao-bing and I ask him, "What can you tell me about this chap?"

"Well, he's a good man to have on our side and he'll do well as a *p'aitou*. The other men respect him but they fear him too. He's probably a member of one of the secret societies that plague Chinese society. There are quite a number and they exert a lot of influence and can be immensely wealthy, even though many hide this from public view".

The steward arrives with the Padre's evening tipple and I settle back to listen as he continues with a concerned expression on his face.

"I know enough to be fearful of them. China has a long history of secret societies. They serve as mutual self-help organisations, a bit like the Freemasons in Europe. In some cases, they get involved with revolutionary groups, probably because it gives them early access to influence if there's any political change coming about. I've even heard that Sun Yat-sen, the man they call the 'Father of Chinese Republicanism', is involved in some way and he's China's very first President for goodness sake. Some of these gangs number in the tens of thousands and operate under a strict code of conduct, which includes a code of silence. It is almost unheard of for a foreigner to be even made aware that the Chinaman he is dealing with is connected. There are plenty of reports of members who fall foul of the code being punished in the most horrible of ways. One of my parishioners told me of an incident where a man was found with all the tendons in his legs severed with a fruit knife. He was just left to die in a busy street. This was meant to be a warning to others and a sign of their power. The police, of course, did nothing."

I listened, fascinated.

"If it's that widespread, do you think we have any of them with us in the Labour Corps?"

The preacher smiles and says, "Quite definitely, Charlie. They'll be into anything and everything. Why should the Labour Corps be different? I've heard they have a strong connection with the French in Shanghai through their consulate, as well as with the French judiciary and the French police. They're into every aspect of organized crime, from kidnapping to extortion to gambling and prostitution, but opium is now the backbone of their organisation. The money from this foul drug is enormous and the corruption it generates is a curse on China, from top to bottom. As I said, it's even involved revolutionaries like Sun Yat-sen. You can't get much higher than that."

The steward returns to tell us that the evening meal is being served so we break off, but I need to know more. In the meantime, I make a note to watch Zhao Xiaobing in a different light.

The latest batch of recruits have been here for three days now and, this being a Sunday, they are roused from their beds by, what to them, is a terrifying and hideous noise. Several of us have ventured out in the pre-dawn to witness the effect that Major Roberts' bagpipes will have on the unsuspecting newcomers. Each Sunday the Scot dispenses with the bugle and replaces the rallying sound with the skirl of his homeland. He adds to the theatre by dressing in kilt and other accoutrements', making for his audience a fearful sight. The old hands pile out laughing to enjoy the spectacle, not just of the mad Major but also of the reaction of their new chums who gawk in wonder and then dance with their fellow countrymen in sheer delight.

After the CO's morning 'O' group I head down to watch as the new lads are given their first drill lesson. Corporal Anderson has his patience stretched as he struggles to get them to learn their left from their right. By the end of his hour-long challenge, he has them turning more or less in unison as the humour of turning to face another man instead of his back fades with constant repetition. One of the other *p'aitous*, a solid looking chap named Sun Jun, takes over for today's physical exercise period and the men relax again and begin enjoying their day. Physical effort seems to stimulate them as they cheerfully compete to outrun, outjump and outdo each other. I decide to leave them to it for a while but when I return any sense of enjoyment has disappeared. Corporal Higgins is drilling the new lot and his technique is not going down well. When one of the new lads makes a mistake, he berates him furiously, despite the fact that they have no idea what he is saying.

Half way through his lesson, matters turn nasty. He gives the command 'Left Turn' and most of the men are now familiar with its meaning and comply. A stocky man, who I have already marked down as being the group clown, turns right by mistake and he doubles up with laughter. Higgins is furious and he storms over to the miscreant. As he yells furiously, the Chinaman becomes helpless with laughter and the Englishman's composure breaks. Not for the first time, he strikes out with his cane, hitting the unfortunate coolie on the head and dropping him to the ground. The man falls in surprise more than as a result of the force of the blow but, as he starts to rise, all humour disappears from his face, now replaced with fierce rage. An equally furious Higgins raises his cane again only to find his arm gripped by the Li Cheng-fang, now kitted out in uniform and looking ominous. Everyone seems to freeze where they stand. Li Cheng-fang just holds the corporal's arm in a rigid grip so that he cannot move. The abused Chinaman staggers to his feet and, at a word from his compatriot, steps back. The incident has been seen by others and I watch as two of our guards unsling their rifles and begin running towards the group.

"Stand fast!"

The words of command are yelled out by Sergeant Major Peters who has also witnessed the incident and the guards immediately come to the Halt. Peters marches forward, takes Higgins' cane from his outstretched hand and nods towards Li Cheng-fang. The giant releases Higgins and he too steps back. Zhao Da-hai comes running up and Peters tells him to send the new lads back to their hut and to wait there until they are called to lunch. They shuffle off, talking animatedly, while Li Cheng-fang and the Chinaman who was struck walk quietly in their wake.

"My office, now!" barks Peters and Corporal Higgins storms away red in the face, still burning with anger.

"With your permission, Sir, I'll sort this one".

I nod to the CSM in agreement, return his salute and watch him march away after Higgins.

"What I liked about Li Cheng-fang's involvement was his composure and his presence".

Relaxing over our evening grog, I relate what I witnessed this morning. The Padre had been told of the incident, of course, and is advocating leniency with Higgins as usual. Peters has put the man on an administrative warning so that any further incidents will lose him his stripes. Hopefully this will teach him a lesson but in the meantime he has been tasked to work with the labourers who have been here the longest and ordered to avoid the newcomers as much as possible. As we don't have that big a staff, it will be hard for him not to cross paths with the big Chinaman and his friend, the Joker, again but time will tell.

"In case you are interested, the Joker's name is Su Ting-fu and it seems that he and Li Cheng-fang have chummed up".

The Padre raises an interesting point. Armies the world over operate on a mutual support basis. Working as a team is essential, not just for the effective use of firepower but also for sheer survival, and, in the British Army, the process of chumming up has been encouraged for centuries. When two men 'chum up', they operate in tandem. When one makes or collects a brew, he does so for himself and his chum. When one man in the tranches cleans his rifle, the other keeps his weapon handy in case of attack. When one man snatches a nap, the other watches and so on. This idea has been passed on to our recruits who take to the process with ease. Li Cheng-fang was looking after his 'chum' when Higgins struck, but his authority confirms in my mind that he has leadership potential and I decide to formally recommend him as a *p'aitou* to the CO.

"Incidentally Charlie, you've become something of a puzzle to the latest arrivals".

The Padre is grinning at me as he says this.

"I went to talk to them and one asked me about the scar and the eye patch you wear. More of interest though was the question another man raised. He saw you blow your nose into your hankie and then put it in your pocket. They are desperate to learn what you do with your snot!"

Chapter Five
Time out in Qingdao

"Thirteen rejects out of forty is not good enough! Rejects are far too high! Waste of resources transporting them all here, taking the rubbish back and then training such small numbers we're left with. We need to tackle the problem in Qingdao. We need bigger numbers and fitter specimens. Doc, I want you to see these YMCA people and sort it out. Take the Padre to interpret for you. Go tomorrow. Charlie, it'll do you good to see that end of the process too, so the three of you go. Stay a couple of nights but get it sorted!"

The CO began this morning's 'O' group with a tirade. I said my 'yes, Sir' automatically but felt a surge of pleasure. A break in routine like this is just what I need.

Doc Hammond drives the truck we're allotted for our jaunt into the 'big city' of Qingdao. The Padre and I cram into the driver's cabin with him to avoid the chill of riding in the tray at the back but before long we need to open the window a bit to let out the steam our rugged-up bodies are creating. As we bounce our way through the ruts that pass for a road in the Qingzhou valley, the Padre begins a history lesson for us.

"You know, we British have got a lot to answer for. To my mind, it all started with our forcing opium onto the Chinese in the middle of the last century. We wanted Chinese tea and Chinese porcelain but we couldn't pay for it. The Chinese demanded silver, which we didn't have, so we introduced them to opium, which we grew in abundance in India and Afghanistan and then sold it to them for silver. The local Chinese took to the drug with relish and soon the country was riddled with addicts. When the Emperor's officials tried to stop the trade, we declared war, not once but twice, and we forced the scourge on to them. After the first war in 1840 we imposed ourselves on the hapless Chinese by demanding and obtaining what we called concessions. We British formed our own dominions along the Chinese coast notably on the Island of Hong Kong where two of Scotland's finest, Messrs Jardine and Matheson, formed a partnership that has dominated the economy of the region ever since, making them both very, very rich men".

The Doc snorts cynically.

"It's called building an Empire, Padre. It's what we are good at".

Undaunted, the Padre continues.

"Yes, it is Doc, and twenty years later the French joined us in the second conflagration during which we actually invaded the capital Peking and sacked the

Emperor's summer palace. We acted like vandals. Other European nations joined in the fun, carving out bits of China for their own benefit as more concessions were extracted from the ever-weakening Qing dynasty. Then at the end of the last Century, the Japanese got in on the act, launching two wars in rapid succession and gaining huge swathes of inland China as a result. Their concessions are based around the railways they have built and the minerals they are extracting. When the War began in Europe, Japan attacked the Germans who had the Shandong province, here where we are now, and they have laid claim to this region as their own. The Chinese have declared war on Germany but they draw the line in terms of sending an army to fight, hence the sort of compromise we have in the Chinese Labour Corps. Well, that's how I see it in simple terms. I'm sure that China will expect to get Shandong back when the War is over. It will be interesting to see how that works out."

As the Padre takes a breath, we pass two interesting and contrasting groups. First, there's a Japanese military patrol, professionally kitted out and marching with first class military precision, while, coming in the opposite direction, is a string of four camels, tethered in line, swaying as they move, with their heads held high in an almost arrogant fashion. Three of the beasts are heavily laden with baskets and sacks of all kinds while the lead camel carries a lighter load and is ridden by an old man in gaudy clothing. A young man who walks beside the beasts calls out a greeting as he passes. I cannot understand what he says but the Padre tells me, "By his dialect he probably comes from Mentougou, up near Peking. There are hundreds of camel drivers there." The contrast between the two groups of Asians is stark. Modern troops versus something Marco Polo must have dealt with all those years ago.

"Tell us about the Boxers", demands Doc Hammond, suddenly joining in the conversation, but the Padre laughs sadly and says, "Too depressing, old man. Another time perhaps. I lost many friends in that uprising. It was horrible".

We are entering the outskirts of Qingdao and the Padre launches forth again.

"Now you will see the clash of civilisations in a big way. Look at the railways for example. This line we are passing was one of the many built by the Japanese. They have built rail lines all through the east of China. Great feats of engineering, but they use the Chinese to do the heavy work. Sound familiar. They are the new colonial power in the world. We white men regard ourselves as superior to the yellow Asian, and yet the Japs are as productive as many Europeans and they are aping our colonial attitudes. They thrashed the Russians just ten years ago. Sank their entire navy at Port Arthur. The local commander refused to believe that Asians were capable of even starting a battle despite the intelligence to the contrary that our people gave them, and the Japs just sailed in and slaughtered them just as they slaughtered their Asian brothers in China a few years earlier. They are a force that we should be wary of, you mark my words".

As we drive into the outskirts of the city there are many more people on the road. The wind is building up and is swirling dust and paper and rubbish into the air. As the traffic builds too, so does my feeling of excitement. I saw little of Qingdao when I arrived last month and I soak up the sights. Gathering crowds are heading towards town. The sun is well past its high point as we go deeper into Qingdao and the road becomes even more heavily congested. I'm interested to see that normal courtesies have disappeared. People push and shove their way forward as they pass by this way and that without regard for others. I look down as we pass men jogging along, bouncing bamboo poles strung across their shoulders from which hang baskets filled with all manner of things. Bales of cloth, chickens in cages, and pigs with their front and rear legs bound tight at the trotters. There are coils of rope and bundles of firewood, clay pots of various shapes, and large coloured vases all heading for some market or other. The traffic increases from every quarter as commuters mix with outsiders and the growing throng becomes an almost solid wall of activity. The noise, the heat, the swirling wind and the frantic activity meld into one. People shout greetings and curses and I hear the Padre chuckle as he murmurs, "Welcome to Qingdao".

We move further into the city and the streets narrow but, unbelievably, the traffic increases even more. Rich merchants ride by, some in automobiles, others reclining as poor men carry poles on their shoulders supporting their well-dressed passengers who sit in suspended chairs. Sometimes there are two men and other times four, carrying those who are richer and more opulent. Rickshaws drawn by breathless, sweating men struggle by, taking less opulent passengers from place to place on their daily business through the throng. More large trucks add to the mayhem as they belch their noisy, fuming way and, after the relative tranquillity of CLC camp, the noise becomes unpleasant and the smell overpowering. I'm amazed to see two women standing on a balcony high above street level. They are dressed in beautiful head-to-toe silk robes and they gaze out over the tops of large hand - held fans that discreetly hide their faces from the throng below. One of them waves to me, giving me a sly, welcoming smile and I feel myself go red in the face. My knowledge of the opposite sex is pathetic. A pitifully thin man, naked to the waist, runs across our path pulling a large-wheeled rickshaw. His European passenger shouts at him in a tongue which he obviously does not understand. The foreigner is dressed in a stained, white suit of clothes and wears a broad-brimmed white hat. I watch as the man hits the driver on his bare shoulder with a wooden cane, indicating that he should turn to the right. He reminds me of Higgins and I feel distinctly sorry for the people of this ancient land.

We are well into the heart of Qingdao when I see a huge sign on the wall of a large building that reads 'Dai-Nippon Brewery'. Ever the guide and fountain of local knowledge, the Padre says, "This is the old Tsingtao Brewery and they make all the beer sold in Shandong and even further afield. The factory was founded by The Anglo-German Brewery as a joint stock company based in Hong Kong about fifteen years ago. The original German and Chinese stockholders owned it all until about August last year when it was 'decided' the company would be sold to the Japanese Dai-Nippon crowd by the Japanese military administration in Qingdao. Nobody asked the stockholders. It's another example of how this new Republic of China is not being respected, in any way, by anyone!"

The Padre continues to give a running commentary as we drive on into a wide sweeping bay. He lapses into a reflective mood as he shares his thoughts aloud.

"Do you know that in the spring of 1898, the German government signed a treaty with the Qing Empire that allowed them to lease a large area around this bay? This was to compensate them for the murder of two German missionaries during the Boxer rebellion."

The Padre speaks solemnly now with a tinge of embarrassment.

"It was a huge price to pay. Each of the other foreign powers that were attacked by the Boxer rebels also used this as an excuse to further humiliate the Qing Emperor. It pains me deeply to say this but China has been subjected to so many unfair treaties over the years that some of our own press are even referring to them as the 'Unequal Treaties'. The Germans were allowed to construct a railway from here in the port of Qingdao to Jinan and to exploit coalfields along the way. This concession has existed from the end of the last century to the outbreak of war, and Germany has taken huge profits out of China. A few Chinese agents and officials have grown rich having their palms greased by the Germans, but for most of the Chinese who built the railways or worked in the mines, their labours were rewarded with a pittance in wages."

Doc Hammond has been silent since he asked about the boxers but he interrupts the Padre's flow in an irritable tone.

"That may be true, Padre, but you must admit that the German occupation was not all bad. Lieutenant Hastings told me that the old main street of Qingdao was widened and, while the homes of fishermen and farmers were razed to the ground, they were resettled in better housing further east. Once they gained control of the area, the Germans remodelled large sections of Qingdao with wider streets everywhere and solid housing areas, government buildings, electricity throughout, a sewer system and a safe drinking water supply. The area also had the highest density of schools and the highest per capita student enrolment in all of China. There are primary, secondary and vocational schools, which have been funded by the Imperial German Treasury as well as by Protestant and Roman Catholic missions. It's not all bad news for the local people."

The Doc has become quite animated and goes on, "Even though the Germans grabbed control of Chinese land, in fairness to them, they have been putting something back into the community. Just look around at all the evidence of them introducing modernity and, best of all, they were paying the bill. I suppose their blasted Christian ideals would be based on the hope for converts to their religion, but don't you think that this was a reasonable price to pay, and a benefit to China in the long term?"

"Steady on Doc. You sound almost apologetic for the Germans. There's a war going on and this is a dangerous attitude to have and certainly not one to voice too broadly".

Ignoring the jibe against his Christian faith, the Padre looks at our companion with concern.

"It's all rather complicated. I don't know if you know this, but when war was declared in Europe, our Japanese allies immediately laid siege to Qingdao. The Germans took to the surrounding hills and defended in depth, but with the help of our Navy, the Japanese captured the city and took many German prisoners. These prisoners of war have been shipped off to Japan but I'm sure a strong German influence remains in the area. The CO was talking in the mess only last week about the danger of German sympathisers remaining at large. They could be reporting on the training of the Labour Corps and even on the shipping that is to take us to France. It's a real concern. And another thing, Doc, in 1914, the German Emperor made the defence of Qingdao a top priority. There was a report in the London Times of him saying, 'It would shame me more to surrender Qingdao to the Japanese than Berlin to the Russians.' We are not the only nation that believes in White superiority. What matter the colour of a man's skin, for Goodness sake?"

The older man looks more than his age as sadness creases his face.

"I'm sure time will change this," he adds, rather lamely.

We become silent as we ride along the sweeping front of the bay. I wonder at the Doctor's anti-religion outburst as I gaze out at squat junks and smaller sampans as they bob at their moorings. I can see families going about their business on board, living their lives under awnings with no need to come ashore except to buy provisions. Content with an existence subject only to tides, wind and weather. Where on Earth are we going wrong with our superior attitudes to others?

"I need a drink!"

The words burst from my mouth as I see the imposing entrance to the Zhanqiao Prince Hotel.

Glad of the distraction, the Padre laughs.

"Too easy, my young friend. This is where we are staying."

We enter a broad foyer with trappings of sheer luxury. Silks, brocade curtains, jade sculptures and ancient Chinese tapestries proliferate, giving us an immediate sense of grandeur. We head for the bar opposite the reception area, guided there by a uniformed doorman who greeted us as we entered. He ensures that we are seated at a quiet table and leaves us in the hands of a waiter who appears the moment we sit down. The Padre is smiling broadly.

"Leave this to me, gentlemen. I'll see that we are registered so, in the meantime, why don't you order some refreshment?"

"I feel right out of place here, Doc", I confess as the Padre wanders off, and Doc Hammond smiles for the first time since we left the camp.

"Not really my cup of tea either, my fine Geordie friend. I had a small country practice in a village just outside Norwich before the world went mad. How I will be able to go back there terrifies me. So much horror".

His smile disappears as quickly as it appeared and, as I don't know what to say in reply, we lapse into silence.

The Padre and the drinks arrive at the same time and he hands us our room keys with a cordial "Cheers" as he raises his glass.

Ever the informant, the Padre settles into his armchair and gives us a potted history of the hotel. It is apparently famed in Shandong Province as a favourite holiday destination of European royalty so it will be more than suitable for three lowly English travellers. There are a number of other patrons enjoying pre-dinner drinks and they observe us with mixed interest. I feel under-dressed and wish heartily that I could be in uniform. One guest in particular is an angular woman in her early thirties. Resplendent in a long evening gown and heavily jewelled, she catches my eye and smiles. I feel my face become hot and my fingers go to the scar on my cheek.

"Steady on Charlie," the Padre murmurs quietly, "Ignore the woman and talk to us. Relax for goodness sake. You're having a holiday."

When I pluck up the courage to look back, the woman is talking to another man, this one dressed in black tie evening wear and they both laugh at something she says and leave the bar, heading further into the hotel. I feel suddenly dirty from the ride out here and plead, "Why don't we retire to our rooms, enjoy a deep bath and meet again down here in an hour to enjoy our freedom?"

That said, we head for the stairs.

Chapter Six
The YMCA

"So, who are these 'YMCA' people the CO is talking about, Padre?"

We are enjoying a very European breakfast despite the Oriental surroundings and, after a couple of stiff whiskeys in the bar last night after dinner, I enjoyed a rare good night's sleep. I'm puzzled about the involvement of the YMCA. Back in Kibblesworth we had a youth club run by the Methodist chapel. There was a YMCA club in the nearby village of Lamesley and we played them at football from time to time but the image of the young YMCA lads back home just does not fit in with what I see here in China.

"The YMCA has been here for years. They run all sorts of educational and social programs for China's youth under a Christian non-denominational banner. The clubs are places where young Chinese can enjoy all sorts of interests and learn useful things while they are doing it. In France, as you probably know, they have built huts where the men can drink tea and relax with a cigarette. They can play chess, put on theatricals and so on and the staff help them to write letters home. Dozens of Chinese students who have been studying in America have volunteered to provide these services here and one thing I find interesting is the zeal these young volunteers apply, given that so many of them are from rich families and would probably never have met a coolie before in their entire young lives.

The Padre chats away in his usual pleasant way but Doc Hammond's reaction shocks him.

"Christians?" he snorts. "I hope they've been taught well because they will need every ounce of their Christian values when they get to Europe. How can you believe in a God, especially a loving God, when our Christian Kings and Emperors continue to slaughter so many of God's innocent creatures?"

We sit in an embarrassed silence. Doc Hammond is red-faced and trembling. I've never seen him like this. In my short time in the camp I have regarded him as being rather aloof, but the last twenty-four hours or so of our close contact has shown me a different side to him. He is obviously deeply troubled by his experiences back in Europe, much deeper than I imagined.

The Padre says nothing. He pours us all a fresh cup of tea and sits back quietly drinking his and staring into space. After a moment or so, the Doctor stands up and walks away without another word.

We locate the YMCA down an alleyway not far from the main road that passes the Brewery. As we enter, a young man greets us in singsong English. He has a stooped, thin frame suggesting a life lacking healthy exposure to exercise or fresh air. His hair is cut European-style and I take his proffered hand cautiously, a hand that is damp to the touch and weak in its grip. He smells of stale sweat and I am not impressed.

"Welcome. My name is Gong Lei but I have taken a Christian name, John, after the Lord's disciple."

The office we stand in is a scene of chaos and disorder, with piles of books, papers, pamphlets and boxes taking up every available space.

When we mention the reason for our visit, he becomes more business-like. "How can we improve our work for you?" he asks, and Doc Hammond launches forth.

"You can start by having the people you send to us medically examined here in Qingdao when they first arrive and stop sending us so much rubbish! How many have you got here waiting at the moment?"

The young man looks shocked at Doc Hammond's tone of voice and begins to stammer, his English becoming ragged. "Yes, there is twenty mens in this house now want work to you soon".

The Padre steps in and asks John gently if he has a doctor in his congregation.

"Yes, yes. We have Father Kailing who is doctor, good doctor with all people happy he look after them. He train in America. Speak very complete English."

"So, can you call Father Kailing to come to meet our doctor, please? This would be most helpful".

The young Chinaman goes to the door of his office and yells out. Another young man runs down from the rear of the building, there is a rapid exchange of Mandarin and he is dispatched as a messenger.

"Father Kailing come soon. Please to see our kitchen please".

We leave his office and follow the smell of cooking to a kitchen and dining area in which a number of nervous-looking Chinese men are sitting. They have heard the Doc's raised voice and they stand up as we enter, showing a mixture of surprise and concern. The men have been eating a meal of rice with cooked vegetables and strips of chicken. The area looks clean and 'John' says something in Mandarin, which makes the men relax a bit. We stand there for a few minutes feeling rather awkward when a Chinaman dressed in smart western clothing enters hurriedly saying, "Good Morning gentleman. My name is Doctor Kailing, although in this place I am known as Father Kailing". His English is as good as John said and he smiles with easy good grace as he offers his hand to us each in turn.

The Padre and the two doctors sit down at a table to talk as the man who calls himself John takes my arm and guides me to a flight of stairs. "Please, I show you more of our home".

We climb two flights of stairs and I'm conscious of a damp, unpleasant smell. It has begun to rain heavily and water is trickling down one of the walls. John notices my reaction and laughs.

"The roof has holes as you see and there is bad wood in many places but the men not worry. We send men to you as soon as we can. They not stay here long time."

We enter a long attic room in which there are a number of thin mattresses spread out on the floor in neat rows. Three of them are occupied by more nervous young men unsure what is going on while others are strewn with personal possessions presumably owned by the men downstairs. John then takes me downstairs to an annex at the rear of the building. There are no windows, just an entry screened with strings of beads leading from within the building itself and a heavily barred door at the far end of the room. I learn that this is where they hold Christian services.

The Chinaman sees me looking at the door and tells me it leads into the street and is kept closed at all times.

"It is for escape if we need," he says in a serious tone. "We need escape door as this place is raided some times. The Boxers are no more a large force but many are still aggressive. Some live near here and they some of the time crash in to stop our Christian services as we worship."

Boxers again? I must press the Padre to learn more about these people.

Back in the kitchen the two doctors are engaged in a deep discussion, leaving the Padre looking pleased to see me.

"They don't need me to translate, Charlie. Doctor Kailing's a nice chap who speaks well of the British. He told us that he has heard back from many of the coolies who have already gone to Europe. They write home and report that they are treated well. The money they were promised is arriving regularly and the families back here seem to be content, so we should be positive in thinking that our task is successful. Come with me. I have something to show you".

We leave the building and the Padre takes me further into the alleyway away from the main thoroughfare and then turns into an even narrower walkway. The ground beneath my feet is broken and potholed. There is a stench of human waste and rotten food. It is pitch dark in places, the light from the now overcast day unable to penetrate the space between the high buildings on either side. The further we go into this warren the worse the stench becomes.

"What the Hell have you brought me here for?" I ask nervously.

"Really, Padre. What are you up to?"

"I'm taking you to an opium den so that you can see for yourself that I'm not exaggerating the extent of the problem".

We walk on past grim-looking characters lounging in doorways, many glaring at us with open suspicion. The Padre stops outside one doorway, says, "This one will do", and then strides inside. I follow him at once, my stomach churning, and I desperately feel the need of a weapon of some kind. Any kind. The dingy, smoke filled place is crowded with people, many of whom are lying on wooden cots, oblivious to their surroundings. The sickly smell makes me want to heave, and the sight of emaciated man and a few women lying there with empty eyes fills me with a mixture of horror and an intense anger. The scene is a nightmare. No one speaks to us and after a few moments the Padre turns on his heel and leaves. I follow behind with a feeling of hopelessness as he strides back out of the alleyway and back to the YMCA.

"Why did I take you there, you ask? You're a good man, Charlie, but you've spent most of your time in the confines of our camp. This is reality for so many of these people and we are to blame. Not you and I but us, the British people, our Empire, despite Doc Hammond's comments. How can we serve these people when we treat them like dirt? We have formed and grown our Empire on this opium foulness, and history will condemn us for it. Not only will we be condemned for this trade and the vast amount of wealth we have gained from it, we will be mocked for using that wealth to destroy ourselves in a stupid, wasteful war. We must all be mad."

What a day. First the Doc loses control and now the Padre. I've not seen him rant like this. He's trembling like a jelly.

When we return, John tells us that Doc Hammond has gone back to the hotel with Doctor Kailing. They have apparently struck up a good relationship and all that I can think of to say is, "Why don't we take our leave and go back to the hotel too?"

My friend and I travel back in silence.

Chapter Seven

Prepare to move

Days drag by as winter sets in and the dry cold begins to cut into me making reveille a daily challenge. I develop rather nasty sores on my lips, which Doc Hammond treats with a local cream. Apart from the sores, I keep in reasonably good shape. Keeping the men occupied is becoming a problem. Li Cheng-fang and the other two p'aitous in Section One start taking drill, and each impresses the CSM. A man called Li Zhang especially. He gives drill lessons like an experienced NCO and Peters suspects that he has had previous military experience. Most of the men are getting bored though and we try to counter boredom in a number of ways. Less drill and more sport is proving successful and there have been a surprising number of talents shown as musicians, singers and actors emerge to provide impromptu entertainments. The men have also surprised us with their own version of physical exercises with a routine the Padre identified as Tai Chi, a sort of slow, complex, individual dance routine. That's the only way I can describe it. Some of the men also practice close-order combat techniques that involve leaps and bounds and head-kicking from a standing start. It has our British troops fascinated. My concern however is in the rise in gambling. Many of the men have money in their hands at a level that is new to them and, while the Padre encourages them to send their money to their families, there are plenty who join in the various gambling schools that seem to be run by Zhou Xiao-bing, the man we suspect of being a gangster. The Padre has raised this with the CO but, no matter how hard he tries, the gambling goes on at a pace.

On a positive note, the Padre's English classes are progressing well and we have a number of the junior Chinese leaders we call *p'aitous* who can hold reasonable conversations in our tongue. I'm delighted to find that Li Cheng-fang is one of the Padre's star pupils and I take every opportunity to talk with him and to expand his vocabulary. The Padre suspects that he has had an education far superior to the other men before arriving here with us. He's a firm favourite of Sergeant Fredricks too and I find the pair surrounded by a cheering mob of Chinamen as they arm wrestle at the edge of the parade ground. This has become a regular Friday afternoon event introduced by Fredricks as a training novelty. He began demonstrating the 'game' by involving Corporal Thompson, a lad from Birmingham with arms as thick as other men's thighs and the ever-impressive Corporal Anderson. The Chinese line up to take on their English trainers as they grasped the technique and the fun of the challenge but the highlight is always the bouts between

Fredricks and Li Cheng-fang. Despite the young Chinaman's obvious strength, Fredricks gives as good as he gets and honours are usually shared evenly. I'm aware that there is the inevitable covert gambling but here the bonding that is taking place is worth the downside.

"Did you win this week?"

Li Cheng-fang is sitting with his 'chum' Su Ting-fu and they both grin as I sit to join them.

"Mr Fredricks a good man," the big man replies happily. "All Chinamen like him".

Su Ting-fu nods his head although I'm sure he doesn't understand much English. His good nature however extends to him offering me his metal cup and I take a mouthful. Surprisingly it is cold sweet tea and very refreshing. The clown, for this is how I see him, chuckles at my reaction.

"Mr Armstrong, when we go war?" Li Cheng-fang has become serious. "We OK now. Go soon, yes?"

It's a fair question and one that has been bothering me for some time. After our visit to Qingdao, the number of recruits has increased significantly and the number of men rejected by Doc Hammond has reduced, so we are well on the way to filling our 'quota'. So much so that the latest recruits have been doubling up as the huts we have for them overflow and bunk space dries up.

"Not long now, Li Cheng-fang. Soon".

The Chinaman smiles but as I say this my stomach tightens in knots. Back to the Front? The realisation that the day for departure is nigh has increased the nightmares. Billy Bissel has again become a nightly visitor and my consumption of whiskey has begun to seriously concern my friend the Padre. I have noticed that Doc Hammond is also aware that our departure is getting close. He is a dour as ever with the recruits but, in the mess, he is even more of a recluse than me. The Padre has tried to talk to him but, after his outburst against the Christian faith, it is to no avail and he remains silent and withdrawn.

The matter is brought to a head one morning when we assemble for the CO's 'O' group. Young Bertram is looking very upset. He has a pile of paper on the table in front of him and he keeps looking at the top sheet in horror.

"Good morning, Gentlemen. The day has at last arrived. We are leaving for Europe in six days' time."

The CO's words are met with a mixed reaction.

"Mr Bertram, hand out the Company structure. Take a moment to study this gentleman and I will take questions when you have done so".

I stare down at the single sheet of paper that Bertram is handing round and the worst of my fears choke in my throat.

Chinese Labour Corps Company Number 21

Commanding Officer Major Roberts

Company Sergeant Major Peters

Number One Section	Number Two Section	Number Three Section
Captain Armstrong (2IC)	Captain Asmiroff	Lieutenant Hastings
Sergeant Fredricks	Sergeant Williams	Sergeant Young
Corporal Thompson	Corporal Bruce	Corporal Elliott
Corporal Davidson	Corporal Higgins	Corporal Black
Corporal Anderson	Corporal Brown	Corporal Collins
3 x 64 man squads	3 x 64 man squads	1 x 64 man squad
P'aitou Li Cheng-fang	*P'aitou* Zhou Xiao-bing	10 x man Police squad
P'aitou Sun Jun	*P'aitou* Wang Lei	20 x cooks
P'aitou Li Zhang	*P'aitou* Yang Fa	20 x general hands

Medical Section

Captain Hammond

Eight man medical team

Three man sanitation team

Others

Lieutenant Bertram - Coordination

Zhao Da-hai – Interpreter

"In addition to the names listed, we will also be accompanied by the Padre"

I look over at the missionary and I'm puzzled. The Padre is smiling quietly. Why on Earth does he want to leave his life's work and go into a war? I know how much he loves the Chinese but his reaction to this news is beyond me. Asmiroff mutters something about me being listed as the Second in Command, but, as a foreign national, what could he expect. Doc Hammond's features have turned grey, Bertram begins to tremble openly but the others take the news in their stride. We are dismissed and I head for the mess with my close friend who will now continue to be my companion. I need a stiff drink and an explanation and in that order.

"Padre, you have me totally confused. We are going to war and yet you look content to be going with us. What's going on?

The missionary smiles shyly.

"All in good time, my boy. All in good time. First I need to challenge my faith".

"Your faith? I really don't follow you there. Why is your faith a problem to you?"

"My faith has never been the same since the Boxer uprisings. I lost so many friends at the time but I carry a deep shame, which is why I try to avoid talking about it. When the violence started, I abandoned my mission and hid until the worst was over. My cowardice has remained with me ever since. I don't like to talk much about the Boxers. They were known as the *Yihetuan*, the Honourable Society of Righteous and Harmonious Fists. A very Chinese name, don't you think? They were part of a nationalist movement that opposed both foreign imperialism and the spread of Christianity in China. They saw Christianity as an offence to Buddhism and a challenge to Chinese culture, saying that we missionaries came here with the Bible in one hand and opium in the other. They spread horror stories to vulnerable, uneducated peasants such as branding our convents as places where women missionaries took abandoned children, saying they will look after them but where the children were murdered, for goodness sake!"

I think to myself that it sounds like the propaganda stuff that *we* are spreading.

"They told tales of people having seen the tiny boxes the poor mites were buried in. In fact, a great number of infants abandoned outside convents are near death anyway. The Chinese believe that if a child dies inside the home, its spirit will transfer to another member of the family and cause mischief. But the Boxer propaganda ignores this and they say that baby bodies had been cut open and the children's hearts eaten for medicine. It's all part of the magic we are supposed to do. Here in Shandong, where I was preaching a dozen or so year ago, many of the peasants and farmers around me believed these tales and joined the Boxers."

I'm concerned that the Padre is now rambling a bit and I'm not sure what he is leading up to, but I remain silent.

"They began killing Christians everywhere. Many of my friends, Protestant and Catholic alike, were slaughtered, as were their families. Even children! The Dowager Empress condemned the Boxers at first, but then she gave them her blessing and the Imperial Army joined in the attacks on us. We were branded as foreign devils and our converts as 'secondary devils'. Thousands of our converts were killed and I despaired. The situation reached a climax and the foreign powers that controlled much of China banded together and defeated the Boxers. They overran China and I came out of hiding to witness European nations engaged in an orgy of plunder, rape and slaughter."

My friend stares out into space but then he turns back to face me as if he's pleading for my understanding.

"I protested at the highest level but to no avail, and I then tried to preach the gospel to whoever would listen. Matters settled down again and my life returned almost to normal until ten or so years ago when war came to China once again. This time the war was between Russia and

Japan. The Russians wanted access to a port that would not freeze over in winter, as it does in Vladivostok, and the Japanese wanted to prevent Russia from gaining any advantage, and so they fought a war. It was a war fought by foreigners over Chinese territory on Chinese soil. A war between two foreign powers, both of whom wanted to exert their influence and their prosperity, but using China as a pawn in their game. This war was not of China's making nor in China's interest and yet thousands of Chinese died as a result. And now we are sending them into another war. Is it any wonder intelligent young Chinese like Li Cheng-fang are wary of us all? What lies ahead of us all?"

All I could think of is, what has this to do with you volunteering to go to France? Obviously, he was not going to tell me.

"I'll take your progress reports, Gentlemen. You first Charlie!"

As so often in the military, weeks of idleness have been followed by frantic activity. The past four days have been a blur but the CO's evening 'O' group is one of contented confidence all round.

"One Section is in good shape, Sir. The men are ready and keen to go. I've eight men in sick-bay who will travel on the next boat but their places have been filled from the newer recruits. They'll get brought up to scratch on the journey over".

The CO nods his approval and moves on to the Russian who gives a similar report on Two Section. Eventually each of us confirm readiness for the move and we are told that convoys of trucks hired for the purpose will begin transporting us to the ship from 0500 hours on the day after next. My men will be the first to leave.

"Well done Gentlemen. This operation is going well. Keep focussed"

With that the 'O' Group is ended and we are left to attend to last minute details.

I head for the mess for a drink.

Chapter Eight
Nagasaki Interlude

The weather is overcast and a storm brewing as we form up in three ranks on the road outside the camp gates, ready to take our first steps on the journey to Europe. I take my place at the head of One Section with Asmiroff behind leading Two Section and Lieutenant Hastings leading the remainder. The roads are lined with some of the staff who are staying behind, some of the recruits still being trained and a large number of curious villagers from the surrounding region. The men are dressed in their Chinese Labour Corps uniforms, while we British, still conforming to political requirements, are in our civilian clothing. Major Roberts marches out to the head of the parade dressed in kilt, sporran and sundry Celtic trimmings, causing a stir among those who are seeing him dressed this way for the first time. He's carrying his bagpipes and, when he gives the order to begin the march, he begins to play. Terrified children scatter in all directions and many of the villagers step back in confusion but for those of us marching we do so with our backs straight and our heads held high.

Trucks are lined up a mile or so down the road and they begin ferrying us to a small railway station where we board a train that will take us the rest of the way. Sergeant Major Peters and his NCOs soon have the men settled and under the control of the *p'aitous,* despite the excitement that fills the air. Within an hour, we're off to raucous cheers, singing and much banging of tin bowls and pots.

From the station in Qingdao we march again to the pipes, down through the curious throng to the docks. Peters organises the boarding of Chinese Labour Corps Company Number 21 on board a huge three-funnelled iron monster and I wonder what the Chinese in our care will make of it all. The Padre and Doc Hammond have made their own way to the quayside and they stand with me as YMCA John and a handful of his recent recruits join us. A dead animal floats by the side of the wharf and there's an all-pervading smell of poorly maintained drains, oil, wood smoke, aromas from numerous quayside food stalls and various other assaults on my being that churn my already anxious stomach.

"You don't look the best, Captain Armstrong. Can I get you anything?"

The Doc's question focuses my mind back onto my duties. I decline his offer and stride off to find CSM Peters to get a report on the men's situation. I find him talking with Lieutenant Hastings and Sergeant Williams from Two Section. There's no sign of Asmiroff.

"The men are settled for the moment, Sir. But they are crammed in tight. I've posted our police to ensure that they stay where they are and don't go wandering off around the ship. The galleys are open but we'll feed them where they are for now. Most of them are shit scared, if you'll pardon the expression, Sir. *P'aitou* Sun Jun told me that the men do not believe that, without the ropes that tie us to the quay, this chunk of iron will ever float, let alone sail out on the high seas".

Happy to leave Peters to his tasks, I climb to the upper decks to find my cabin. As I do so, I see that one of the other Companies has arrived. We are to sail with the two other Companies, 19 and 20. All together we'll be around sixteen hundred souls, so space will be at a premium. Our first stop will be in Nagasaki in Japan where we will refuel before taking the longer journey across the Pacific to Canada. When I queried our route with the CO, he told me that an early attempt to transport the Chinamen to Europe via the Suez Canal had ended in tragedy. A vessel called the Athos had been sunk in the Med with over six hundred Chinamen on board. All were drowned. To make matters worse, the only record of the names of the men on board sank with them.

Lieutenant Bertram meets me as I climb and shows me to my quarters for the voyage. I'm sharing a small four-berth cabin with poor lighting and one porthole that looks out onto the deck. 'First in - best dressed' so I climb with a clear conscience onto the top bunk near to the outlet. There's a knock on the door and I find Bertram again, this time with a steward and my kit bag. My trunk will stay stowed away in the hold but I'm delighted to shed my civilian clothes and once again put on my army uniform. As the sun sets and the light fades, I feel the throb of the ship's engines and I rush to the side. We gently ease away from the quayside as my stomach sheds its contents into the swirling harbour waters. Just like my first voyage across the English Channel and at the start of each voyage since, I learn that I am far from effective as a sailor.

It's two days before I find what the Doc laughingly calls my sea-legs. He and the Padre have been tending to my needs since we sailed. The fourth bunk has been allocated to Asmiroff but the Russian nobleman has somehow managed to secure himself a single berth near the Captain's quarters. This is a mutually convenient arrangement as it gives us more room and we do not have to suffer his arrogance.

I decide to take a tentative turn around the deck, where I'm met by a sympathetic CSM Peters.

"Good to see you looking better, Sir. You're not alone in getting mal de mer as the French put it. Most of the men have been in a shocking state. It's funny but the thing that seems to have helped the most is peanuts. There are sacks of them on board and we have been letting the lads eat as much as they like. The only problem was with the shells but the *p'aitous* solved that themselves. Sun Jun scrounged some empty boxes and told the men to put the peanut shells in there. Any man found throwing shells anywhere else was put on latrine duty. The latrines are disgusting so it was a great incentive not to litter. The *p'aitous* have been working their socks off and doing a good job all round. We can be proud of them. Between us we have a good routine going and the men are content. Boredom is the curse again, especially as there is not much room for exercise".

"Well done, CSM. The weather is fairly calm at the moment. What do you think about lifting restrictions for a short while and letting the men get some fresh air?"

"As you wish, Sir. That'll go down a treat".

Peters goes below, the hatches are lifted and the hardiest of the men venture onto the lower decks and look around in amazement. I watch with amusement as the men wander around like tourists on a strange and exotic island. The men examine the entrance to the engine room with great interest, the decks are explored as far as permissible and the various bollards and winches are examined and discussed, as they debate, argue, agree and disagree on a use for each newly-found piece of apparatus. As I watch, the Padre joins me and tells me that he has been in the sick bay for most of the time since we sailed, looking after some of the more seriously ill on board. Li Cheng-fang is among the men up on deck and he calls out, "Good morning Captain Armstrong. You look much sick. Have you eat much?" He looks at me in horror as I retch over the side of the ship. Feeling guilty, I hurry away from him, leaving my friend the Padre to cover my embarrassment.

Time passes and a cry goes up from the front of the ship. Some of the men on deck have spotted land ahead. They crowd the rails like excited children and as we get nearer, we watch sampans pass us in droves as they head out to the fishing grounds. Seagulls begin flying overhead and I can feel the excitement growing all around me. The ship slows to a crawl, still a distance from the dockside, and there is a loud rattling sound as the anchor is dropped. The interpreter, Zhao Da-hai, sidles up to me with a smirk on his face.

"This Nagasaki, Sir", he sniggers, implying that I would not know where I am. "We in Japan. Many days sickness more ahead, yes?"

He turns and walks away, and my dislike for the man continues to deepen. We slowly swing with the tide on a thick chain, and we settle in a gentle swell as the throbbing of the engines ceases. I realise how much that sensation has become part of my waking existence in so short a time, and I lean at the rail, gazing out at a new wonder.

A number of small barges come towards us, laden with coal. Ladders and ropes are lowered to boats lined up around us and coal is manhandled on board in a continuous line of baskets that are heaved up by Japanese workers in a speedy and effective manner. Their industry is good to watch and I look over at our men who are also taking in the scene. Sun Jun sees me watching and calls out, "Japanese work and we look. This very good, Mr Armstrong. We better important!"

I gather from this that he regards himself as some kind of superior passenger being served by the Japanese, which I find strangely pleasing.

The Padre joins me and says, "I'm going ashore to get some medical supplies, Charlie. How would you like to come with me?"

I don't need to be asked twice and shake his hand with delight.

We make our way to the sick bay, where the Padre collects a list of medical supplies that the medical staff have requested. Then it's off to the side of the vessel where crew members are waiting for us. The sailors indicate a treacherous rope ladder that swings freely down the side of the ship, and we climb over the rail and down the swinging steps, arriving at the deck of the waiting tender with jaws and other, more delicate areas, locked shut. We bounce in the swell of the harbour and my poor stomach begins to heave again. A coxswain at the helm takes control and we are soon thudding over the water to the quayside. Once on dry land, it is all I can do to stop myself from kissing the ground in relief.

A Japanese Major is waiting to meet us. He bows formally and introduces himself as Doctor Akihiro.

"I am with the Japanese Imperial Army and I'm at your service to assist you procure the medical supplies that your cable requested," he says in a clipped but polite fashion.

I tell him that I sent the signal on behalf of our Padre and I introduce us by name. More bows.

There's an Englishman waiting with the Japanese officer and he greets the Padre warmly.

"Welcome to Nagasaki," he says, "I'm Reverend Latham. I'm the minister with the Presbyterian Church here in Nagasaki. I want to add to the Major's welcome and assist in any way I can."

Formalities over, Major Akihiro ushers us to an open topped military staff car, the driver of which is standing rigid to attention, holding open a rear door. He bows deeply as we climb in and I gaze around with interest as he takes us into the centre of the city. It's an Asian city of course, with ornate wooden buildings and lanterns hanging everywhere, but there is much more of a Western feel about the place. There are many more automobiles and motorised trucks than we saw in China, and a tramway runs down and across streets as we journey on. We drive past wooden houses with ornate, sculptured trees and ornate gardens made of stones. There are bamboo shades, wooden lattice work and open, windowless shops displaying the trades of watchmakers, furniture carvers, lantern makers and tea emporiums. Women totter along on wooden clogs. They are wrapped in colourful robes that cover their bodies from shoulder to ankle in discreet fashion and have a curious-looking affair tied in the small of the back. I smile to myself thinking that they look a bit like a soldier's bum-pack.

Major Akihiro is watching me carefully, so I switch my gaze away from the woman to a man who is also dressed in robes and with a strange looking haircut. His head is shaved from his eyebrows to the rear of the crown but the sides and back are just clipped. Weird! Many others are dressed in Western clothing and the street lighting and traffic has a modern feel to it. I'm left with an impression of a society that is different to any I have seen before, but one that is certainly progressive. Much more so than the chaos we left behind in Qingdao.

As if reading my mind, the Japanese doctor says, "We have our traditions, Captain, but Japan is becoming a modern nation. Like you Europeans have done, we are developing an Empire and our economy is growing rapidly. You will be aware that after we defeated China recently, we acquired the island of Formosa. Like other Imperial powers, we also hold sway in many parts of the region, including Shandong where you have just come from."

His stilted words are part history, part lecture, but said in a challenging way. I think that these Japanese may be a force to reckon with at some stage in the future. They're certainly a lot different to the Chinese. Major Akihiro continues to talk and he makes a lot of the fact that Japan and England are allies in the war.

"One of my sons is at present on the island of Malta. He is serving aboard a destroyer of the Japanese Imperial Navy. We have an entire fleet in the Mediterranean in support of your Royal Navy. I am very proud of my son."

As he says this we arrive at a large, impressive and very modern looking hospital. Major Akihiro is obviously proud of the facility too and rather grandly escorts the three of us through the main entrance. Staff dressed in crisp, white uniforms bow towards us at every turn. We seem to be something of a novelty and I wonder if I should be bowing back all the time. We're taken into a pleasant sitting room where we sit in comfort while tea and very English-looking sandwiches are presented to us.

"I have ordered the supplies you requested be brought to the vehicle and kept there for your return to the ship. Everything you asked for is available to you. When you have finished your tea, I would like to take you on a tour of our modest hospital and then, perhaps, some lunch in town and a short trip around the city before you return. Would that be to your liking?"

I'm impressed.

Major Akihiro escorts us back to his waiting vehicle and we drive off once more into the city with the Japanese doctor acting as the perfect host, taking us to a pleasant hotel where we are bowed towards a table for lunch. Reverend Latham recommends a variety of dishes that will suit the English palate, much to the amusement of Major Akihiro, who looks on with an indulgent smile on his face.

"I insist that you try our sashimi," he says innocently, and I have my first taste of raw fish. All I can think of is the challenge of holding it in my stomach as I face the ferryboat back to the ship.

All to soon we are back on the quayside and Major Akihiro bows formally as he says goodbye with his driver bowing several times in the background. Once again, I'm not sure how I should respond and wonder if I should bow back or shake hands or what. Years of training kick in and I snap to attention and salute smartly. The two churchmen embrace and, with our medical supplies transferred from the vehicle to our transport the Padre and I return to the ship. Back safely on board I take to my bed once more, having first thrown up my beautiful lunch into the bowl of the nearest toilet.

Chapter Nine
Canada bound

"This seasickness of yours has advantages, Charlie. You are not drinking as much".

The Padre's right but that's only half of it. I've no stomach for the whiskey but dreaming about Billy Bissel is another absence. All I can think about as I lie in bed is holding my insides inside. There's no room for grog *or* nightmares.

Once again, I slowly get my sea legs and, two days out from Nagasaki, I stagger up on deck to see the CSM and start doing my duties. We no longer need the pretence of being civilian employers and we now wear our uniforms at all times. Many of us wear campaign ribbons on our tunics indicating that we have been engaged in combat. The Padre makes an interesting observation that veterans tend to be more considerate towards the Chinese than those with bare chests who in some ways still treat them like livestock. Even so our orders are to keep our charges fed and watered but restrict them as much as possible to their confined spaces below deck. As our journey begins to take on a dull routine, Sergeant Major Peters reports that squabbling among the pent-up passengers is increasing significantly. The p'aitous are earning their extra pay.

Hastings has formed sanitation squads within Admin Section and they've maintained a level of cleanliness that pleases inspecting officers as we do the rounds every five or six hours. I'm particularly pleased to watch Peters as he encourages the men with his positive and pragmatic attitude. He's strict but fair and is obviously well regarded. I roster young Bertram to go with Peters as often as possible in the hope that he learns from the experienced older man. The refuse baskets into which any rubbish, especially the all-pervasive peanut shells, are to be deposited are regularly emptied overboard and the men enjoy fresher air with the opening of hatchways to the outside. Many of the men are still unwell but in general the situation is slowly improving. Unfortunately, as spirits slowly begin to rise we are faced with the revival of an old problem. Gambling schools spring up all over the ship.

The CO's response is surprisingly swift and heavy. A number of gamblers are arrested and taken to a cage that has been built in the open on an upper deck. Here the miscreant gamblers spend their time sitting like chickens or ducks, staring out through the bars while others mock them as they walk freely past. Those who persist in spitting are also taken into custody and they join the gamblers in the cage. Twenty-four hours of this humiliating punishment seems to work, and for once the problem of gambling is virtually eliminated. Even the habit of spitting, a habit the men have formed over a lifetime, is brought under control. This is all well and good but the boredom persists and I talk to Peters, asking him to join me in thinking of another way for the men to amuse themselves. Peters has already organised some physical exercise programs but, with the limits that cramped space impose, these are minor distractions. One of the *p'aitou* finds out from a Chinese crew member that there is a store of musical instruments on board. When he tells Peter's this, the CSM and I prevail upon the ship's Captain to sell some of them to the musicians we have amongst us. I'm delighted to discover that we have some excellent talent on board, and space is created where the men can sit each day and listen to a performance. Competition among those who can (and those who think they can) play music is continuous and the journey is lightened.

The *p'aitou's* initiative reminds me of the benefit we enjoy teaching them English. The Padre spends most of his time with Doc Hammond tending to the sick but I enlist Hastings, who speaks fluent Mandarin, and Bertram to work with me to give the *p'aitous* as much practice as we can.

Once we start lessons, I'm approached by Sergeant Fredricks and Corporal Anderson who want to help and soon we have quite an intense school in operation. It's at the end of a lesson that Fredricks and I have run that he raises an issue that has been in the back of my mind for some time.

"Sir. With respect, Sir, can I ask you something?"

When I nod approval, the old soldier continues, "We're taking these lads into a war like no other. You and I have both seen what is happening up close and it's bloody 'orrible, if you'll pardon me for sayin'".

He obviously has more to say so I wait patiently and he blurts out, "They need basic weapon training, Sir, just in case".

The CO's reaction is just what I expected it to be.

"I understand your concern Charlie but it can't be done. For one thing, we don't have much on board by way of weapons but, even if we did, it's going dead against what we were ordered to do in the first place. These men are civilians and they are employed, contracted not enlisted, to do civilian work. They will be deployed behind the Front so they will take their chances like the civilians who still live all around them".

"How're ya gannan, marra?"

The Padre smiles as he hears my broad Geordie greeting.

"I presume that is some kind of pleasantry, Charlie. How are you?"

We sit down side by side, mugs of tea in hand, on a bench on an upper deck reserved for the English staff. The air is fresh but the noon sun takes the worst of the chill from the air and I welcome this chance to have a chat with my overworked friend.

I decide not to mention my meeting with the CO as I'm sure the missionary would be appalled at the idea of giving his flock any military training, and I reply, "I'm well, thank you Padre, if rather bored. The men are handling things as we expected and Peters and his NCOs are doing an excellent job. Thank God for decent sergeant majors. He has a strange sense of humour at times, our Mr Peters. Yesterday, I heard Corporal Thompson ask him what we were fighting this war for. He answered, 'money!' Thompson looked shocked and said, 'what about honour and glory, sir?' 'That too, laddie. All the things we don't have any of'. He then walked away, laughing his head off. I had to think long and hard about that one."

The Padre sits there grinning, and I feel totally relaxed for the first time since I climbed on board this bloody ship.

We have another week to go until we arrive in Canada and it can't go quickly enough.

"How are you getting on with our two Lieutenants?" chuckles the Padre.

"Hastings is a good lad and will do well. He runs his Admin section effectively and listens to his sergeants as I've told him to. His police do a good job in a fair way and the men accept their role, although the gamblers grumble a lot. As you know, the medics have been flat out in sickbay and the cooks have also had a busy time of it. The Caterer told me this morning that some of the men are deliberately committing minor irregularities in order to get kitchen duty as a punishment. It seems that they actually prefer being busy. As we've said before, they have a different mindset to our soldiers. Hastings told me his sanitation squads have taken over from those set up by our foremen. The *p'aitous* themselves took the initiative on Day One, but now we've a routine in place and Hastings has enough to keep him occupied. Bertram is the problem child."

The Padre is immediately concerned, and asks, "How do you think he is going to cope with France?"

"He has as much military spirit as my left big toe", I reply angrily. "When he's with the men, he says 'what do you think' ten times as often as 'now do this'. I keep telling him he should give orders, not ask for opinions or make requests. Peters sees him as a major problem, and has ordered the sergeants to keep him under their wings, but Higgins, for example, openly scoffs him. The poor bugger cannot always see it either, which makes the other corporals laugh openly. He commands absolutely no respect whatsoever from our lads. Higgins continues to be a pain in the arse, Padre, if you will pardon the expression. Every unit has a 'Higgins' I suppose. We'll just have to put up with him. Sergeant Major Peters is on his case so let's just leave it at that".

The Padre shakes his head and says, "My tea's now cold and so am I. I need to get back to the sick bay"

The days pass as days do and we prepare for the next phase of the journey, the crossing of Canada. The entry requirements for our Chinese passengers were telegraphed to the ship and we began complying by having every man's head shaved bare, ensuring that they bathed and that each man is wearing a clean uniform. On the fifth day of December 1917, with our men as clean and presentable as schoolboys on their first day at school, we arrive in Canada.

Chapter Ten
Crossing Canada

Sergeant Major Peters and I meet with our counterparts in the other two Companies and we go ashore after the ship ties up well before dawn at William Head on Vancouver Island. The six of us are ordered to liaise with the Canadian authorities to ensure a rapid transfer of the men from the ship to the railhead where they are to be transported across the vast plains of Canada. Two men, a Canadian immigration officer and a Captain in the Canadian Army, are waiting to meet us and we are taken into a hut on the quayside. The heat inside is like an oven, with a metal wood stove burning fiercely.

"Great coats off," laughs the Canadian officer, and we strip down to sit at a small table.

Once mugs of coffee are handed round and the pleasantries are over, the serious business of moving the first of the passengers ashore begins, and it begins badly. When I suggest that, as we are structured in three companies, each over five hundred strong, they disembark unit by unit, the Canadians accept this as a logical move. But when I continue, "OK then so I'll bring my men ashore first," the Immigration officer's reaction has me reeling.

"Your men? I thought you were bringing a boatload of Chinks!"

There's an awkward silence as we stare at the Canadians. I break the silence saying coldly, "Right then. There'll be five hundred of us in the first detail ashore. How do you want this handled?"

The Canadian Captain returns my stare and replies just as coldly, "We want this handled with speed and discretion. My orders are to see that the Chinks are moved to the railhead over in Vancouver with as little exposure to the public as possible. The last thing our government wants is for Joe Public to learn that tens of thousands of Orientals are coming into the country."

And I thought our lot were prejudiced.

It takes less than an hour for us to finalise movement details. This done, we grab our greatcoats and return to the ship. No one mentions the racial outburst but I can tell my companions are as disturbed as I am. When we are alone, Peters busts out, "They're not livestock, for Hell's sake! I feel our men could be in for some rough treatment."

Everything around us is covered in a thin layer of snow. This does not seem to bother the hardened men of Shandong who are used to the cold - on the contrary they look delighted to be off that dreadful ship and into crisp clean air. The sea journey has left many of them weakened but the chance to move around in the fresh air is clearly an excellent tonic. They form up and march from the quayside to a place that the Canadian immigration official calls the 'Quarantine Station'. As we march along, the fields seem to be strangely empty. It's still very early in the day but I'm aware that the emptiness in the fields extends everywhere around us. There are no people to be seen which is puzzling and I think to myself, "Why the secrecy?"

We eventually arrive at a building with a large red cross painted on the wall and we are confronted by the Canadian Captain and a squad of Canadian troops. The men are to be examined by Canadian doctors and I tell Peters to get them processed as quickly as we can. When I go into the building to check on what is happening, I find that the Chinamen are lined up in rows as three men in white coats, wearing white masks covering the lower parts of their faces, walk along each rank, looking each of the men in the face. Occasionally they indicate to one or other of them to stand to one side. Nurses place thermometers in the mouths of those selected and, when they are checked, the men are told to return to their lines. All except one man who is taken away by one of the men in white coats. There's a general murmuring of dissent from the rest of the men in his company when this happens, and I step forward with Zhao Da-hai to tell them that the man is unwell and he is going to be examined further by this doctor. As I'm doing this, Doc Hammond makes a timely entrance and he follows his Canadian colleague into a side room. A few minutes later, the two doctors emerge with our labourer who returns to join the others. Doc Hammond sidles up to me and murmurs, "False alarm. They are being rather paranoid about this European 'flu outbreak, but our chap just has a gut ache that is causing him to sweat. Nothing to be concerned about".

Peters takes charge again, moving the men outside into the cold. The Canadians have set up trestle tables and I see that the men are being fed a hot meal. They are also receiving as many apples as they can carry.

"This is all they will get today so tell them to makes the best of it"

The Canadian Captain remains aloof and dismissive, obviously not caring too much about the welfare of the new arrivals.

"They'll stay here tonight and we'll start ferrying them over to the city tomorrow to put them on trains that will take them across country to Halifax. As soon as they've eaten, we'll take them to one of the reception halls we keep for Chinks where they'll spend the night. We've arranged for you English guys to bunk down in our transit lines but the

Chinks will have to huddle together. There's no bedding to spare for so many of them. Your other two companies are to get the same when they get here, so there'll be plenty of bodies. The stink will stop them freezing".

It's just turned eight in the evening and the last of the men are ensconced in the 'assembly hall'. Fifteen hundred men packed in like tinned fish with hardly room to move, but at least the closeness is warming their freezing bodies. Peters and the CSMs from the other two Companies have sorted territory and have managed to arrange for the at least some of the men to lie down in shifts. The Chinamen are remarkably stoic in the circumstances. I think our lads would be close to rioting at this point. There's a staircase to an upper gantry near the door, so I climb up a few steps with Zhao Da-hai and get him to yell out for silence. He interprets as I try to put a positive note to my voice.

"Get what rest you can and enjoy the warmth. In a short while you will be taken on the next leg of your travels. There will be a short march and then you will get onto boats that will take you into the city on the other side of this island. The city is called Vancouver. You will then be put onto a train for a long journey across Canada to another ocean!"

Zhao Da-hai sounds nervous but his stilted voice carries well and the men settle down to wait. I have their trust and hope that it is not in vain. If the Canadians are keen to get our people moving as quick as they say, the move to the train should not be delayed in any way.

To Hell with the Canadian's offer of a bunk in the transit lines. I have the comfort of my greatcoat and I've spent worse nights in the trenches.

"CSM. I'm going to stay with the men tonight".

"Yes, Sir. So are we".

Peters grins at me and I look down to see the other two CSMs have moved in with their respective charges.

"I've a feeling we will get a short night here, Sir. I've ordered everyone to be ready for a move at any time ".

Sure enough, just after midnight the Canadians are back and we are told to prepare to move. We assemble the men in company formation and march them back down to the quayside. Several small vessels are waiting to take us across the water into Vancouver itself. There's a bright moon shining and the city looks deserted. Mugs of tea are served as we take the short trip and this mollifies my foul mood a bit, but I'm less than impressed with the way things are run here. Once we reach the city, we leave the ferry area and form up outside on the road. We then march through deserted streets. We march silently down the middle of broad avenues, past empty churches with their doors closed to the elements, tall brick and stone buildings, many with ornate carvings, and rows of shops with large glassed windows. The city is modern and orderly but it's empty.

Eventually we arrive at a huge railway station. There's a long line of railway carriages hooked to two large engines way down at the far end of the platform. The carriages bear the markings of the Canadian Pacific Railway. Our 'liaison' officer appears, together with a man in another uniform who is introduced as the commander of the railway guard that is apparently going to travel with us as well. There'll be three sets of guards in place for each carriage: we British, a contingent of Canadian soldiers and, now, railway guards.

My rising anger disappears as I notice the Joker Su Ting-fu approach Corporal Anderson who is talking to two of the Canadians beside the steps to one of the carriages. Anderson looks at him warily as he approaches but, when Su Ting-fu slams to attention and throws a salute worthy of a British Guardsman, the Canadians just stare back in confusion. Anderson tries not to laugh, but the Canadian soldier on guard returns the Chinaman's salute, while the railway guard looks on with his mouth hanging open. Many of Su Ting-fu's companions burst into laughter but, before the Canadians can react, Su Ting-fu retreats back into the safely of the sea of oriental, indistinguishable humanity that is still being shepherded on board.

I'm delighted.

Eventually the train is fully loaded and we begin to roll forward. We are once more on the move.

The windows of the carriages are covered over with some sort of white paste on the outside, which stops us from seeing out. There's a Canadian soldier standing nearby so I ask him what it is we are not supposed to see. He looks at me strangely and says, "Sir, that's not to stop you seein' out. It's to stop people seein' in. There'd be all Hell to play if people knew that a hoard of Orientals was criss-crossin' the country".

Admin orderlies arrive with boxes of food and, once Peters lets me know that the men have been fed, I settle down to eat. I'm sharing a carriage with the other officers in our Company but they are all on duty elsewhere. The Padre and the Doc are making sure the few sick men we have with us are settled, Hastings is carrying out his Admin duties, Bertram is nowhere to be seen, and the Russian has secured himself a berth with the three Company Commanders. Once again it serves a mutually pleasant purpose. In the meantime, I have the carriage to myself and I take a swig from the bottle of whisky I managed to wheedle out of the 'liaison' officer when we arrived in Vancouver.

Suddenly everything goes pitch dark and howls of fear bellow all around me. Panic sets in and I go out into the corridor and yell for calm. Seconds later, the blackness disappears and one of the guards calls out that we have just been through a tunnel. He's laughing uncontrollably and then he sneers at the men saying, "They're all like kittens! Off to a war and yet terrified by going through a tunnel. Frightened of the dark, are we?"

Before he can say more, we enter another tunnel but, this time, lights come on in the carriage and I can see men who are fearful but in control. When we emerge from this tunnel, there's a burst of embarrassed laughing and, as a third tunnel is entered, the situation becomes a matter of mere annoyance. Once again however, the Canadian attitude is far from helpful. What is their problem?

The train stops frequently during the journey. Sometime people get on and others get off but, as far as I can tell, they are just changing guards. We are the only passengers and once again the Chinese are being treated badly, this time by the Canadians.

The Padre's not happy either.

"I raised this very issue with a vicar I met in Vancouver while we were at the station. Chap called the Reverend Bill Ramsay who had heard of our arrival and came out to see what was going on. He's very concerned about the anti-Chinese sentiment that he says pervades Canadian society. He related the history of Chinese immigrants who helped to build Canada's vast railway system and how badly they were paid and treated. By his account, Chinese workers have been pouring into Canada since the mid-1800s when gold was discovered in a place called Fraser Canyon. He said that during this gold rush, many Chinese settlements were established in and around Vancouver and, in the 1880s, a huge number of Chinamen were contracted to build the Canadian Pacific Railway".

"It sounds a bit like our scheme".

The Padre nods and continues.

"They slowly moved further East, building Chinatowns in the larger cities as they went. He says that one of the Canadian Pacific Railway construction contractors, an American, enlisted a number of Chinese labourers from California to help build the railway. Most of these men deserted the railway construction to work the goldfields for themselves, and so he hired more Chinamen, mainly from China's Guangdong province. He apparently brought over 5,000 labourers as 'guest-workers', but many of them deserted too and moved onto the goldfields. It seems that the Chinese were only paid one dollar a day for their efforts, while white, Negro and native Canadians were paid three times as much".

"Well that's not fair", I throw in. "At least we are paying a fair wage for a fair day's work.

"Yes, Charlie" the Padre replies irritably, "Now, if you would kindly stop interrupting. In addition to poor wages, the Chinese, unlike other workers, had to buy their own food and pay for their own equipment. This meant they were unable to save any money to send home to their families, which was why so many deserted the railway company to seek their fortunes on the goldfields. Those who stayed to work on the railways were given work that was not only hard, it was very dangerous. Many died from accidents, misuse of explosives, rock falls and so on. He believes that the Chinese were being exploited and their desertions to work for themselves in the goldfields were understandable. After the railway was completed, many Chinese were left with no work and were no longer seen as being of any use to either the Railway or the Government. Many were also too poor to return home but, despite the horror stories, many new Chinese immigrants continued to come here to join their families and clan members, and so the Government passed an act of Parliament that levied a tax of $50 on any Chinese citizen entering the country. When this failed to deter them, the rate was increased to $100 and then again to $500. This is about ten years' income for a Chinese labourer, yet this is the amount of the levy that exists today. It's being waived for those serving in the Chinese Labour Corps as we're are seen as being part of the war effort, but only on the basis that we ship our people across the country as quick as possible and in virtual secrecy".

The Padre pauses for breath and then launches forth again.

"It goes further than that. Bill Ramsay told me that two of his parishioners who are Chinese tried to enlist in the army. They were born here and have Canadian citizenship but they were refused! He says that under the law in British Columbia, Chinese men, whether naturalised or not, are not allowed to serve in the armed forces. Last August, the government introduced conscription when voluntary enlistment fell below required levels, but Orientals are still not conscripted. Like you, I ask myself, what are they afraid of?"

There's a discreet knock on the carriage door and there stands Sergeant Major Peters. It's time to check on the men again.

"We must talk more on this subject, Padre", I tell my friend with a smile. "You're a treasure trove of information".

As I walk along the corridors I become angry.

"We are well out of any habitation, Sergeant Major. Let's get some of these windows up".

"A lot of them are nailed shut, Sir. Leave it with me".

As the windows are being freed, the Canadian guards protest and the situation turns nasty.

"Hold it, Mr Peters. Leave it there for the moment. I'll talk to the CO later and see if we can get this done without the risk of a punch-up with our so-called allies. Go and get Zhao Da-hai and we'll keep on doing our rounds".

Zhao Da-hai is not happy but then neither am I. My grasp of Mandarin is now getting to the stage where I can tell if Zhao Da-hai is distorting the meaning of the words we share with the men. I can also tell by their body language that he is being devious. I decide that I'll get Hastings to do the rounds with us at some point to see what he can find out.

The train has stopped at a deserted station and all the doors are opened to ventilate the carriages. I can see a sign that reads 'Ignacio', which seems to be a small town on a wide empty plain, the empty land stretching beyond for miles in every direction. Some of the men crowd around the few windows we managed to open and, as we walk down the carriage corridor, I can hear shouting and laughter. It's Su Ting-fu playing the fool once again. Standing back from the open window but with a view over the heads of the other labourers, he chooses his time carefully. Half a dozen Canadian soldiers march onto the platform opposite, and they're brought to a halt by their corporal who then disappears from sight. The guards stand rigidly to attention, determined not to display any slackness in front of those gawking at them from the train.

Su Ting-fu yells out, 'Squad! Squad, Right Turn!' and the soldiers obey, turning as one to face the grinning Chinese.

"Stan'at ease!" yells the prankster in perfect imitation of one of our English drill instructors.

The squad obeys with precision. Su Ting-fu then follows this with more drill commands just like those he had learned during his training. The Canadians follow the commands precisely and the drill continues for a few minutes more until their furious corporal comes racing down the platform. He has witnessed his squad's antics and he is not happy. Looking round in vain for someone to abuse, he turns instead to the squad and tears into them. The Chinese are laughing themselves hoarse as the red-faced corporal marches his men out of sight. It's a bright interlude in an otherwise drab journey, a journey that seems to be taking forever. It's time for another of the Padre's stories.

"Tell me more about this opium business, Padre. You were very harsh on our role in this affair. Not very patriotic, like".

My companion settles back comfortably and begins.

"Let me tell you about two of our patriotic countrymen who founded one of the most powerful companies in the Far East. They were both Scotsmen and they were traders back in the 1820s. William Jardine was a Scottish doctor and his partner, a fellow Scot called James Matheson, was a graduate from Edinburgh University. They formed a company called, not surprisingly, Jardine, Matheson and Co. Their fortunes were mainly based on the trade in opium, although they also traded in tea and cotton. When we took possession of Hong Kong after the first Opium War, they set up their headquarters there and they prospered mightily. They also deal in insurance, shipping and railways and a host of smaller enterprises. Lately they've been expanding into Shanghai, building cotton mills and a brewery and so on. They're very successful, incredibly rich and totally ruthless."

The Padre spoke in his best preacher's tone of voice and I said mischievously, "I wonder if they'll have a job for a Geordie war veteran with one eye and a smattering of Mandarin?"

"Good grief, Charlie. Did you learn nothing from that den I took you to last month? Those wretches soaked in the Hell of addiction are a direct result of the trade these Scotsmen are steeped in. Our very Empire is steeped in this trade. How could you even begin to think of joining them? Really, Charlie, you disappoint me!"

Realising I've overstepped some line, I desperately look for a way to change the subject. He's sitting beside a newspaper, one he bought in Vancouver and has read from cover to cover, so I ask him, "What did you find so interesting the paper, Padre? You have certainly got your money's worth from it".

My friend glares at me and then shakes his head and smiles.

"What am I going to do with you?"

He picks up his paper and says, "This may interest you. It's a story about Pu Yi, you know the boy who is still, I suppose, Emperor of China. Last July, he was restored to his throne in all its glory by a decree issued by a warlord called, it says here, Zhang Xun. This general surrounded Peking with his army and Pu Yi, who's just nine years old don't forget, became ruler of China again. That was the intention, but after a few days, a plane dropped three bombs on the Forbidden City and all the Emperor's supporters abandoned him. The poor child has gone back to living his meaningless life, just as before. What do you think of that?"

I grinned, glad to feel a more light-hearted mood.

"Three bombs to end a conflict? We can learn a lot from the Chinese, don't you think?"

At long last, eight days after leaving Vancouver, we arrive at the port of Halifax on the Atlantic coast and we leave the train with relief. Several of the men from one of the carriages have become ill during the journey and we have them taken to an aid station. They all have some kind of breathing problem and are being isolated from the rest of us to prevent whatever it is that ails them from spreading. They can join us later but, in the meantime, the rest of the men are formed up and marched to a field three or four miles out of town where we bed them down in lines of round, bell-shaped ten-men tents.

The next three days are spent camping out and the good-humoured nature of the Chinese quickly returns. The Admin boys have the camp ovens set up quickly and they serve up hot meals and a constant supply of tea. Sergeant Fredricks has acquired three footballs and a long, thick rope.

Our charges run madly around, chasing any ball that comes close, with Fredricks making the most noise and then he forms teams for tug-o'-war. This is as happy as I have seen the men since we left China.

"Just look at them".

I'm sitting with the Padre and Lieutenant Hastings, having morning tea in the open. Young Bertram has joined us, looking as lost as ever. Not for the first time I wonder how on Earth is he going to cope with the Front?

"Listen to the men. It's a pity we can't just stay here."

Lieutenant Hastings looks shocked when I say this. He can't wait to get to France but I ignore the younger man and think to myself, "I've been there, son. You have the horror to come".

Bertram just sits there, staring into space.

"Why don't you two go and join in the fun with the men. Have some fun together. Do some more bonding. It will do you both good in the long run."

Hastings grins and leaps up while Bertram obviously takes my words to be an order rather than a suggestion and slowly follows his fellow lieutenant out into the fray. The Padre shakes his head sorrowfully.

"What can we do to help that young man?" he asks of no one.

"They'll have to cope for themselves soon enough, Padre. I've my own nightmares to cope with".

The Padre leans forward to place his hand on my arm, and says, "There's a doctor at the mission here in Halifax. Why don't we go and see him before we sail? I know you've been seen by Hammond but why not get a second opinion?"

I feel angry again and snort, "Nothing's going to change. We're going to France and that's that!"

The Padre jerks back at my reaction and blurts out, "Charlie, I'm not going to go to France with you. I'm going back to England to see the woman I love".

Chapter Eleven
The Atlantic

All I can do is stare at the preacher open mouthed.

He blushes deeply and pulls a crumpled telegram out of his pocket.

"This arrived a couple of weeks before we left Qingdao. It's from a lady called Margaret Jenkins. That's her married name. It's rather a delicate story really."

The Padre takes a mouthful of his tea looking very uncomfortable and stammers, "Basically I suppose - what I mean is - Oh, dash it Charlie, I've been in love with this woman since I was a teenager."

Once his decision to talk is made, he continues rapidly.

"I was born into a devout family as you can probably imagine. We lived in a small village called Barnsworth in Yorkshire in the north of England and, from an early age, I wanted to follow my uncle and become a missionary, to spread God's will and the message his son Jesus Christ gave to us. As the disciple Mark ordained, 'Go into all the world and proclaim the good news to the whole creation', and I've tried my best to do that. I grew up with this calling, and my future seemed to be clear, until I met a young girl who moved into the village when I was sixteen. We became close friends and I fell in love with her, but all she wanted at that time was my friendship. Her name's Margaret and she encouraged me in my religious studies, but made it clear she wouldn't take on a life of missionary work, and I was faced with an agonising decision. Should I pursue the feelings I had for her, or remain true to my faith? It was a terrible time, deep as I was in my teenage years, until the question was resolved for me by my sweetheart herself. Margaret began going out with another boy."

Fortified by another mouthful of tea, the Padre continues.

"I focused on my studies with increased vigour, and the day came when I was accepted by my church to go to China as a missionary to spread the gospel. My sweetheart married the other boy and we parted, agreeing to remain friends and to write to each other, even though I felt a deep sadness at the thought of leaving her. I arrived in China way back in 1884, determined to put my past life well and truly behind me and to focus on my calling. God was kind to me at first as I fell in love with China and the life I had to lead. The language came easily, and the people I met accepted me in a friendly manner, even if they laughed at the way I dressed. Life was hard but fulfilling. Eight months ago, I received a letter from my mother. In it, she told me the girl I fell in love with all those years ago had lost her husband when a Zeppelin air ship dropped bombs on London. Sadly, Margaret and her husband were there on holiday I suppose. Imagine! The Germans are taking their war to England and deliberately killing innocent civilians. It's barbaric! Margaret is now a widow, still living back in our village in Yorkshire. I wrote to her when I heard the news, offering her my sympathy and my continued friendship, and she wrote back to me in a lovely letter. It was no more than a letter of friendship, I know that, but we have kept in touch since. This telegram tells me that she is willing to meet me again, so the timing for me is ideal. This is the real reason I joined the Labour Corps in the first place. I have lived with hope, and God has been kind. I need to renew my faith but I also need to find out how Margaret feels about me. I intend to court her and to ask her to marry me. If she will share my life in England, and then possibly back here in China, I will know my faith has been rewarded!"

The padre puts his head in his hands and sighs deeply.

"So, there you have it, my young friend. As I say, this telegram is from Margaret, telling me she would like to see me again so I'll be leaving you when we arrive in England. I know you expected me to be with you all the way to France, but now you know, I hope you will not think badly of me."

I don't think badly of him at all, just amazed. I could sense back in China that he wasn't telling me the full story as to why he wanted to join us to go to France, and now I know. The sly old dog.

The defiant sound of Major Robert's bagpipes leads us as we march directly from the camp onto a quayside where there's another ship lying in wait to take us across the Atlantic to Liverpool, ever closer to France. The discipline we have trained for and the chain of command we have in place sees the men once more stowed on board, again in cramped conditions, but now we sail onwards as experienced travellers. Routine is quickly established.

As the ship is preparing to sail, a Chinese government official comes on board. He tells us he's employed by the Chinese government to inspect the conditions in which we are taking their citizens to the war in Europe. I'm able to tackle him shortly after we begin to move away from the dockside, but it seems that he has little authority, he's merely a functionary. He can observe and report back to the government in Peking, but that is the extent of his role. He seems to be more concerned with the risk of disease than any other matter and he soon leaves me to hurry away to the safety of his cabin. To me we are now facing more pressing risks than catching this cold that is spreading. The Royal

Navy is imposing a very effective blockade of the German coast and few of their surface ships are getting in or out without being detected but their submarines are getting through. The CO has told me to warn the men of the danger but first I have to persuade them that such things as underwater ships exist!

I gather all the *p'aitous* together and tell them, "I've told you already that you will see things on your travels that will amaze you. You now know about ships made of iron that sail *on* the sea but there are also ships that can sail *under* the sea. In France, you will see machines that will fly like birds in the sky and guns that will fire explosives that will travel far out of sight. You are now on an iron ship and we sail on water, right? All of these other things I talked about, and more besides, are real. These are not stories to be used to frighten children. They are not stories of sea serpents or dragons or whatever they are real dangers. We have drills when dangers are near and these drills are to protect you and your men. You must take them seriously".

Several pairs of eyes look back at me seriously and I'm sure that they are taking it all in.

"We are now sailing in very dangerous waters, much more dangerous than any we have sailed in before, and they will get more dangerous as we get closer to Europe. You can begin by telling the men about the danger of showing lights on deck during the night. They've been told more than once but please, stress the danger. You can also tell the men that lifeboat drill is not a game, as many of them seem to think. Tell them to take the drill seriously, as their lives may depend on knowing the drill inside out if we are attacked and we start to sink. There were many people in China who were friends of the Germans in Qingdao and they would know of our journey. They could pass this information on to our enemies who may be waiting for us. If this makes you frightened, then good. Frighten your men enough to make them take our warnings seriously".

I'm pleased to see them nodding and talking among themselves. They may still be sceptical about the existence of submarines but they seem to take my serious tone to mean than there is at least some form of danger that needs protection against. Hopefully they will get the message through to the men. The *p'aitous* have enough English and I keep my words simple but I get Zhao Da-hai to interpret to add emphasis and watch as he does so. When he talks, his words are received in a sullen manner. There's a problem here and I need to find out why. Is it him or the words he uses? Later! The main thing is to get the men to take the drills and so on seriously. I'm satisfied that I have done that, so I dismiss the men telling Li Cheng-fang, Li Zhang and Sun Jun to stay behind as the others leave. Zhao Da-hai wants to stay too but I tell him to leave. He looks positively fearful.

"OK you three. What's going on with Zhao Da-hai? Ever since we left Qingdao I know that there is a problem. What is it?"

The three Chinamen look back at me with expressionless faces.

Li Cheng-fang speaks up saying, "There is no problem, Mister Armstrong".

Sun Jun and Li Zhang nod their heads in agreement. They return my stare without blinking and I'm at a loss to take it further. This may be a job for the Padre before he leaves us and, after a long silence, I dismiss them and go in search of the preacher. When I find him on another deck, I tell him, "I've spoken to a number of the men as discreetly as possible but all I can say is that the dislike they felt for Zhao Da-hai back in the camp has increased significantly and I'd even go further and say they almost hate the man. No one will tell me why, but it is not a good situation, Padre. For once they will just not take me into their confidence. I'm not sure what to do".

I'm faced with another problem that puts Zhao Da-hai out of my mind. Ever since we left Halifax, there has been an increase in the number of men who have become sick with this flu' thing that is worrying the medics so much. It is much more serious than I thought as one of the patients died last night. How do you die from a cold? But that is the reality. We have stricter quarantine put in place and the CO orders that the dead man's body be buried at sea. This almost causes a riot and the Padre implores the CO to change his order.

He later tells me, "The Chinese want their dead sent back to China so that they can rest with their ancestors. This is a very important cultural issue, Charlie. I need your support to get the CO to recognise how important it is. We could lose so much of the respect we have built up so carefully over so many months".

When I go to the CO, he accepts my argument that a burial at sea could affect discipline but he refuses point blank to return the body of the man who has just died to China.

"This will not be the last of them I fear. We're not returning our own dead to their families so why should we make an exception for the Chinese. He can be taken ashore in Liverpool after we dock and be buried there. The Padre can see to this before he leaves us. He's told me you know of his plans to desert. Bloody cheek, if you ask me. He's used us, Charlie. Bloody cheek of the man. That'll be all".

I take the news to my friend, but as I approach him he looks quite frantic.

"Zhao Da-hai has gone missing. It's being said that he has fallen overboard!"

Li Zhang is by far the most reserved of the three *p'aitous* in Number One section but it is he who gives us a hint as to what might have happened.

"Sir, maybe you ask Zhou Xiao-bing about Zhao Da-hai".

I gather all six of the *p'aitous* in the Company and ask them outright what they know of the disappearance. Hastings and the Padre are with me but the six men before me speak enough English to understand my question.

Zhou Xiao-bing, the gangster, answers me in a tone dripping with arrogance.

"He should not had too much rice wine. Bad things happen when you drink much, 'specially on slipping ship floor."

The others remain silent and no amount of prodding from me or from my fellow Englishmen, who ask the same questions in Mandarin, brings any other answer.

I dismiss the six Chinamen but watch Zhou Xiao-bing as he goes to join his brother and other members of his squad. They sit together uneasily, some smiling as if sharing in a conspiracy, others looking fearful. A young ladylike coolie sits down close to the gangster's side. He says something with a sort of giggle but his humour ends abruptly in a yelp of pain as Zhou Xiao-bing sinks his fingers into the young man's thigh.

Not for the first time I think to myself that there is a depth to these Orientals that I may never understand.

Chapter Twelve
Liverpool and beyond

The Padre looks to be in a pensive mood as we sail slowly up the Mersey River into Liverpool. It's the thirtieth day of January 1918, and I join the preacher as he leans on a rail looking out at the city skyline.

"Welcome home, Malcolm".

He ignores my familiarity and says, "I'm to go with the body of the lad who died and see to his burial here at a place called Aintree. Once that's done I'll go on to Yorkshire, so we'll be saying goodbye shortly. I'll miss you, my young Geordie friend, so you take good care and look after yourself".

As we shake hands his grip tightens. "Charlie, we've never really talked about this but how strong is *your* faith?"

This takes me unawares and I can only give a soldier's answer.

"No atheists in the trenches, Padre. You know that".

There are tears in his eyes as he turns to walk away.

Large crowds gather at the pier to watch as our men come ashore and form up. The reception we receive is welcoming with flags waved, people clapping, and even a few cheers.

There is none of euphoria of the early days back in 1914. Then women threw flowers, older men cheered with chests bursting with pride, their hats waved in triumph and small boys ran alongside joining in the excitement of the day.

"It will all be over by Christmas", we were told.

"Play your part while you can".

As we march smartly though the streets to Lime Street Station as a formed body of men, English and Chinese together, with Major Roberts leading us, bagpipes blazing, the contrast to reception in Canada is remarkable. These crowds are much more sombre but the British public, despite the occasional Trade Union banner calling for no foreign labour taking 'our jobs', are clearly desperate to make us feel welcome. I suppose that we are seen as being here to make a difference and, as we march with pride, the crowds have every right to cheer. At last our men are being treated with the respect that they are due, and backs stiffen significantly.

When we arrive at the railway station, Major Roberts dismisses the officers and hands the Company over to Sergeant Major Peters. The platforms are packed with people, many in uniform, some obviously returning from the Front with injuries, while others kiss their loved ones as they bravely head off into the War. Tears are being shed all around. There are tears of joy for those who are welcomed and tears of grief for those who depart. A train has been allocated specifically for our Company, and all five hundred or so men are lined up to be loaded on board. While this is happening, I buy a newspaper and find a seat in a small café on the platform, drinking 'English' tea with milk and sugar and eating a large pork pie.

Any feeling of guilt as I shirk my duty is buried in the joy of being back in my homeland doing something ordinary. I can see Peters from where I sit, and the man has everything well in hand as I would expect. The way that our NCOs link in with the Chinese foremen is a pleasure to watch. Squads are allocated to carriages and filled with men who settle in with commendable discipline. Within an hour, everyone has been accounted for and ensconced onto the transport that will take us closer to the battlefields. We will go south to Folkestone where we will get on a ferry to take us over the Channel. The jelly in the pork pie now in my stomach curdles up into the back of my throat at the thought. South to Folkestone! My entire being is screaming out to board a train going north to Newcastle. My eye socket begins to ache terribly and, for a moment, a feeling of sheer misery becomes overwhelming.

"There you are, Sir. Sergeant Major Peter's compliments, and could you please join us on board. We leave in five minutes."

Lieutenant Bertram stands fidgeting in front of me and I bawl out, "Stand to attention when you address me!"

The young subaltern almost faints on the spot. No longer feeling self-pity, I growl," Follow me and for God's sake try to look as if you are in His Majesty's Army and not just dressed up for a bloody pantomime."

There are no blacked-out windows on this train and I join my fellow passengers gazing out as field and village flash by. We were able to catch glimpses of the vast, empty snow-covered plains as we travelled across Canada but this is England in winter and, despite it being cold, wet and miserable, it's surprisingly welcome. I realise how much I have missed it all these months. The pleasant feeling doesn't last though. We're nearing the end of our journey with memories of the Front flooding in and I become increasingly anxious.

There are continual delays as we travel but the Admin Section does a great job in keeping up a steady supply of tea and food. The food is mainly in the form of sandwiches made from thick slices of bread smeared with jam, which the Chinamen take to with gusto. If they miss their rice, they make no mention of it. In the absence of the Padre, I turn to Lieutenant Hastings for news from and about the men. If I'm honest with myself, I'm also looking to him for companionship. At one point in our tedious journey across England I find him alone in the compartment set aside for our Company officers.

He stiffens to attention when I join him but I smile and offer him a snifter of whiskey from the flask I've managed to acquire. When he declines, I ask him to tell me more about his background and he begins, reluctantly at first but with increasing ease, to talk about his earlier years growing up in China.

"My father is production manager for a cotton spinning and weaving company in Shanghai. It's a subsidiary of the Jardine-Matheson Group who are based in Hong Kong. He came out to China thirty years ago for a spot of adventure, having learned his craft in the mills in Lancashire and he fell in love with the life. I feel the same way actually. Shanghai's my home, I was born there and I'll go back when this is all over".

"I've heard of this Jardine-Matheson outfit from the Padre. I thought they were opium traders".

Hastings becomes quite defensive and replies, "They started that way but now the group is involved in all manner of commerce. Before I joined the Chinese Labour Corps I was being trained in the insurance business, but we are also involved in shipping, railways and all manner of other businesses.

"Just out of interest, why did you enlist?"

"China is changing. She has a great future to look forward to but first she must get rid of the shackles of foreign concessions and stand on her own feet. Take Shandong province for example. This has been a German concession for years and now the Japanese are taking the place of the Germans. We look like having tens of thousands of Chinese in the Corps working for the British and another huge number working for the French. This must carry some weight when the Germans are beaten. China has declared war on Germany and, even if we aren't sending troops, the Corps are just as good in a way as we will be doing all the logistical work needed to help defeat the enemy. We must have a good say when the war is over and the spoils are shared".

The lad's eyes are sparkling and I'm amused to hear him use the words 'us' and 'we' when referring to China and the Labour Corps.

"The National Government seems to be in a bit of a mess though, don't you think?"

Hastings shakes his head dismissively.

"Teething troubles, Sir. Sun Yat-sen is a remarkable man who will do great things and take us out of the feudal past and into the modern future".

He's got the bit between his teeth and I decide to ask him about the gangster in our midst.

"Mr Hastings, I'm concerned about the antics of Zhou Xiao-bing. The Padre reckons he's part of some secret society. What do you think?"

"Definitely. The men are fearful of him and of his brother. I suspect that they are both members of the Honourable Qing Bang Society, the so-called Green Gang. My father deals with them regularly. He pays them, bribes them if you like, to get his goods moved through the docks. It may not be the English way to operate but it's certainly the way of China. They lead by fear whereas *p'aitous* Li Cheng-fang and Li Zhang, for example, lead by earning the men's respect. We have selected them because we recognise their obvious leadership qualities. These qualities come naturally from the fact that they are both cousins in an old respected Shandong family. I've heard that the family lost its fortune years ago but, even as poor farmers, they still have the respect of the other men because of their family history. Li Cheng-fang joined us to help restore his family's wealth but his cousin, Li Zhang, joined us to hide from the authorities. Rumour has it that he deserted from the army when Yuan Shikai deposed Sun Yat-sen as president and … ".

"Steady on Hastings. You are losing me. Stick to what this all means for us and our roles when we get into France".

"Sir, in simple terms, I believe that the interpreter Zhao Da-hai was blackmailing Li Zhang and that his death was somehow organised by Zhou Xiao-bing. I have no proof, so I've kept quiet, but if my suspicion is right then this will mean that the family of Li Cheng-fang and Li Zhang will owe a debt of honour to the Qing Bang Society, this criminal Green Gang, who can call in a favour whenever it suits them. It's the Chinese way, Sir. That's how things are done".

The railway station at Folkestone is crowded too but Sergeant Major Peters takes control and once more the labourers from China form up and march away into the streets. The general public, who no doubt see men marching to and fro every day, go about their business and give them scant notice as they pass by. There are no cheers in this town.

"The men are settled, sir. All is well."

Peters stands in front of me in the late afternoon sun. We are to stay in here in Folkestone for two days and the men are now billeted under canvas in a large camp in town.

I thank Peters who salutes smartly and leaves me with my thoughts.

The transit area that will be our home is in a large field of ten-man tents, with adequate, well-established catering, latrine and administration areas staffed by regular personnel. There is even an hospital on site and I find that I have little to do. The light's beginning to fade and there's a tent set aside to serve as an officer's mess, so it's there that I head for. I order my first English beer in nearly three years, with a double whisky chaser, grab a copy of today's edition of 'The Times' that is lying on a table and I find a seat well away from the other patrons.

The front page carries the story of a Member of Parliament who has been fined four hundred pounds for hoarding, another expressing concern over a spate of forged Bills of Exchange hitting the market, and a report of a march through the streets of London by four companies of the Jewish Regiment. The men, 428 in number, with 12 officers, were greeted enthusiastically by the general public and then given a rousing welcome by the Mayor and Mayoress of Stepney, before being farewelled as they headed off to the Front. More lambs to the slaughter, I mumble to myself. I then spot an advertisement in the personal column that reads, "Young officer, wounded, commercial ability, go ahead and energetic, seeks outdoor appointment as representative of high class commercial house. References. Reply Box 562." My morbid state of mind leads me to think of my prospects after the war, and I ask myself, "Do I really want to return to the coal mining business?"

There's an article in the body of the paper about the situation in Russia. Wartime censorship makes for scant news of real worth, but I scour the piece avidly. Following the Bolsheviks' overthrow of the Kerensky government and the installation of a Communist one under a fella called Lenin, Russia has ended its war against Germany. Asmiroff will love that but ... Shit! The end of the war for Russia means that Germany will have tens of thousands of troops that they can redeploy from the Eastern Front to the battlefields that we are heading for. The article says that the war in the East ended in December, and it's now February 1918. Our side must be close to exhaustion. Additional troops on the German side will mean they have, or their General Staff will think they have, a great advantage, which means that they must surely launch an offensive soon. Where are the bloody Americans? This is all too depressing. I'm off to my bed.

It's our second day here and, just after breakfast, the CO calls an 'O' group.

"Well, we've managed to get this far without too many problems, gentlemen. Keep up the good work. Captain Asmiroff has left us for the moment and the bloody Padre has deserted so we will press on as best we can. Charlie, you and Mr Hastings will have to share the load left by Asmiroff until I find out if the beggar is coming back to us or, if not, until I can arrange for a replacement. Doc, I want full medicals for the men before they go into France. Facilities here will be far better than those closer to the fighting, so take advantage of it. Everyone must be prepared to move at two hours' notice. The channel crossings are in a shambles and we may have to take pot-luck. Any questions?"

Damn and blast Asmiroff. What is he playing at? As this thought crowds into my mind, Peters speaks up. "The boots our men were issued in China are beginning to show wear and some already need replacing. Have I your permission to get this fixed while we're here, Sir?"

"Certainly, CSM. Get whatever you need and refer any difficulty to me. Anything else?"

We sit silently so the CO ends the meeting saying, "Fine, gentlemen. In that case, you're dismissed. Charlie, stay behind a moment".

Once the others have left, the CO turns and me and barks, "You've started drinking heavily again. What on Earth has got into you, Charlie?"

Major Roberts sits in front of me with a look of concern on his face.

"Look here, laddie," Roberts says softly in his Scottish brogue. "I have a high regard for the way that you have come to terms with your injury. I'm also impressed by your success with the Chinese, but I'm concerned by your isolation from your fellow officers. You've always been a bit of a loner but since the Padre left us you never mix in with any of the other officers. 'Officers should work hard and play hard' has been my motto since I was commissioned way back in '87 but they should do so together. Bonding is an essential part of being a success in the army. Being alone in the army and especially drinking alone as you do is unhealthy. You're close to the Chinese and you care for them a lot but you're too remote from your own kind. Your treatment of that wimp Bertram is understandable in a way but there again you should be supporting the lad or else how's he going to change? According to your record, you have always been a first-class officer and yet now I see you dreaming and talking to yourself and yer breath stinks in the morning. Not good enough, Charlie. If you need to talk, I can do the job the Padre did. Just ask me, alright?"

I feel my face flushing red with embarrassment and reply, "I'm not sure that I understand what you mean, Sir."

"Look son."

The Major with a chest full of campaign ribbons becomes agitated.

"I've seen enough of men who have been through Hell and come out with or without physical injury to know that inside, deep down inside, there are injuries that no one can see. You were fine when you had the Padre as a support but now ... well, if you have to talk about things, don't talk to yourself. God's breath man, di yee want to be put away?"

The Scot lapses into a heavy accent in frustration.

"You're a good officer. Get yer blasted act together, why don't you."

I thought I was ready to face my demons but the CO's outburst has left me feeling weak at the knees. All this time I have been confident that I am performing my duties to the best of my ability. True, I don't mix with the officers from the other two Companies or with Asmiroff, who's a pig anyway, or with the Doc who's every bit a loner as I am and the two Lieutenants are wet behind the ears, although Hastings is proving good value at least, and as for the drinking and talking to myself ...

A wave of panic is flooding over me.

"I need a drink".

I actually hear myself say that!

SHIT!

Luckily there's no one around to see me vomit my insides out, just as I did when first on board ship.

But this isn't seasickness.

There's a canteen nearby run by the YMCA of all people and I go in to order lemonade. The sweet gassiness makes me want to throw up again but I hold it down and order another glass. The young man behind the counter serves me without saying anything and, despite the shake in my hands, I pay him with as much composure as I can muster and head for my tent. There's a half empty bottle of Dewar's White Label under my bed. I hold it in my hand for a few long seconds and then pour it into the ground. It's not yet ten in the morning but everyone is out and about, so I throw myself onto my cot and fall into a troubled sleep.

Chapter Thirteen
Over to France

We're again on the march. In the early morning frost, we march back into Folkestone and down to the docks where another large ship is waiting to take us on board. There are numerous British soldiers already on board but ropes that restrict our men to the rear of the vessel keep them apart from us. The sun is shining brightly when we cast off, but even so, there is a chill wind as we sail out to sea, and those of us who cannot find shelter inside the vessel huddle together on the deck. The Chinese have their padded jackets but my British greatcoat proves as always to be warm, effective and welcome.

We are all issued life jackets but the Chinamen fool around and make light of the matter. The men are roped off from the British soldiers as I expected, but they are also being kept clear of the side of the ship in case of floating mines. We are sailing with three other ships crammed with troops and an escort of two warships. Overhead there is a blimp with a basket hanging underneath. There are people in the basket and the Chinese are gazing up at the airship in amazement and jabbering like schoolboys. I wonder what they will think when they set eyes on aeroplanes for the first time.

In no time at all we are riding at anchor outside the port of Calais, which is crowded with vessels of all shapes and sizes. We have to wait for over four hours before we can enter the quayside and put our feet onto French soil. The men are eventually brought ashore and are formed up quickly in what is now a routine drill. The quayside is soon behind us and we march out of town and up a very steep hill. There's a transit camp the size of a large village, made up of row upon row of tents. Hundreds of troops are staying here and the camp Adjutant directs us to a far corner where we pack in twenty or more men to a ten-man tent. We're told that the kitchens are closed and that we'll not eat until the next day but I see that the British troops around us are packed in just as we are and they're as hungry as we are. The blankets in the tents are crawling with lice so I order Sergeant Major Peters to have the infested bedding piled outside on the ground and to leave them there. The men will be better off sleeping on the camp stretchers provided in their clothes, using their padded jackets for warmth.

After a reasonable breakfast of eggs, bacon, tomatoes and toast, which the men dispatch with speed and good humour washed down with black tea by the gallon, we are off once again, this time by train to a town called Noyelles-sur-Mer. On the way from the station, we pass a sign written in English that reads, 'DO NOT SPEAK TO THE CHINESE.' Underneath, also in large letters, someone had written, 'WHO THE HELL CAN?' As we enter the camp, we pass a stinking line of latrines. There's a notice in English and Chinese, which reads, 'These latrines are reserved for Europeans and are not available for use by Chinese." It's an unpleasant welcome to the Chinese Labour Corps Headquarters and I feel my anger rising. Travel weary yet excited, the men enter the camp, one that is constructed of a series of wooden huts and lines of large tents. A high wire fence surrounds the area and soldiers carrying rifles man the gates. Not again, surely! When are we going to treat the Chinese with some kind of respect?

The CO has called an 'O' Group for an hour's time so I get myself a berth in the officers' lines and then head off to find the CO's office and join the others. Still no sign of Asmiroff, and a young, cheerful Chinese lad is sitting beside Lieutenant Bertram who has his note pad out as usual as we wait the CO's presence. I let my thoughts wander and wonder if our men realised what was really happening when we crossed the Channel. They took the wearing of lifejackets as something to laugh about. Their naivety is touching at times and I watched the disappointment on their faces when they were stopped from going to the ship's rails.

They probably thought that the ropes that held them back were some perverse restriction on our part, whereas they were held back in case the ship hit a floating mine. And once again I wonder what they made of the airship. I laugh out loud at the thought and then pretend I'm clearing my throat as those around me give me strange, enquiring looks.

After five or so minutes, the CO comes in office and we stiffen to attention.

"Sit easy, Gentlemen. Welcome to Noyelles-sur-Mer, the Head Quarters location for the Chinese Labour Corps in Europe. Let me begin by emphasising that our men are to be isolated as much as possible from contact with any non-Chinese, apart from our own officers and NCOs. The official line is that this is due to strict rules of censorship. This is what you are to tell the *p'aitous* and make sure they get that message through to the men under them. The reality is that the upper brass just don't like the idea of them being here despite the fact that the Corps is doing a great job in so many areas. The bastards just don't like the Chinese, never have and probably never will".

Should he be talking like this, I wonder? His face has gone red, so his anger is certainly real.

"Let me introduce our new interpreter, Ma Long".

The young Chinaman beams at us. He seems to be an improvement on the last chap and I smile back.

"Ma Long has been here over a year working for the YMCA and will be an excellent source of local knowledge as we settle in. He's from Hong Kong where they speak Cantonese but his Mandarin is fluent so he will fit in well. Charlie, you and Mr Hastings can introduce him to the *p'aitous* when we finish here. Now I've had some preliminary contact with HQ and we are to stay here in transit for three days and then move further inland. Charlie, you and Mr Peters will be points of contact during our time here. Introduce yourself to the Adjutant, a chap called Aspen. Once you've done that you are to keep an overall eye on things. Still no sign of Asmiroff and I'm not getting much joy in replacing the beggar, so you'll have to keep on as you've been doing. Any questions?"

I'm tempted to raise the unpleasant signs we saw when we arrived but it's better to do this on a one on one basis with the CO when time permits, so I shake my head in response. It's too early for any real problems to have emerged, so the meeting ends and Peters and I grab the new interpreter and head back to the lines.

We find Captain Aspen, a harassed young Ordnance officer who looks near to exhaustion. He greets us in a perfunctory way and tells us that the Labour Corps has been established here for the past two years. We're told to send the men to a large barn of a building where they are to be given yet another medical examination. Mr Peters and Ma Long go to work organising both our staff and the *p'aitous* and, once again, the men line up and strip to the waist in front of medical staff. This time there is nothing superficial in the way that the medics go about their business. Three British doctors in white coats, but in the presence of their own interpreters, examine each man in turn. Each is examined physically but also asked questions about how they are feeling. Questions are asked such as, are you feeling sick in the stomach, or do you have headaches, and so on. Aspen tells me the doctors are seriously concerned about the flu epidemic, which, he tells me, is decimating the Front and they see the Chinamen as potential carriers.

"Carriers? We've only just got here. I've been told it's called the Spanish Flu, not the Chinese Flu! It's our men who are the ones at risk!"

After three days in transit at Noyelles-sur-Mer, we march further inland to the town of Abbeville, where we climb onto trucks. The trucks take us a few miles even further into the French heartland on this never-ending journey to the town of Amiens. On the way, we pass through a town called Vignacourt, where there are lots of other Chinese labourers. Many of them call out greetings and I'm pleased to see that they all look relaxed and happy as they work. As yet there's no sign of any fighting.

We arrive in Amiens late in the day and drive past a huge railway junction in the centre of the town. There are dozens of rail lines merging into a huge marshalling yard and hundreds of different kinds of rolling stock. I can see the men gazing out in awe.

After a short while, we dismount from the vehicles inside a large camp at the edge of Amiens, set up in a similar way to the training camp back in Qingzhou. Again, we have a wire fence surrounding the camp and there are the inevitable guards at the gate. We are allocated huts and we ensure that the men settle in to rest while they can. They are tired but very excited, as we now face the real tasks they all signed up for. They'll soon be working and I'm confident they'll be ready and able to do so.

As we're getting the men settled, an unpleasant Welshman approaches, giving me a perfunctory salute. Speaking with a pronounced superior lisp, he introduces himself as Lieutenant Evans and tells me that he is the Camp Adjutant.

"I'm to give you a tour of the camp and point out where your Chinks can and cannot go. If you'd like to follow me".

My hackles rise and I bark, "Try adding 'Sir' when you address me Lieutenant. Do not call my men 'Chinks' and try to use the word please. I'm not under your command".

The Welshman takes a step back and flushes with anger.

"As you wish, *Sir*. Would you please follow me".

The tour is quite basic, with the principal point made that the Chinese are to be restricted to certain areas and are not to leave the camp unless on work detail or by the express permission of a British officer.

"The Camp Commandant's policy is that such permission is not to be given lightly".

Hiding behind the assumption of higher command, Evans adds, "It is also his policy that your people are not to fraternise with the French civilians who work in the camp, nor are they to look to any form of entertainment outside the camp".

The bugger actually smirks at me and continues, "If any of your people have any grievances they cannot sort out among themselves, they can present written petitions to the British staff. Any such petitions should be placed in locked petition boxes that are provided in each hut. These rules have been made by CLC Headquarters and have worked a treat so far, Sir".

He ends his words in a sneering tone and I control my anger, thinking it best to go along with the situation until I have a better feel for the place. We have had no need for petitions so far and I will certainly not be encouraging such procedures, rules or no rules.

We stop outside a large hut and once again the Welshman irritates me by saying, "What the Chinese do have is the YMCA. That's about all I need to show you, Sir. I have other duties so do you have any questions … please?"

Once he is gone, the new interpreter Ma Long speaks up.

"There are many good programs here in YMCA. Please, Sir, you have time we go in and I show".

The hut is large, warm and well served with chairs, tables and a canteen serving food and drinks. There are a few Chinese enjoying the facility and we are made feel welcome with broad smiles all round.

"I worked here before I get job helping you, Sir. We run many programs to help Chinese people who come to here. The Young Men's Christian Association have brought many men and women to France from many countries to give talks, provide rest facilities and set up entertainment. We also have cinemas for anyone and everyone. All of Chinese labourers are given specific attention by us in YMCA. We have been active in China for many years and many non-Chinese volunteers can speak Mandarin and Cantonese, some even in dialects of various remote regions. All can write Chinese language characters, which is same for all Chinese. Members of YMCA can help your men who cannot write letters to families China. The good Lord has blessed us with this facility, so we should all be truly thankful".

Ma Long ended with words that made me think of saying grace before a meal and I smiled at him saying, "This sounds like an excellent set up, Ma Long. I'm sure the men will benefit greatly". With that, it was time for a late 'supper' of tea and a stale sandwich, then to my bed.

Welcome to the Front.

Chapter Fourteen
Down to business

It's Monday, the eleventh day of February 1918, and as I wake, I remember Ma Long saying that this is the start of the Chinese New Year. He explained that the Year of the Snake comes to an end and the Year of the Horse begins. It just serves to emphasise to me how different our two cultures are. The Chinese tradition is to greet the New Year with fireworks, and I remember the noise of fireworks that turned out the guard back in China when a wedding in the nearby village began at two minutes past seven in the morning. Apparently, this was the precise moment the local fortune-teller deemed the 'auspicious time' for the couple to marry, and the celebrations started with firecrackers and what sounded like a full-scale infantry assault. We laughed about it later but the guard commander at the time became the butt of many jibes.

There'll be no fireworks for our Chinese this New Year, but then I realise that the noise that woke me from my bed was an artillery barrage and not that far away either. I look out and see bright flashes that fill the sky. Perhaps the Chinese Gods are celebrating the New Year for us? I feel strangely homesick for the first time in many weeks and I realise with some surprise that it has taken almost four months for us to get from the training camp in Shandong to this, our new home in France. What I find really surprising is that I miss China! The reality is that we are closer to the Front than I would have liked. Thinking back to the briefing we were given last night, the shelling must be around St Quentin, eight miles or so to the east. My body and mind shake briefly in unison.

"So, the killing continues."

The thought leaves me feeling rather sick in the stomach. Two years in China have passed. Two years of contact with Chinese labourers who have a humour, stoicism and an acceptance of their hard lot in life that is so reminiscent of my former life with Geordie miners. In China, I found a form of peace, but, here in civilised Europe, the killing goes on as it did before. Desperately fighting off the need for a whiskey, I throw on my uniform and stagger slightly as I head to the mess for breakfast.

After breakfast, I sit down with a copy of the Adjutant's briefing guide, written for British officers who are to work with the Chinese. It's the same 'guide' the unpleasant Welshman read from and I find it disturbing. It begins with the statement 'the Chinese coolie has an inherent contempt for foreigners'. I hear myself laugh out loud at this, and I sarcastically wonder why? Any contempt they feel must come from our intrusion into their homeland and our superior attitudes towards them all the bloody time. They have every right to feel as they do. I think back to the medical examination the men received when we arrived. I heard the doctors and nurses who carried out the examination referring to the men as 'Chinks'. They openly compared the fitness of the Chinamen with an earlier batch from South Africa who they referred to as 'Kaffirs'. Perhaps this arrogant racism can be excused due to the horrors of the war they endure on a daily basis, and they would be deep the worst of the horror, but it would be no wonder if the men became sick and tired of our superior attitude. If the Chinese are to function effectively, they *have to* be treated with some degree of respect. It's up to us to make sure this happens.

The guide also notes that the Chinese labourer comes to France, 'purely and simply for money, with no interest in the war'.

That's perfectly reasonable. They are contracted as labourers, not soldiers or diplomats.

It goes on, 'a labourer will adopt a rigid adherence to his contract. He is agreeable to modifications, e.g. a change to piecework, if the change was advantageous to him'.

Just like any trade union lad in England. The lads in the pit would relate to this, no bother.

I chuckle at the next bit, which reads, 'the Chinamen are unequalled as a judge of human character. What is seen as being necessary is the best procurable class of white overseer to obtain the best results'.

Well, they have that right. They're a canny lot and no mistake, but a good officer will get great results from them, I'm sure.

My reading is interrupted by Sergeant Williams from Asmiroff's section.

"Pardon the interruption, Sir, but the CO has called an 'O' group. Ten minutes in his office".

I thank the Sergeant and throw the 'guide' to one side. I've got the gist of it and I'm ready to defend our blokes whenever necessary.

The first 'O' back 'in country', is a farce. Company 21 has arrived three days ahead of expectation, and work details are still being planned for us. The Adjutant, Lt Evans, is there and he cops a blast from the CO, which does little to cheer the Welshman's unhappy frame of mind.

"We'll just have to stand the men down for the day."

Another day getting used to conditions here won't hurt I suppose, so the CO's order is not much of a problem but it shows a lack of attention to detail by the hapless Lieutenant. Sergeant Major Peters and I leave to tell the men and I decide to retrieve the Adjutant's Guide and read more of what the British Command think of our charges.

It observes that the Chinese have a fondness for litigation and lodging complaints. They can be 'sworn,' but 'evidence must be accepted with considerable reserve'. The Chinamen are characterised as being 'not addicted to crimes of violence or drunkenness but are all inveterate gamblers and indulge freely in immorality with women, if opportunity offers'.

I grin to myself as I read this last bit. The author obviously thinks they're a disgusting lot but that bit earlier about the need for 'the best procurable class of white overseer' is very true. If I've learned nothing else, I know that if we want the best out of these men, we must employ the best to lead and to manage them. If we don't, much of our efforts in France will be wasted. Thinking back over the past two years, it has taken time for us, both officers and NCOs, to develop any mutual respect with the Chinese, and some, like Higgins or the useless Bertram. still have a way to go. It takes time but time is something the war-weary frontline British, like the medical staff yesterday, don't have. This is going to be harder than I thought.

I decide to start a diary.

Wednesday, 13 February 1918. Eleven days without a drink. Weather dry but chilly. Sober breakfast and off to the 'O' group to see what this day has in store.

The Adjutant and his staff have been busy catching up on work schedules for the men. Lt Evans briefs the CSM and me that some of the men are to be sent to work in the railway marshalling yards, loading and unloading the constant stream of freight trains, while others are to be detailed to repair roads, lay railways lines or to build huts and repair buildings in different locations. All these tasks will be done here in Amiens. A third group is to work at an airstrip outside a nearby town called Vignacourt. The Adjutant has a better attitude now following the roasting he got from his Commander and he tells Peters and I that Vignacourt is a sort of rest area. There are apparently a lot of men there who are having a well-deserved break from the front-line fighting. The town is beyond the range of the Hun's artillery and is deemed to be quite safe. We are a bit stretched for supervision and, as this is the smallest task in terms of manpower needed, I decide to give the task to Lieutenant Bertram to see how he can manage. I allocate Corporal Anderson and Li Cheng-fang, the huge young Chinaman, who is by far the most competent of the *p'aitous,* to go with him.

Having delegated the airstrip task to Bertram, I leave him to it, but not before taking Li Cheng-fang to one side.

"Look, I have been talking to one or two of the officers who have been here for some time. What I am about to tell you is important and you must pass it on to the other *p'aitous* and make sure all the men understand. As you know, your contracts say that you are not to be engaged in fighting and that you are to be treated like civilian contracted labour, but from what I hear, after your government declared war on Germany in March last year, this part of your contract is not being strictly applied. What it boils down to is that any act of indiscipline on your part could, and probably will, be dealt with by military means. If any of you do anything wrong, very wrong, you may be judged as if you were soldiers and not coolies"

The big man is listening carefully and I'm sure he understands but I want to be absolutely sure and so I say, "Li Cheng-fang, if your men do any very bad thing, they may be shot".

He looks back at me, shaking his head from side to side as he takes in what I have told him.

"Yes, Captain Armstrong. I understand and I tell others also. I must tell my men to learn more of the weapons you use. Will you help us to do this?"

Where has that come from!

"Li Cheng-fang, that's not really what I meant. I want to tell you about indiscipline, doing bad things, and what could happen if any of you misbehave, not about the chance of you fighting. If you want to learn about using guns, I can do it I suppose, but we would have to be very careful. No one must know. That's all for now, but first tell everyone what I have said about what will happen if they do very bad things".

I'm still thinking of Li Cheng-fang's reaction as I watch him join Bertram and the others as they form up to tackle the ten-mile march to the airstrip they'll be working on. A truck carrying the gear they'll need for the time they'll be there will follow later. That little chat didn't go the way I planned. Weapon training? It makes some sense but they'll have my guts for garters if I let it happen I suppose. I'd best talk to the CO.

I put Li Cheng-fang's idea of weapon training out of my mind as I try to focus on the work to be done at the railway yards. I've decided to give this task to Sergeant Young with support from Corporals Thompson and Davison. They'll have just over forty men with them and two competent *p'aitous* in Sun Jun and Li Zhang, the army deserter as I now think of him. Sergeant Major Peters will oversee the start of this task and, once they march off, I join

Sergeant Williams. He'll take care of the last task, the road works and so on.

"You'll have Corporals Bruce and Brown working with you, a full squad of sixty men and *p'aitous* Zhou Xiaobing and Yang Fa. I'm coming with you to see to the start of the task. Do you have any questions?"

Williams is a good NCO and I get a crisp, "No, Sir. Sounds good. Ready to get stuck in, Sir".

He's grinning from ear to ear and obviously keen to get working at last, just like the rest of us, so I smile back at him. We've been allocated three trucks to get us going so we climb on board and head off to find the Logistics Command Centre. Once there I stand by as Sergeant Williams is briefed as to the details of the work to be done and leave him with confidence that he does not need my rank to get things done. The need for our assistance is huge and we are well received. I decide to head back to base and see if I can find the CO. Li Cheng-fang's question still looms large in my mind, but the Commander's reaction is swift and clear.

"Are you mad, Charlie?"

The CO roars at me and looks at me as if I had propositioned his wife.

"Give the men weapon training? Give them arms too, I suppose? Bloody madness".

Well, that was that.

At around mid-afternoon, the caterer comes to see me. "That truck that was sent out to the air strip, Sir. The gentleman in charge loaded all the necessaries for a camp canteen, Sir, but he forgot to load any food".

Corporal Anderson arrives back as light is fading.

"I understand that you know about the problem at the air strip, Sir?"

The young corporal looks a bit sheepish but I tell him to sit and give me the full story.

"It was an easy enough march to a town called Vignacourt. Lieutenant Bertram made contact with the loggies, sorry, Sir, the Logistical Support Unit, and we were given directions to the airstrip that's on the edge of town. It all went like a dream really and we fronted up late this morning. We were expected and the Lieutenant reported to a Captain Gregory who in turn handed us over to a Sergeant Major Grant. We were allocated a row of ten-men tents on the edge of the field and told to set ourselves up. Li Cheng-fang and I got the men settled in the tents they gave us but, honestly Sir, the bedding that was there was filthy. It was riddled with lice. We had enough stretchers so I told Li Cheng-fang to have the men stack all the bedding in one of the unused tents and then tell them to sleep in their clothes for tonight. Those padded jackets they wear are as warm as our great coats. I was rather hoping, Sir, if we could snaffle our bedding from here and take it up to them. They're going to be staying up there for a week or so as I understand it".

Anderson then turned red in the face. He was obviously very embarrassed.

"It wasn't until early afternoon when we set up the field kitchen that we found out that we didn't have any food with us. Lieutenant Bertram told me to come back here and report the matter to you, Sir. I managed to hitch a lift, Sir. I think the Lieutenant was going to try to scrounge some supplies from the fly boys, Sir".

The poor lad shuffled his feet and would not look me in the eye.

"Not your fault, Corporal. The caterer briefed me this afternoon. I've managed to get a truck and we'll take food up to them but we can't move until the morning. Hopefully Lieutenant Bertram will succeed doing as you said. It's not a good start. Look, you get yourself a hot meal and an early night. I'm coming with you tomorrow. We'll load up and move out after breakfast. Dismiss".

Anderson threw me a very relieved salute, turned smartly and almost ran out of my tent as I went in search of the CO once again to brief him on this development.

We set out after breakfast as planned, with orders from the CO to have Bertram report back to him in the truck on its return to base. He has been relieved of a very short command, to be replaced for the moment by Sergeant Elliott, the paymaster from Admin section. We're still missing Asmiroff and Bertram's uselessness is biting deep and hard. We don't have sufficient experienced leaders on the ground yet. I've been ordered to go with the truck as well and to smooth over any bad feelings with the airstrip commander.

The ride is an interesting one. There's plenty of the devastation I remember only too well from before, with fields ploughed by artillery fire, trees denuded and stark and, in places, long strips of white tape indicating where the road used to be. We drive as best we can with ambulances going to and fro, horse-drawn carts moving slowly over the ruts, and men on the move in various conditions. Some march in file, equipped and determined. Others straggle as if lost, and one file of eight men goes passed, each holding on to the shoulder of the man in front. Only the lead man has unbandaged eyes.

So, they are still using gas, I think to myself with disgust.

As we enter Vignacourt, I'm surprised to see relatively little damage. The streets are narrow and cobbled. Stone steps lead down to the streets from neat doorways and there is even a park with a band playing from a rotunda. The airstrip is located on the edge of town. It's a broad open field with wooden huts and large hangers to one side. Near the entrance is a wired compound with a scattering of ten-man bell tents, and we receive a cheer from our men as we pull up. Morale seems much better than I expected.

The hapless Bertram greets me with a salute I would normally berate him for. He looks so miserable however that I return his greeting and walk past him to where Li Cheng-fang is waiting quietly with a broad smile on his face.

"Good morning, Captain Armstrong. It is pleasing to see you, Sir".

I want to boost his status with the men and so I call Sergeant Elliot over and ask the Chinaman to show us around, leaving Bertram and the corporal to one side. We have a brief inspection of their tents and the empty field kitchen and I'm impressed to see that they have dug deep and effective latrines. I tell the young giant to organise the offloading of the wagon, re-join Bertram and ask for a report.

"We were fed last night by the airmen and again at breakfast this morning. The CO is Captain Gregory, Sir.

His office is over in the middle hut. Sir, I'm sorry about leaving the food behind. It will not happen again".

He's on the verge of tears, which only makes me angry.

"It won't happen again Lieutenant because you are relieved. Sergeant Elliot here will take over. You are to return to base with the truck and report to Major Roberts as soon as you get there".

I then turn to Anderson and tell him to give the clean bedding we brought with us to Li Cheng-fang for distribution while Sergeant Elliot and I visit Captain Gregory.

We find the airman in one of the hangers. They are obviously busy but the Captain shakes my hand, returns Elliot's salute and takes me to his office. We are joined by his Sergeant Major, a cheery chap called Grant, and I advise them of the changes we have made. That done, we finish the coffees we have been given and return with Mr Grant to our men. The kitchen is already producing tea and hot biscuits and there are smiles all round as Grant and Elliot discuss the work to be done. With Li Cheng-fang's involvement, men are allocated to tasks and our work gets started. There is transport going from the airstrip back into town after breakfast tomorrow, so I secure a ride with that and tell our truck driver to take the empty truck we came in back to base. Bertram climbs into the front of the truck and disappears without another word.

As dawn breaks next day, our breakfast is interrupted by the deployment of three aircraft, which are wheeled out of their hangers and prepared for flight. The Chinamen gather in awe to watch. Out from the huts come three pilots wearing leather coats, flying goggles and long white scarves. The aircraft engines fire up and the planes taxi to the makeshift runway. As the pilots rev their engines and take off, there are yells of amazement from our men. Most of them have never seen aircraft before and they are staggered.

Su Ting-fu is dancing around waving his hat madly, and an awestruck Li Cheng-fang asks me, "How those machines fly like birds?"

"I did tell you that you would see some wondrous things, Li Cheng-fang. Ships that sail under the sea, machines that fly, and there will be more".

Yes more, I tell myself, like guns that fire huge shells that land and kill without warning and mines that blow up as you walk. Fortunately, our men have not been exposed to that as yet.

Trying hard to focus on the joy the planes have caused rather than the reality of this bloody war, I watch as the men begin work and then join my lift back into town.

As Company CO, Major Roberts, is reviewing our first week in country with me.

"My main problem, Sir, is Lieutenant Bertram. He is just not cut out to be in the military. No one is taking any notice of the lad at all and I can't see it changing. Without Asmiroff, he is worse than useless."

Roberts sucks on his pipe, then replies, "Bertram can work here with me until we decide what to do with him. Disappointing. God knows when Asmiroff will get here. I've no word on the man. What about the work details?"

"Going well, Sir. Li Cheng-fang is doing well out at the airstrip and the other two foremen in Number One Section, Sun Jun and Li Zhang, are getting good reports. I've spent most of my time with them since we arrived. They are doing well. We have them down at the railhead working with the French railway Johnnies and they are also involved in road repairs with our logistics people. Everyone needs extra hands, so our men were given a good reception. The men work well, when they get the chance, but we waste an incredible amount of time marching them to and from their work sites. The admin is cumbersome and having to bring them back here each night reduces their value considerably. Is there any possibility we can billet them closer to where they're needed, just as we have done with Li Cheng-fang's group?"

"Not a chance, Charlie. My brief from above is to keep the Chinese under tight control. No fraternising with the troops or with the civilians if it can be prevented. There's a large YMCA facility here in the camp, and now that HQ has accepted their presence, they look to them to keep a tight grip on our people. Bloody ridiculous, if you ask me, but there you are. Anything else?"

I look up from reading my notebook and reply, "There is one problem, Sir. Our people at the airstrip have been given blankets that are filthy and the men risk being infested with lice. They've been allowed into the showers at the airstrip, which helps, but the Q people here are ridiculous. According to them, none of the bedding issued to the men for their huts should have been taken out of the camp and they insist that the bedding the men are now using should be returned. Any chance you could pull a string or two?"

The CO nods, but says wearily, "You know as well as I do that things are not going to get much better than this. Lice, short supplies and bloody-minded quartermasters are going to be the norm, and we'll have much more to worry about as time passes. Is that the lot, Charlie? Well done, old man. Not a bad start. Tomorrow's Sunday, so take your foot off the pedal and relax a bit. I'll see you in the mess later, won't I."

The CO's last comment was more of an order than a question. He hasn't mentioned my drinking since he took me to task and probably thinks I'm now cutting myself off from the others even more since I gave up the grog.

Chapter Fifteen
Amiens YMCA

My diary is open at a clean page headed Monday 4th March 1918. As we wait for the arrival of the CO to begin another 'O' group, Asmiroff walks in and sits down as arrogant as ever. He returns my amazed stare with a curt nod of his head and turns to look out of the window. Not a care in the world. Lieutenant Hastings is sitting quietly with a sheaf of notes, but there is no sign of the problem child, Bertram. The interpreter, Ma Long, is also absent, which only happens when the CO is going to talk about things he does not want the men to know. Sergeant Major Peters and his sergeants sit, notebooks open at the ready, as professional as ever waiting for the orders of the day. When Major Roberts enters the room, I call out, "Gentlemen!" and the Englishmen straighten to sit at attention. Asmiroff slowly takes his gaze from the window and smiles at the CO. What is going on?

The CO is in a 'no nonsense' mood and begins, "Right! Listen in! Welcome back, Captain Asmiroff. You *will*", he pauses for effect, "resume command of Number Two section. See Captain Armstrong as soon as we finish here, and get up to speed."

No nonsense there.

"For your information, Lieutenant Bertram has been assigned to work as liaison with the YMCA here in camp. He will be better served working there to assist in keeping up the morale of our men."

Asmiroff sneers at this but Sergeant Major Peters looks relieved, a reaction I share deeply.

"Before we get into tasks for the coming days," the CO continues, "be aware our Intelligence people are warning of a German build up, thirty or so miles to the east, beyond St Quentin."

He unrolls a crude sketch and pins it up on a board.

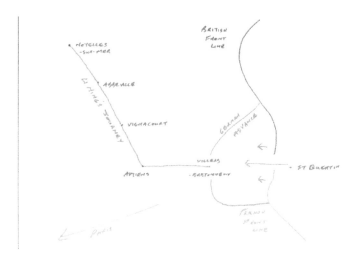

Amiens Map

"Now that the Russians are out of the war, we can expect to face another fifty or more divisions of German troops that are heading towards us. That's anything up to a million men, gentlemen. Another million Huns! They know this will give them numerical superiority, but only for a while. The Americans have joined in, at last, and are being shipped over at a high rate, but so far, only around 300,000 have arrived in France. They are keen but unbloodied, so how this will work out is yet to be tested. Added to this, we have a conflict in England. Old Lloyd George has refused to send Field Marshal Haig any fresh British troops. He is actually ordering some of our troops to leave France and to go to Italy! Our boys are being thinned out, and St Quentin is where we link up with the French. This is the obvious weak point in our lines."

The CO points to the map with his cane.

"I'm told this is where we can expect the heaviest assault, if the Hun does mount a big push. What it means for us is that we may find ourselves slap, bang in the way of a major enemy offensive."

His words are greeted with a stony silence.

"Any questions?" he barks.

"If we are not going to arm our men, we should at least get them issued with gas masks."

My words cause eyebrows to rise, but Major Roberts snaps back quickly, "Out of the question as you well know, Charlie. They're non-combatants and our instructions are crystal clear. They're civilians and should be kept as far back from the front line as possible. If we are over-run, and I stress, 'IF', then they'll have to take their chances with the other civilians in the area. I know how you feel, Charlie, but the matter is closed."

"Any other questions? Fine. All yours, Captain Armstrong."

With that, he leaves and I direct Captain Asmiroff to the desk that young Bertram has been using.

"That's yours, old chum. Now listen in, all of you, and I'll go over the tasks for the week ahead."

Asmiroff glares at me but moves to Bertram's empty desk and sits down as arrogantly as ever.

As Second-in-Command, it's my job to organise the work schedules. It takes a little time to brief the others, but all goes well and another week begins.

"Change of plans, Li Cheng-fang."

I've decided to brief the man without the help of the interpreter who has still not appeared. The Chinaman looks unfazed and smiles at me.

"You are being assigned to a Logistics unit and will work at the rail depot in the town centre. I will come with you for the first day and Sergeant Major Peters will keep track of what you are doing, but you will be working directly under the command of another British unit. Do you understand?"

"Yes, Captain Armstrong. No problem".

Li Cheng-fang now grins openly as he uses one of my favourite expressions. I've been speaking slowly and clearly to see just how much the Chinaman understands. I've long suspected that he either has had some prior tuition in English, or he's a genius at languages, or he studies non-stop. Whatever it is, his grasp of English is remarkable

"Right laddie. We'll move at 0830 hours tomorrow morning, so have your men ready. In the meantime, have each man draw heavy gloves from the Q store, and have them carry their mess tins and wet weather capes when we move out. The forecast is for heavy rain this week. They will not need anything else as the railway marshalling yards are just thirty to forty minutes' march away, so you'll be back here for the evening meal. Is that clear?"

"Yes, Sir. Zero eight thirty, big gloves, mess tins, and coats for raining. No problem. I go now to Q store with men."

We set off on a cloudy day and the march into town is uneventful, until suddenly there is a rush of air above us and a huge explosion shatters a nearby building. The men freeze in fear. Sergeant Major Peters screams out, "Keep moving!" and the men automatically do as he says. At the railway station, I tell Peters to halt the men and keep them standing at ease while I find out who we will be working with. When I return, the men are chattering amongst themselves and it is obvious that the shell that landed as we marched has unsettled them. Ma Long is with us and, when I return to the men, I call him forward to interpret.

"Listen in! That explosion you heard was a German shell. I've been told that they only fire one a day to annoy us. These railheads are vital to us, but the Germans obviously think that they will need them too, so the shells have never come anywhere close to here. You'll be quite safe working here."

Except when we are marching here or returning back to Amiens, I think to myself, "And if the Germans think they'll need these railheads, I wonder when are they coming to get them?"

Despite my fears, the men seem reassured and begin their usual happy banter when waiting for orders to move.

I look around and marvel at the size and complexity of the rail system. A French Lieutenant and two railwaymen approach Mr Peters and me, the Lieutenant saluting smartly. They are the people we are to work with, and the task of moving freight begins. Boxes are to be taken from the rail wagons onto waiting trucks and horse drawn carts, which will leave for various destinations, making room for more waiting transport. It is to be a constant stream. We warn Li Cheng-fang that much of the incoming freight is dangerous and includes large numbers of artillery shells, as well as boxes of ammunition and grenades, and Peters and I watch as he moves among the men stressing the need for caution, admonishing the few who usually fool around. Today, however, no one thinks to take matters lightly. The memory of the morning shell-burst has left many of the men rather thoughtful. The men are divided into teams and off they go to different parts of the station.

As I am about to leave, a number of ambulances arrive, together with a convoy of open trucks, all of which are carrying wounded men. The casualties are assisted from the trucks or carried on stretchers from the ambulances, and taken on board a waiting train. There are so many of them, I think there must have been a fair bit of activity nearby that we have not been told about. I pose this question to one of the medical staff, who looks at me strangely and says, "Sir, this is the regular train. It's taking casualties to the West to make room for our hospitals and casualty clearing stations here in and around Amiens. There's a regular flow, Sir, even though the fighting is quiet at the moment."

This is a quiet time? There are hundreds of sick and wounded men!

We work in the railway marshalling yards for two weeks, returning each day to our camp on the outskirts of the town. When not working, the men are restricted to the camp and not allowed outside the area. Camp activities take on an important role and are constantly in my mind. The men are tired at the end of the day, but they still need to be distracted from mischief. I have accepted the inevitable where gambling is concerned, and it goes on unabated, but the YMCA hut provides a welcome alternative. It has plenty of seating and a continual supply of tea and biscuits. There are piles of newspapers, magazines and books and a separate room inside the hut, which the men are using to write letters home. Some of the reading material has come all the way from China, but some are printed here in France. The Chinese Labour Journal, *Huagong Zazhi*, is the most popular with the men as it features both educational items and essays of interest. The men are proud of what they are doing. They see themselves as worthy of their new Republic and want to better themselves. The Journal carries topics such as science and the arts, news items, short stories and opinion pieces, which reflect opinions many of the men seem to accept. Hastings is a great advocate of this facility and tells me that the men are improving their knowledge and improving their wellbeing.

I meet Lieutenant Bertram in the YMCA writing room one evening. He is keen to tell me that after the farce of his 'command' at Vignacourt, he has been transferred to work as a liaison officer with the YMCA.

"I'm learning to speak and write Chinese," he brags proudly, "and I'm helping a large number of the men to write home. The men can write two letters a month if they wish. They are subject to military censorship of course, just as our letters are, but the men are happy with this. This YMCA service is excellent."

He is transformed, now filled with enthusiasm.

"There's so much we can do here to make the lives of our men easier."

His reference to 'our men' both surprises and pleases me.

Li Cheng-fang floats the idea of growing some of our own food and I greet his idea with enthusiasm. I tell Bertram to procure seeds, which, to my surprise, he manages to do in no time at all. Soon we have vegetable gardens everywhere.

The men collect horse dung for fertiliser, and competition between huts provides incentive and more good-natured banter. Bartram also helps the men to buy extra rations to supplement the food that they are given. The Chinese are not allowed to shop themselves, except for the odd occasions when out on work details if the guards are sympathetic. They rely on the YMCA people and Bertram in particular to assist in buying apples, fresh eggs and other treats that are in short supply. These treats cost dearly but the men have little else to spend their local money on. Most of them appear to be happy that the bulk of their earnings are going back to China.

A short, self-important American, who introduces himself as Mister Graham Flaxton, is waiting for me when I return to the camp in Amiens one evening. He tells me he is from the YMCA central office in Paris and is visiting all their facilities near the front line.

"I've received a letter from Brother John, the young man you may know as Gong Lei. He is in charge of the Qingdao YMCA, as you may remember, and he tells me that you met him last year when you were preparing to sail with the Labour Corps."

I nod my agreement to his questioning tone.

"Ah, good," he continues pompously.

"Brother John has told me in his letter how keen the men are to read the Bible, and to learn from it about a better life for all mankind, through the words of our Saviour Jesus Christ. I can assist you in this."

He speaks with the fire of a zealot, and I decide it's best to be cautious.

"The men are always keen to learn, Mr Flaxton. Leave your Bibles with me and I'll see that they are placed in our YMCA canteen. Those who wish to do so can help themselves".

The American hesitates for a moment and I anticipate an argument but my words have been firm and he accepts them with a bow.

Despite my friendship and respect for the Padre, I've formed the view that the Christian religion is nothing more than superstition, but I can see benefit in his offer of 'assistance' at once. Half of the Bibles he has with him are in Chinese but the rest are in English. It'll give the YMCA staff another source of material for their work. I then ask my patronising and pompous visitor," Why have you come to France at this time? What's your purpose?"

Flaxton beams, puffs out his chest and launches into a monologue. He relates how the YMCA is taking a leading role in the provision of education, social and entertainment programs for the Allied fighting forces.

"Everyone has support from the Red Cross, but our aim is to provide specific assistance to the Chinese Labour Corps," he tells me.

"Subscriptions have been raised among Chinese people back in China to fund the bulk of the programs the men can get involved in. This is in line," he continues rather grandly, "with China's pursuit of a new national identity, and their efforts to join the world community as an equal member. You know, there was a lot of early resistance from the British High Command to the idea of the YMCA even being here. Nevertheless, we have prevailed, despite this lack of support and YMCA venues have been established in many of the camps, which have been set up to contain our friends from China. It's all for the good. For example, just last month a young YMCA interpreter, called Sun Qing, was able to defuse a potential riot, after a group of Chinese labourers went on strike over a petty misunderstanding. Not being aware of the reasons for their anger, the Colonel in charge of the British troops on the ground ordered his men to fix bayonets. Sun Qing spoke to the men in Mandarin and was then able to brief the British Colonel on the reasons for their anger. The misunderstanding was cleared without resort to violence."

He pauses for breath; or is it for applause I wonder?

"It was news of this incident that prompted a change of heart by British Commanders and, good Sir, I'm happy to tell you that General Headquarters has, this very week, invited the YMCA to set up canteens and recreational programs among *all* the Chinese Companies with the British Expeditionary Force. Many illiterate labourers will now be able to use the services we provide to write home and to get letters from home interpreted for them. Do you know, we are sending up to 50,000 letters every month to China? I'm sure the YMCA, funded as we are by the national headquarters in China, will make the experience of the Chinese workers in Europe less miserable and more fruitful."

There's obvious merit in what he has to say although I am sceptical about his claim of so many letters going out to China. On the other hand, the *p'aitous* have indicated that many of the men are beginning to get homesick and to worry about their families back in China. Anything that can help them at least to send and, more to the point, receive, news will be welcome. For many of them, their lives are now dominated by long hours of hard work seven days a week, followed by boredom in the evening when work ceases. Young Bertram mentioned various social activities he had in mind. He seems to be quite capable of helping the men to write simple letters, and to read their replies, so I smile at Mr Flaxton and thank him for his efforts.

"No need to thank me, Sir," Flaxton goes on to say. "The Chinese YMCA aims to move beyond the early missionaries who went out to China to proselytise the gospel. We will still spread the word of the Lord, but we have been told to downplay the theology, and to emphasise service and education above the need for conversion to the faith. Once China develops into a modern nation, led by a middle class, I am convinced that Christianity will naturally find its place among its' people. The Lord's work *will* be done."

He finishes speaking with great conviction, but inwardly I cannot envisage China becoming like Europe, with a middle class and a religion that promises nothing now, and everything in a life after death. But I keep up a smiling façade of acceptance and I'm beginning to warm to the world of the YMCA.

I find myself sitting alone in the office allocated to the officers of Company 21. As is so often the case, Asmiroff is nowhere to be seen and Lieutenant Hastings is doing the rounds of the huts, checking on the wellbeing of the men. The CO has his office next door but it stands empty as he too is off doing some task or other. I'm able to relax with the latest edition of *The Times* newspaper, even if it is a month old. I've poured myself a hot coffee and I shrug off the feeling of guilt as I take a scalding sip.

"Three-thirty on a Wednesday afternoon and plenty of work to be done. What am I doing here?"

I console myself by thinking, "I didn't finish until well after midnight last night and I'm up to scratch in most things. A short break won't matter too much."

Thus mollified, I take another sip and return to my newspaper.

Page one lists Killed-in-Action notices and 'In Memoriam', all too depressing by half. I flip to page nine and see that 'The London Symphony Orchestra, under Mr Boult, last night at Queens Hall, performed, among other pieces, Mozart's 'For Harp and Flute', played by Gwendolen Mason and Louis Fleury'. It seems the 'solo work of the Mozart, especially the un-harp like counterpoint for the harp, was neatly done but the orchestral work lacked 'crispness'.

"Jolly bad show," I say to myself with a plummy upper-class accent and then I chuckle quietly as I have absolutely no idea what the reviewer is on about. I take another sip from my mug and turn to the Stock Market report.

The possibility of action being taken by Japan in the Far East led to some further selling of bonds and prices closed appreciably lower. Chinese bonds shared in the same weakness.

"The possibility of troops facing each other here in France may also induce weakness," I mumble aloud before draining my mug and staring at the wall.

"Oh, shit!"

I throw the paper to the floor and sigh despondently.

A growing number of the men are being affected by the illness they call the Spanish Flu. We begin to suffer deaths due to the illness itself, and from accidents at work caused by men in a weakened state handling heavy goods at the marshalling yards. We are faced with a major problem as a result. British Army policy insists on burial of the dead here in France. The Chinese hold a strong fear that, if they are not buried in their homeland, their spirits will never be at peace. The *p'aitous* band together and ask me how families will be able to pay respect to the dead, down through the ages to come, if they are interred in foreign soil? I'm not sympathetic.

"Think of the millions of dead in this war. It's not possible for us to even take the bodies of our own fallen back to England, close as it is, and the idea of sending your dead back to China is impossible."

The Chinamen accept the logic of this reluctantly and ask that at least as many of the dead as possible be buried with dignity and in one place. I've been told there's now a cemetery being planned at Noyelles–sur-Mer, which will be solely for Chinese dead, and they greet this news with resigned smiles.

"I've also been told that the graveyard is to be designed by a Chinese expert from your Embassy in London. It will be built on a slope with a stream of water running below and ...."

Sun Jun cuts me off with a shout of delight.

"It will agree with the spirit of feng shui."

"Whatever you say, Sun Jun. Does this make you happier?"

They nod and smile in agreement and I feel that another problem has been diverted.

On a happier note, the men are able to engage in games at the YMCA which don't involving gambling, and Bertram has been able to organise performances and even get some of the men to perform traditional operas. Many of the men love to sing, even if others may find their singing hard to bear. These concerts prove popular, both those involved in the production as well as those who make up the large audiences. Even those with dubious voices receive good-humoured support. I'm interested to see that they also provide entertainment for us British.

Relationships between our two races continue to improve with time, although the military style of administration remains in force. The Chinese are still restricted to the camp at all times except when working. The camp is surrounded by wire mesh but a *tin* fence surrounds the main camp in Noyelles–sur–Mer! The men there can't even *look* at the people outside! Despite this, many of the men brag about sly contact they have with the French civilians. One of Sun Jun's men came back to camp bearing four hats, all covered in flowers. Another brought a garment that confounded everyone in his hut.

"It's full of what we think are fish bones and wire", says *p'aitou* Sun Jun when he showed it to me. I couldn't help bursting out in laughter. They were women's corsets.

It's during a camp performance that I meet Henri Isakson. He's a YMCA interpreter, but Henri is an unusual employee of the YMCA. Henri's not English or a Christian. He's a French Jew.

Henri and I become friends after a fashion. Each of us recognises in the other a desire to right the wrongs that fester in the hearts of the prejudiced. He speaks good English as well as his native French but in addition, having worked in a bank in Shanghai for several years, his Mandarin is good enough for the YMCA to recruit him. They've stationed him here in Amiens where his knowledge of three languages is of great benefit. We sit drinking tea one evening and I ask him to tell me about himself.

"Well for a start, I'm a Jew," he begins. "We're hated and persecuted everywhere. Every ill that befalls the Christian world is somehow our fault."

Henri's the first Jew I have ever met and I'm interested in his story.

"There are Jews who are French, English and German. There are Jews all over the world, even in China. Thousands of Jews are fleeing the revolution in Russia and going into China as we speak. Yet Jews are being accused of starting the very revolution they are fleeing from. We can't win. Jesus was a Jew, but we had him crucified, and the Christians have never forgiven us for this. You know about Dreyfus, don't you?"

To my shame, I can only reply, "Well yes, I've heard his name. French traitor, wasn't he".

"Charlie, that makes my point. Listen. Alfred Dreyfus was a competent army officer in the French army during the last years of last century. There was a spy in the Army general staff, and Dreyfus was accused of being that spy. There was no proof that he was betraying his country, a country he loved and served well, but he was charged and convicted of treason and sent to prison. He was a scapegoat and was picked on purely because he was Jewish. No other reason. When the real traitor was caught, the Army heads were embarrassed about having convicted an innocent man, so Dreyfus was left in prison, and it took a huge outcry from the public to bring about his release. Even then, most people in France continued to hate the Jews. It was the blatant injustice this exemplary French officer endured, just because of being Jewish, which persuaded me to leave France in 1906 and to go to work in China".

The Frenchman's face is becoming red with anger as he continues.

"When war broke out in 1914, I joined the YMCA in Shanghai as a part time volunteer, and when a call was made for interpreters in 1916, I saw this as a chance to return home. Being tri-lingual was more important than my faith, and I was taken on to the YMCA full-time staff. For me, the main thing is that it has given me the opportunity to return to France. When I got back here however, I soon realised the anti-Semitism, which had prompted me to leave in 1906, has not become any less widespread. If anything, it has increased significantly. As I said, following the Bolshevik revolution in Russia last year, we Jews are being blamed for that too. We are used by many in the Allied Command as an excuse for this and any other 'unfortunate' event."

Henri then tells me he holds his counsel and works quietly, despite his seething anger at the injustice surrounding him. I like the man, I can relate to him easily and I feel that he and I may become friends.

I'm sitting alone again in my office. Another day has passed and the war goes on. Today I was at the railway yards again when the train to the West, as I now think of it, was being loaded with sick and wounded who were being shipped out to make room for more casualties yet to arrive. I find myself singing a song I hear one of the injured singing over and over. At first, I thought he was singing that popular song 'If you were the only girl in the world', but he was singing words different to the original.

'If you were the only Boche in the trench
And I had the only bomb
Nothing else would matter in the world that day
I would blow you up into eternity
A chamber of Horrors just made for two
With nothing to spoil our fun
There would be such wonderful things to do
I would get my rifle and bayonet too ....'

I rest my body across my desk and fall asleep where I sit.

Chapter Sixteen
The Reality of War

Oh, how I hate this war! I hate the mindless slaughter, the pain and injury and destruction we are causing to the enemy, to the civilians around us and to ourselves and yet through all of this our men, my men, my Chinamen endure. They endure the hardship of their labour and their conditions but they also endure the restrictions we impose and the insults and the lack of regard. My admiration for them grows day by day

Spring is late and the weather remains cold. I sit talking in the open with the three *p'aitous* from Number One Section. We have chosen well as all three of them have grasped a good command of English and, while I continue to work on my Mandarin, I think the Chinese are more adept at learning a foreign language. They've certainly done much better at reading our language than I theirs as I find the Chinese written characters totally incomprehensible. Conversations, such as we are now having, tend to be in English. The young interpreter, Ma Long, is with us just in case the briefing gets too complicated but so far we have managed well without his help.

"Number One section's going to be sent to a town called Villers-Bretonneux in a day or two. You'll be helping to make the defences on the edge of the town much stronger. If the Germans take that town, they can attack us here in Amiens and if *we* fall, they can turn north and cut off the entire British army. It would be an end to the war but in their favour. Villers-Bretonneux is the key. We must hold there and you and your men will help us do that."

I stare hard into their eyes one at a time to stress the seriousness of what I'm saying.

"This is more than a normal labouring task. This one is very important."

Two days after this briefing, I take Number One Section by truck to the outskirts of Villers-Bretonneux and then have them dismounted. We form them up to march the rest of the way into the town centre and I have Li Cheng-fang take the lead. Sun Jun and Li Zhang lead their men in squad formation behind Li Cheng-fang's squad but I march off to one side and tell Sergeant Fredricks to bring up the rear with our three corporals and Ma Long the interpreter. It's a gesture that continues to surprise and to please the men and they march with straight backs and heads held high led by one of their own. We march through mud and across ground that may once have been fields. It is torn up into mound after distorted mound of sodden soil. Denuded trees point claw-like to the sky or pile one fragmented piece on top of another. We follow what could be the remains of a road, lined in places with grimy white tape and as we move on, we are passed in either direction by open carts drawn by horses and mules, motorised carriages with red crosses emblazoned on their sides, long stemmed horse drawn cannons, men on horseback and men on bicycles. Men in uniform trudge towards us, their heads slumped forward, shoulders sagging. All of this traffic emerges out of a smoky haze, laced with a drizzle of rain, only to disappear again into the same nightmarish fog.

Marching further into the town, we come across badly damaged buildings, some totally destroyed. The cobbled streets are strewn with rubble and refuse of all kinds. Civilians cluster around water points with pans and buckets, collecting the precious fluid. Soldiers move this way and that in apparent disorder, some in shirtsleeves, some in full uniform, some bearing rifles and webbing, some carrying shovels while others carry stretchers on which lie wounded comrades. I see the occasional officer dressed in a smarter way but to my eyes, everyone looks just as confused as the next man. In doorways and on street corners I see bemused civilians, men stoically smoking pipes, women dressed in dirty white aprons, all with looks of despair. This is not a happy place.

Suddenly around a corner in the road comes a huge tank. The Chinamen stop in confusion, their ranks disintegrating. I bellow at Li Cheng-fang to keep on moving and he does so with a semblance of order restored. Gone is the pride however. Some of the men look terrified. The tank passes us by and we continue into the town. Eventually we come to a clearing in which a large canvas tent has been erected and I order Li Cheng-fang to halt the men. When he does so, I tell him to fall the men out while I go to find out what we are to do next.

Inside the tent I see a number of harassed men in uniform who, I presume, will be allocating tasks for us to perform. After a quick briefing from an exhausted looking Major who allocates an equally exhausted sergeant to act as our contact, I call Sergeant Fredricks and Ma Long to join me.

"This is the logistical headquarters for the town and you will report here each day for tasking. Today you will be divided roughly into three equal groups. Your first task is to go with this sergeant to collect the stores and equipment you will need for your work. All the items you will be issued with must be returned at the end of the day and then collected each morning before you start work again. Each group will be issued with shovels, picks and wheelbarrows and will then go, with British guides, into the town. One group is to clear rubble from a building that still has much of its roof intact. The building is unsafe, so, for God's sake Ma Long, tell the men to be careful. The second group is to clear mud and debris from the roads leading to the West. This road is vitally important and must be kept free of any obstacles that may hinder its use by vehicles. Sergeant Fredericks, you will take charge of Li Cheng-fang and his squad. You'll be restoring damaged trenches two miles further to the East of the town".

Fredericks looks at me with an unspoken question written all over his face and I answer him with a nod of the head. Yes, we will be working directly on the front line.

"These trenches are very important, which is why I want you to concentrate your time with Li Cheng-fang's squad. Any questions?"

Fredricks replies, "Understood, Sir", and I leave him to work with his fellow NCO.

While our people are getting organised, Ma Long asks about the tank we passed when we entered the town. Knowing that the men would be curious, if not fearful, I gave him an answer.

"It's a new invention called a tank. It's made to force gaps through enemy defences. They give us a big advantage and the men have nothing to fear from them".

What I didn't tell him was that unfortunately the machines are few in number and prone to breaking down often. They have not had as big an effect as first hoped for. We caught the Germans off guard at first because they didn't know how to counter this new weapon. Then they started firing their big guns, their artillery pieces at the tanks from very close range with good effect. The enemy is quick to learn and they've been making tanks of their own, so we're back in balance and the killing will go on. I try to look positive and cover the fact that it is just one more thing that is making me glum. I'm concerned that we are too close to the front and I can feel that my hands are trembling a bit.

Ma Long doesn't appear to notice my mood and asks cheerfully about the horseshoe that was hanging from the front of the tank.

"That's all a bit of superstitious nonsense, really. The horseshoe is supposed to bring good luck. It just shows how desperate some of the troops are."

Aware that I'm sounding bitter, I ask the interpreter, "What about your people, Ma Long. Do you have things you take with you into battle to bring you good fortune?"

"Yes, Yes, Captain. We have banner of Zhong Kui. In our history stories, Zhong Kui was exemplary soldier in the Song dynasty who, many say, was able to 'break through any obstacle and still go bravely on'. Perhaps your tanks get rid horses shoes and fly Zhong Kui's banner instead".

He bursts out laughing at the thought and I cannot help joining him. I have a fleeting image of our tanks riding into battle like some modern-day Genghis Khan.

I decide to go with Fredricks and Li Cheng-fang's squad to see for myself what they will be asked to do. I'm still concerned that we are too close to any possible action. We arrive at the trenches later in the morning and I look at the never to be forgotten sight of ditches that go for miles, out of sight, in all directions. A man could walk forever without putting his head above ground level. They're lined with wooden planks and the floors are covered with wooden boards. Duckboards meant to keep the soldiers feet clear of the mud and water seeping in from all sides. Duckboards that often proved inadequate for the task leaving the fighting men in misery. I was told that we would be working in third line trenches and that two more lines of trenches lay in front of us but I can hear the sound of battle ahead and my fear increases. This is too close. If the front line gets overrun, I tell myself, our people will pull back to the secondary trenches to our front but God help us if *they* get overrun. These trenches right here where we stand will become the front line and they are in a shocking state. There are more trenches running at right angles to this line, linking the front, secondary and these third line trenches, the communication lines. They'll be handy if we have to get the men out in a hurry. I'm not comfortable with the idea of leaving our men exposed like this and decide to stay with them for a while longer than I first planned.

The trenches are deep enough for a soldier to stand erect and not expose his head to any approaching enemy, but, set into the trench walls, are steps to allow the defending troops to raise up high enough to fire over the sides. The tops of the trenches are lined with hessian bags, filled with soil. Many of them have split open and the rain has turned the contents to mud. At intervals, there are shelters dug into the rear walls of the trenches to provide cover but many of them have collapsed. These trenches are in a shocking state and it's not long before the men set about the task of repairing them with enthusiasm. This task is much more constructive.

At day's end, we march back to the logistics tent in town. We return our stores and equipment and, when all three squads are together again, we march out of town to meet up with the trucks that will return us to our camp in

Amiens. We have been away from the camp for about ten hours but have spent almost half that time moving to and fro and in collecting and returning stores. Our first day here has seen a lot of wasted effort. I need to raise this with the CO. The sheer waste is ludicrous. When we get back to camp, I can see that the men are tired, some still agog at what we have seen during the day but for most, they just need a good wash, a feed and an early sleep. I feel just as tired, my mind filled with concern about our nearness to the fighting, but this all disappears as a familiar voice calls out to me as I enter the Mess for my evening meal.

"Charlie, my good friend. How are you?"

It's the voice of the Padre.

We head for a quiet table and the steward arrives to take our order.

"There's no tonic for your gin, Malcolm but I'm told that the wines are first rate".

The Padre orders a red wine and then his eyebrows rise as I order a coffee. He's surprised to see me order a non-alcoholic drink but he surprises me in turn by lighting up a cigarette.

"So, I've stopped drinking and you've started smoking. Plus ça change, as they say here. Things change. Now talk to me. How was your visit to Yorkshire?"

The Padre smiles and avoids answering me immediately by telling me that I have my French phrase back to front, but then he begins to talk quietly and sadly.

"I met with Margaret and her family and they made me welcome. In fact, I stayed with them as their houseguest for nearly a week but it became obvious to me that Margaret's feelings towards me were those of a friend and no more. I must confess, Charlie, I tried very hard to pluck up the courage to ask her to marry me but my nerve failed. I couldn't recognise any similar feeling in her. We've agreed to keep in touch and perhaps in time, when her sadness over the loss of her husband has faded a bit, I may try again, but then again, perhaps not."

"She must be mad," I reply, "But her loss is our gain. Oh, it's *so* good to have you here!"

We sit and grin at each other, lost for words in the pleasure of being reunited.

After we have eaten our meagre evening meal we retire to drink coffee and the Padre expresses concern for my tired demeanour.

"I'm fine, Padre, fine. Especially now you're back. The work goes well but there is so much to do. Asmiroff's disappeared for a while but the arrogant sod is back at least.

His men work well even if he lacks interest in them. He's working them at the marshalling yards as I was doing earlier. There's some scuttlebutt about dodgy dealings with some food supplies or other but the French police are looking into it. You'll hardly be surprised to learn that Zhou Xiao-bing, our pet gangster, is involved. The Frogs'll sort it out. Young Bertram was a bloody disaster, as we expected, but the CO has him working in the YMCA and that's going well. Hastings's a good lad and Peters has the others well in hand. My lot are happy and our protégé, Li Cheng-fang, is exceptional, as we would expect. We've just started working on the third line defences in front of Villers-Bretonneux. Everyone is expecting a major push by Jerry any time now. We're as ready as we'll ever be but it would help enormously if the blasted Americans would get their act together. They may be leaving their grand entrance a bit late. The Australian's are in our area, which is comforting. They're a hard bunch."

The Padre smiles as he listens to me cover the main issues succinctly as if at a CO's briefing.

"Yes, Charlie, but, how are *you*? Are you sleeping well and, be honest, how are you coping with being back at the Front?"

"One day at a time, Padre, one day at a time. The food rations for the men are a worry and there's an issue with lice.

Everyone's now crawling with them. They're impossible to get rid of. Bias against the Chinese is another bloody problem. There's a book going the rounds of 'useful phrases' to be used when dealing with Chinese labourers. Written by Major R. L. Purdon, whoever he is, it includes useful phrases such as, 'why don't you eat this food?' and 'the inside of this tent is not very clean' and 'you must have a bath tomorrow'. Not a word about positive phrases like, 'you did well today' or even a simple 'thank you'. When will we learn? On top of all that, Amiens gets shelled from time to time. Nothing serious just unsettling. Unless you're bloody unlucky, of course."

The Padre lights another cigarette and changes the subject.

"Charlie, I spent yesterday visiting the sick and wounded in hospital in Noyelles-sur-Mer while I waited for transport here the Amiens. This is my first time at the Front remember. I listened to some terrible stories from the medical staff and from the patients."

His mood changes and he begins to relate stories of horror far beyond his previous experience in life, stories that are obviously upsetting him greatly.

I would rather keep the conversation light but the Padre is almost desperate to talk further.

"These men spoke of months, and in some cases, years of front line fighting. They told me tales of lost comrades and of the dreaded sound of an officer's whistle ordering them out of their trenches with bayonets fixed. They're told to move forward over cratered land, over barbed wire and over landmines. Over dead and dying comrades some screaming in agony. Ordered to charge forward in the face of fire from rapid-fire machine guns and into the accurate, deadly, experienced fire from enemy rifles. All this under a barrage of artillery shells, sometimes their own, landing without warning or exploding above them, spraying those still alive with mud, shrapnel and the blood and the flesh of the fallen. How could a loving God allow such carnage?"

I'm horrified at the preacher's words and I watch as he lights yet another cigarette.

"All of this would be just a start, a nightmare interlude, until they reach the enemy lines or heard the order to pull back. If they had to fall back, it was to be under the same fusillades of gunfire and bursting shell, and they told me of running in panic to the safety of their own trenches once again, past dead and dying friends. They would reach the safety of their own trenches and have to listen to the screams of the men they had left behind in what they call No Man's Land. All this in the knowledge they would have to do the same thing again and again, next time and the time after that and on and on."

The Padre's hands are really trembling now and my earlier joy turns to one of deep concern. Perhaps he should have stayed in England after all or at least, if joining the Labour Corps in the first place was just an excuse to get back to see his Margaret, perhaps he should have gone straight back to China when that encounter failed.   The preacher continues to pour out his reactions to the hospital visit.

"If our troops managed to reach the enemy trenches, it would be to fight with bayonet or with clubbing rifle or with grenade or trenching tool until the mayhem ended and they either had victory or, more likely, a last-minute call to abandon their great effort and retreat once again to their own lines. It's horrible! Mindless! Inhuman!"

"Malcolm, I know. I've been there, remember."

"Yes, you have. I haven't. And you have never spoken about it. I listened to men talking about life in the trenches, with water constantly lapping at their feet, of the cold in winter and the suffocating heat of summer. But it's my job to listen and to provide comfort. I'm not sure that I can do this. They speak of the screams of wounded men left in No Man's Land and of the truces being struck by the men themselves on either side so that dead and wounded could be collected in safety. They have a life shared with lice, flies, rats and the stench of death. They talk of the constant terror of gas attacks when wispy clouds of chemical smoke float across the battlefield, causing any unprepared or unsuspecting soldier to fall gasping for breath. Men dying a horrible death or surviving with burned lungs and blinded eyes. One man told me of how sometimes the gas came from shells fired by their own guns! A change in wind direction blowing foul poison away from the intended target and back into our own people! How can God let this happen?"

He suddenly begins crying quietly.

I feel extremely embarrassed, not knowing quite what to do.

"I know all this. It is precisely what I have been dreading coming back to, Padre. This is what war is all about. This is reality. Easy does it, old chap".

I struggle to change the subject and ask him, "What now for you my friend?"

"I will continue my work and serve my fellow man. My contract with the Labour Corps is apparently still in force. They're a bit disorganised, I think, and my contract wasn't cancelled when I left the ship in Liverpool. When I reported back for duty, their only concern was getting me on transport to come over to France and I am still on the nominal roll of CLC Company Number 21 so we are together again. I'm so glad to see you again, Charlie. You are a valued friend."

As he's perked up a little I ask, "Let me get you another glass of wine."

He drains the glass he's holding, gathers his reserves and says, "Yes, of course, Charlie. Forgive me. Let me tell you of a different encounter. I met one of our men from another Company when I visited the hospital He asked me why Englishmen all speak their language in a different way? He thought that England must be a vast nation just like China to have so many accents. I told him that England is smaller in area than Shandong province but I also told him that we have the largest Empire in the world and our influence is spread everywhere on Earth. I actually found myself saying, "The sun never sets on the British Empire".

He blushes slightly when he says this. It's true of course, but saying it sounds like bragging. Something the Padre I knew doesn't do.

He then smiles at me and continues, "I told him that when it comes to speaking our language, officers in the military are expected to speak what is known as the King's English. This is the manner in which the upper class speaks but, I told him I have a friend who is an officer, a Geordie, who can speak in ways many Englishmen cannot not follow".

He's smiling again and his mood is much lighter.

"I warned him that he will soon meet men from Australia and others, I hope, from America and they all use the same words but spoken in a different way. Though I can tell you, Charlie that I continue to be surprised at the progress many of the men have made with our language. Just look at Li Cheng-fang. The big man is a star in the Company. I'm amazed that he can understand you, for example, when many of our fellow officers pretend they can't."

The preacher suddenly has a fit of coughing and as he looks so tired we part for the evening. I head for my bed, still pleased he has returned but wondering what else has changed in him. His stress is contagious.

The following days see a repeat of the same tasks with the same wasteful time lost in travelling from the camp to our respective workplaces. Li Cheng-fang's squad is now thirty strong, repairing and renovating the trenches. A British corporal stops to watch the men work. He sees me watching him and quickly calls out, "These trenches will be very important if we have a forced withdrawal from positions further forward. Get your backs stuck in". He has a worried expression on his face. British soldiers now work alongside our men such is the increased sense of urgency. They guide the Chinese in the construction of firing platforms, strong points for the placement of machine guns, areas of shelter where the soldiers can rest or take cover during artillery attacks and first aid posts to give initial assistance to the wounded. Communication lines are strung out in all directions and command posts are established at regular intervals. More duckboard flooring is laid and the damaged hessian bags are repaired, filled with fresh soil and stacked on the edges of the trenches.

The middle of March has brought an easing of the freezing temperatures and we have clearer skies. As we toil away one morning, the men pause to watch a number of aeroplanes fly over from our rear towards other aeroplanes flying towards us. They stand with mouths hanging open at the sight. Without warning, the planes begin to chase each other as a dogfight breaks out. They swoop and they dive, one chasing, another evading sometimes both being chased by a third. The machines spiral around in the pristine blue sky above us and for a very brief moment I enjoy the spectacle but the illusion is soon shattered. The sound of machine-guns comes from above as the airmen shoot at each other. To the horror of the Chinamen, one of the machines begins to burn and they watch aghast as it falls like a broken kite into the ground. As it spirals down, the noise of its frantic, screaming engine ceases abruptly in a ball of fire. A second or so later, there's the sound of an explosion and then a waft of heat. Two more aircraft are destroyed before we see the rest break off contact and head back to their respective sanctuaries. Sergeant Fredricks yells out for the men to start working again but they do so in stunned, unhappy silence.

The Padre is a bit pensive when I tell him the day's news. We have resumed our habit of finishing our evenings together when my duties permit but now I finish the day with a coffee rather than grog. Aerial dogfights are nothing new to us but the effect on the men has been heavy. I tell him of their reaction to the downed 'plane, but he drops a bombshell by telling me, "They have something else to occupy their thoughts. The gangster Zhou Xiao-bing's brother, Zhou Xiao-jin, is in jail. I've been to visit him prison and I understand that he's being held on rather serious charges. I've told Zhou Xiao-bing about his fate but I'm not sure if he knows just how much trouble his brother is in. Who knows if or how many more of our men are involved. I thought Li Cheng-fang might want to talk to him. What do you think?"

What I think is that I really don't need this sort of problem now.

"Yes, OK Padre. You may be right. I need to find out more about what he is said to have done. I'll sleep on this and talk to Li Cheng-fang in the morning. Leave this with me."

I decide to raise another issue that has been bothering me.

"Listen here, Padre. As you seem to get about a bit, what can you tell me about this mongrel Asmiroff? He goes missing; the CO is kept in the dark and then he suddenly reappears, as large as life and not a word said. What do you know about all this?"

The Padre sighs and says, "It's all about him being some kind of aristocrat. He has connections with some of our nobility and he has been briefing our General Staff on the situation in Russia because of this revolution they're going through. I can't see his opinion being of much use as he fled the field but he has this aristocratic pull. It will be interesting to watch how he fares from now on. We are being inundated with large numbers of so called White Russians, all of whom say they want to get to grips with the Bolsheviks. If you ask me they are looking for a means to an easy future now that most of them have lost their estates and the privileges that go with them. Asmiroff may actually be in trouble.

On that confusing note, another day is ending and I part from the Padre to spend a night in fitful sleep.

Chapter Seventeen
The Ludendorff Offensive

Work continues at an increased pace in Villers-Bretonneux with over sixty of our men now under my command working side by side with British troops in repairing the trenches. We are expecting a major attempt by the Germans to advance at any time and the work in the trenches has been given the highest priority. This morning, as we work, we come in contact with yet more men from the Colonies who have entered our world. Troops from Australia have begun arriving in large numbers. They look to be a tough lot with cheery dispositions. When they pass by, one of them yells out, "Jesus, fellas. Bloody Chinks. The bastards are everywhere." I don't react to the soldier's words but think bitterly, "More racism! Is there anyone, anywhere, who has a decent word to say about the Chinese?" I just smile back at the man who shouted, thinking that the Australians are just the latest Allied troops we are to come into contact with as this war continues to eat up so many men from all over the world.

There's a letter waiting for me when I get back to the Mess that night. It's from Kibblesworth, written in my brother Norman's handwriting. I open it with a sense of fear. Norman's not much of a one for writing unless it's serious. The letter tells me that Billy Bissel's brother, Jack Bissel, came back home from the Front with a bullet wound that shattered his knee, a wound that was turning rotten. He also had a shocking head cold. Our Nanna knows the Bissel family well and helped Jack's mother tend for her returned son. He died after being home three days from the head cold. Spanish Flu. Our Nanna caught it from him and she died a week later. Before she died she passed it on to our Grandad and him, being near on sixty years old, couldn't cope with it. He too died within a week. Norman tells me that he's all right but being very careful. There's a lot of this 'flu illness in the village but what can he do? He ends his dreadful news with the hope that I'm all right and to look after myself. It's not for a couple of hours later that I begin to sob.

My diary tells me that it's the twenty-first of March 1918, the day the German Commander, Field Marshal Ludendorff, launches an all-out offensive. His army has been bolstered by the arrival of over one million troops from the Eastern Front, following the withdrawal of Russia from the war and he attacks before we can deploy the overwhelming resources, both in men and materiel, of the Americans. Just as our General Command expected, their main offensive is aimed at the point where our lines meet those of the French. Their aim is to drive a gap through towards Amiens, swing to the North and isolate and destroy the British Army. Ludendorff must reason French will then sue for an armistice. Three other offensives are launched against our lines to the north of the Somme at the same time but these are considered to be only diversionary. Billy Bissel inspired nightmares become more regular. Surely this carnage must end soon.

Ludendorff orders a change in tactics from those used in earlier battles. His men are ordered to attack and, once through our lines, to keep on advancing. He deploys his fittest and most battle-hardened men in the vanguard of the assault. Referred to as storm troopers, they are the best available out of his exhausted army. We learn from prisoners we take that their orders are not to consolidate gains but to advance into our rear areas and destroy our support elements and reserves. A second wave made up of second grade German troops is deployed to mop up any pockets of resistance after the first wave has crashed through. That's the theory anyway. What actually happens is not as planned and quite remarkable.

In many instances, once the German troops get past the front-line defences, they come across large quantities of food and wine and they stop fighting for three days while they gorge themselves. The Allied blockade of German ports has had a devastating effect on Germany's ability to feed its troops. Many of them are literally starving. After three days, the German command manages to get the poor buggers to restart the attack and a section of the fighting falls on the centre and left of the French First Army. They are a regiment of newly arrived troops who have taken over some of the line to the south of Villers-Bretonneux. Part of the French line falls back, but a counterattack regains much of the lost ground. As is so often the case in warfare, the situation becomes very confused. Despite the fact that Ludendorff fails to establish clear objectives, the initial German advance achieves significant results. On a fifty-mile front, we fall back in disorder with German successes poised to take the Channel ports in the north, enter Amiens in the centre and to capture Paris to the south. A German victory is a distinct possibility.

As the German offensive builds up momentum, we are drafted to move ammunition forward and to assist in bringing huge numbers of pitifully wounded soldiers back to Amiens. For the first two weeks of the offensive, we work all hours with no time for effective rest. I find no real time to grieve for my grandparents as I can hear the sounds of the guns clearly and my fear grows again. Too many times.

I've been here before too often. We are eventually able to hold firm and the German offensive stalls but I'm sure they will attack again and I feel a sense of panic. I try to focus on the task at hand and push the men to double our efforts repairing the third line trenches.

The CO hands us each a copy of the latest piece of bumph from Head Quarters, although what our Prime Minister expects those of us here in the thick of it to do is anybody's guess. Of course the Americans need to be here! Perhaps if we pray harder?

LLOYD GEORGE TO THE UNITED STATES OF AMERICA

We are at the crisis of war. Attacked by an immense superiority of German troops, our army has been forced to retire. The retirement has been carried out methodically before the pressure of a steady succession of fresh German reserves, which are suffering enormous losses.

The situation is being faced with splendid courage and resolution. The dogged pluck of our troops has for the moment checked the ceaseless onrush of the enemy, and the French have joined in the struggle; but the battle, the greatest and most momentous in the history of the world, is only just beginning.

Throughout it the French and British are buoyed with the knowledge that the great Republic of the West will neglect no effort, which can hasten its troops and ships to Europe. In war, time is vital. It is impossible to exaggerate the importance of getting American reinforcements across the Atlantic in the shortest possible space of time.
The Times, 29 March 1918

We are now perilously close to the fighting and I'm deeply concerned for the wellbeing of my men. I climb up onto a platform in the trench I'm working in and use the pair of binoculars I've scrounged to look to the East. Li Cheng-fang stands beside me and I'm surprised to hear him remind me that he and his fellow countrymen have not come here to fight. My anger boils within me.

"You listen to me, Li Cheng-fang. You're an essential part of our defence force right now. Whether you like it or not, there's no way you'll be allowed to move to the rear away from the front line. The situation we are in is critical. Get used to it, laddie."

The giant stares back at me. He may not understand all of my words but I have no doubt that he grasps my meaning.

I open my diary at the fifth day of April 1918.

'The Hun is getting very, very close. Off to the trenches with Company 21 again. We leave at 0500. They're handling the extra work and longer hours well but Li Cheng-fang is right. We shouldn't be taking them so close to the fighting. No choice, unfortunately. We have to do what we must do'.

We have been here for just an hour when I hear frantic cries of 'Stand to' and I see soldiers around me leap to their firing positions and begin to fire from the tops of the trenches. I yell to the men to take cover but this is easier said than done, and some of them begin to panic. Our position is precarious. It's far too late to run with safety. We have to stand and fight. Twenty paces to my right, I can see German troops leaping into the trenches and fierce hand-to-hand combat taking place. I begin to shake and bite my lip hard to steady myself. Men are slashing wildly at each other with bayonet, helmet, shovel or whatever else they can use as a weapon. Once more, I'm knee deep in foul murder.

A young British soldier falls beside me. He's been shot in the face and is quite dead. I pick up his rifle and climb onto the platform we had moments earlier been repairing. There are men lying dead or wounded all over the mud in front of me. Others are charging up behind them. Hundreds of them, all charging forward, screaming like banshees, bayonets fixed and intent on killing. I look to my front and see men beginning to fall as British machine guns cut them down from the flanks but one man suddenly looms large into my view. He is screaming madly and running straight at me, with his rifle held at the waist, bayonet gleaming. I feel the ice that was so familiar not two years ago course though my body. The enemy soldier is much closer and his screams fill my ears. He's almost upon me and I see his face twist in terror as I fire.

The Hun is no more than a young man who is now lying within an arm's length to my front. His helmet has come off revealing yellow, wavy hair. His blue eyes shine with agony as he lays, face forward, his hands gripping the lower part of his body where my bullet has torn a bloody hole in his uniform. His boots are drumming the ground as his body convulses. His rifle lies useless by his side, the tip of his bayonet now level with my face as I stand there staring. My victim's screaming changes to heavy sobs and I look again into the poor man's eyes. Man? He looks to be no more than sixteen or seventeen. Far too young to die like this.

Su Ting-fu, the man we call the Clown, is the first of my men to follow my lead. He strips a rifle from a wounded British soldier and begins swinging it around like a club. Why did we not teach them the basics of weapon handling, I groan to myself. Several others join in the mayhem while some of my men turn tail and flee. Many around me are writhing horribly and then a young soldier passes me mumbling frantically to the object clutched in his hands. He's carrying a pigeon.

There's a terrible, loud noise over to my right as a shell bursts above us. Another shell explodes closer still and I'm sent flying backwards into the trench. Not again, please. As I stagger to my feet there's another shell burst and I feel the warmth of blood pouring down my face. My knees lose their strength and suddenly I'm being lifted across the broad back of a huge man. It's Billy Bissel. But why is he speaking Chinese? There are steps leading out of the rear of the trench and I'm being carried like a sack of spuds up and out of this Hellhole.

"OK, mate. We can take him from here but you had better come with us too."

I'm being lowered onto a stretcher and then bounced heavily as the pain hits me. Billy's telling me that I'm going to be all right, but he's not Billy Bissel and I sink into blackness.

I turn my head away from the bright light that is drilling into my eye. As I focus, I see a nurse fussing over the man lying in a bed next to me.

"Lie still now. You've been hurt but it's not serious and carrying that wounded officer has not helped. Everyone is talking about your bravery, Mr Chinaman. You're a hero! Just take it easy now. The Doctor is coming soon"

I try to lift my head to get a better view but the effort sends a sharp pain through my skull and I yelp out.

"Well now. Welcome back, Captain. I was just telling your saviour here how brave he was bringing you out of danger like he did. Everyone's talking about it".

My eye focuses on the man in the next bed. It's Li Cheng-fang. What the hell happened? The effort is too much and I drift back into the peaceful darkness again.

"Charlie. How do you feel? Charlie, it's me".

The voice of the Padre brings me back into a world I'm not sure I want to be in. My mind fills with the noise of battle and the gurgling sound the young soldier made after I shot him. I can see his face, contorted in agony and I hear again the sound of bursting shells. What was Billy Bissel doing there? I think of him and my mind turns to my Nanna and I feel tears streaming down my face.

"Steady on my friend. You're safe now and in good hands. Your wound is not as serious as we first thought and the medics say you'll be out of here in a day or two. I'll see that you are taken good care of".

The gentle, soothing voice of the Padre envelopes me and I try to go back to the darkness but I suddenly remember the man in the next bed.

"Where's Li Cheng-fang?" I manage to croak.

"He's fine too, Charlie. Easy does it. He has a slight wound in his side, a fragment of the shell that knocked you out. It didn't stop him carrying you to safety though. He's been treated here and is now back in camp resting. We're all very proud of him, in fact we are proud of all our men. They acted with bravery, especially Su Ting-fu who fought like a madman apparently. He helped Li Cheng-fang to get you up across his back and get you to safety. The Line held. We were fortunate. Now rest, Charlie. You need to rest".

A day has passed and I have been sleeping easily, or so they tell me. Now that I'm awake, I'm more or less ignored as the medics see to other more urgent cases. There seem to be plenty of them. A harassed looking doctor stops by my bed, makes a quick assessment and says to the orderly by his side, "This chap looks much better. Get him back to his unit as soon as you can. We need the bed".

Chapter Eighteen
A hero's welcome

"Good morning, Charlie. How are you this morning?"

The Padre has brought me a cup of coffee. He also brings me news of the fighting, which is much more to my liking. Ludendorff's supply system apparently failed to keep up with his so-called storm troopers and his offensive stalled completely. The town of Villers-Bretonneux where we were working became pivotal in the campaign. German storm troopers managed to get into the town but a magnificent counter attack, in which Australian troops play a major part, drove them back. I'm delighted to learn that the attack on Amiens came to a halt.

"That's good news, Padre and I have some too. No permanent damage this time. The head has cleared quite well but I don't remember much about what happened. I've been told a number of times about Li Cheng-fang's actions in saving my skin. How is he? And what about the other men who were hurt?"

"Li Cheng-fang's fine. He's here in camp and wants to see you. If you are up for it, I'll bring him around later after the evening meal. As for the others", the padre pauses, "well, I wasn't completely truthful with you yesterday. Two of the men were killed and four injured. Two of the injured are not in a bad way and are now resting and the other two have been taken to the hospital for Chinese labourers that has been set up at Noyelles. My word, Charlie, it is *well* set up. 1,500 beds and over three hundred medical staff. Chinese speaking physicians, excellent equipment and good quality nursing. Fellow called Douglas Gray, a doctor, has come over from the British legation in Peking and he's the CO there. He insisted on the Chinese having the same standard of medical care as the British and by George, he's been successful. Our men are excellent hands."

The padre takes out a packet of cigarettes then puts it back into his pocket.

"Oops. Force of habit. Mustn't smoke in front of any patient and you should be no exception."

Damn his concern about smoking in front of me, I'm shocked to hear of the death of my men. They didn't come here to fight. Did I take them too close to danger? Damn this bloody war. I'm heartily sick of it. And I want to know about Li Cheng-fang.

"How badly injured is he, Padre?"

"The initial wound was apparently not that serious. He took a piece of shrapnel in his side but the chap who removed it did so in the frantic heat of handling mass casualties. I'm afraid he rather butchered the young man.

He's getting good treatment here in camp now but apparently, there could be complications. The shell splinter took a piece of his cloth shirt into the wound with it and it has become infected. He can walk but he may have to go back into hospital for a while yet. The problem is finding both transport and bed space. If the infection can be treated here, he's better off staying with us. I went to see him before coming in to see you and the first thing he said was to ask how you are. He doesn't see himself as having done anything special. You're his friend and he looked after you. A simple philosophy we could all benefit from adopting, don't you think?"

It is 0800 Friday April 12th and I'm back on duty ready to hear the CO's daily orders.

"Briefly, gentlemen, and for the benefit of Captain Wallace, the strategic situation has improved. The Germans came within 400 yards or so of taking Villers-Bretonneux. It was a bloody close call. Mainly as a result of a counter-attack by a thousand men of the 36th Australian Battalion, the Germans were pushed back. They forced two entire German divisions to retreat from the town. Magnificent effort. Our people believe that Ludendorff has now brought his entire offensive to a halt. We'll see how long that lasts, but where are the bloody Americans? That's the key.

Ludendorff's still trying his luck elsewhere, however, for the moment, not here in our sector. So, what this means to us is we press on with bolstering defences. Captain Asmiroff, you will continue to command Number One section as well as Number Two. You have your tasks for the days ahead?"

The Russian nods his head and says, "I have, sir."

He looks as arrogant and disinterested as ever and I wonder what effect this morose, unfriendly man will be having on my men.

"Next item. There is a report that the Germans dropped bombs on one of the Labour Corps camps in the north near Calais. The men came out in the open to see the airplanes. Many of them had never seen fighting aircraft before and apparently, they stood gawking upwards like children. When the bombing started there were several deaths and injuries among the Chinese, caught unawares and in the open as they were and they went berserk. Several of them broke out of the camp and attacked some German prisoners of war who were being held nearby and they killed a lot of them. Not much we can do about this but it serves to warn us of the need for tight discipline. Be aware, gentlemen. Our Chinamen may be docile with us but they too have their limits"

The CO pauses, staring hard at each man in turn and continues, "Sergeant Major Peters, you will focus your time assisting Captain Asmiroff with the tasks allocated to Section Number One."

"Lieutenant Hastings … what have you got for us?"

The lieutenant looks serious and announces, "Four more men have come down with this blasted 'flu and another of the men hospitalised with the infection died last night. He was only admitted three days ago."

Major Roberts snorts angrily, "All the way through the Army we're losing far too many men to the 'flu. It's a bugger! Civilian deaths are massive too. It's a huge epidemic and it's getting worse."

He looks hard at me, obviously aware of my news from home.

"You young man, are excused duties until further notice. I want you rested and restored to fitness as soon as possible. In the meantime, you *will* take things easy. That's an order. Now, does anyone have any questions?"

No one says anything and so the CO concludes the meeting and we all move outside. As Asmiroff strides away without a word, Lieutenant Hastings salutes me with a warm smile and says, "Good to see you up and about, sir", before walking away.

As everyone else heads off to their duties, I take Sergeant Major Peters to one side and ask him, "How are the men coping, sergeant major?"

"They were badly shaken by the deaths of their mates and they're certainly not happy about going back to trench work. Captain Asmiroff has taken a hard line and morale is a bit of a problem, but we're coping well. They're really concerned about illness. So many of them are being affected by this 'flu epidemic. Just like us, they don't know what to do to protect themselves against it. Not much we can do there except to make sure they get medical treatment a.s.a.p. They miss Li Cheng-fang but, on the good side, they're incredibly proud of what he did. The other two foremen, Sun Jun and Li Zhang, are good blokes and we've spilt Li Cheng-fang's group between them. Other than all that, they'll be happy to see you up and about and will be even happier when you're back on deck, Sir."

I dismiss him with a 'thank you' feeling a bit lost. Inactivity is not something I need right now. I decide to head for the officer's mess, which is empty, and I order a cup of tea. There are papers and magazines lying around so I settle in for some light reading, picking up a copy of *The London Illustrated News* dated Saturday February 16, 1918. The cover carries a drawing depicting the burial of the first U. S. troops 'killed in action' in France, followed on page two by an article on 'The Threatened German Offensive by a Major W. Wittall'. Old news and opinions. I begin flipping the pages until a headline catches my interest. 'Names in

Everybody's Mouths: People of The Moment'. There's a portrait of a Mister Trotsky declaring the war with the Central Powers is at an end and another announcing the appointment of Lord Beaverbrook as Minister of Propaganda. Meanwhile, Jemadar Gobind Singh of the Indian cavalry received his VC recently from the King at Buckingham Palace. The citation shows that he 'thrice carried messages over a mile and a half of open ground swept by enemy gunfire, his horse being shot under him each time'.

"Jemadar?" I murmur to myself. "A second lieutenant in the Indian Army. I wonder if I should recommend Li Cheng-fang for a gong too?"

I glance cynically at photographs of the King's procession to open parliament. More pomp and posturing. It's a bit of a contrast to here where his loyal subjects are striving just to survive. There are two drawings from the Middle East. They depict successes against the Turk, one with the benefit of air power and the other an old-fashioned cavalry charge, swords drawn, by a Yeomanry Squadron against Turkish bayonets.

"All very *Boy's Own* adventure stuff and nothing like what we went through in the trenches last week," I murmur aloud again.

The pages continue with various war related stories, proud family photos of young officers killed in action, French politics and the sacking of the Russian Tsar's Winter Palace by the Bolsheviks. Not much in the way of light reading. Even the two books that are reviewed provide little interest. One is a war story and the other a tale of spies.

It begins to pour with rain, it's only 10.30 in the morning and my head is starting to throb. The mess steward asks me if I would like anything and I almost ask for a whisky. I could murder a stiff drink right now but instead I ask for another tea. My thoughts begin to wander. The loss of my grandparents is sinking in harshly. My Nanna taught me to think in a broad sense about what I will do with my life, but I followed the path of so many Geordies with a life starting in the mines and moving to the only alternative our villagers knew, that of the Army. I doubt that I could ever go back down any mine without the ghost of Billy Bissel coming with me. At first the Army gave me great satisfaction and dreams of the future but that has long since disappeared. The senseless slaughter I have seen and taken part in has all but destroyed my love of the uniform. Just as Billy will block any notions of mining, the image of the young German I killed only a couple of short days ago has sickened me. I need to find something else, something of greater value to do with my life. A return to Kibblesworth or even to England is not one I'm looking forward to. As I sit lost in thought, the Padre comes into the mess.

"There you are, Charlie. And drinking tea, no less. Well done my friend".

He sits down with a smile on his face and says, "I've just come from seeing Li Cheng-fang. He's doing well. The infected wound is responding to Doc Hammond's treatment and his prognosis is a positive one. Li Cheng-fang is looking forward to our meeting this evening, although he tells me that he has something of great importance to share with you. I have no idea what it is but that mystery will be solved when we meet. How are you bearing up on 'excused duties'? Knowing you, I imagine that you are already getting restless".

I smile back at him and keep my thoughts to myself.

Later in the evening I greet my rescuer as he and the Padre come into my office, and the Chinaman shakes my hand in the English way but with great vigour. He is beaming and laughs loudly when I protest and pretend that he has torn my arm off. We have the room to ourselves as the other officers I share the office with are elsewhere and we gather three of the more comfortable chairs around a low table. The Padre sets down a large pot and three mugs then pours us each a hot coffee. Milk has become scarce but we have plenty of sugar. Quite a contrast to a mere six months ago when he and I would finish our evening with gin and whiskey. The peaceful life we had in China seems like a dream.

"My injury is now very better. I thank Doctor Hammond who is doing very good for me".

Li Cheng-fang's English may be fractured but he speaks with confidence and his English leaves my Mandarin to shame. I'm surprised though when he starts talking about what happened in the trenches. I'm sure that this is not the 'matter of great importance' the Padre mentioned but I sit back and listen.

"Just before we injured, I see soldier with bird in his hands. He crazy?"

I smile and tell him that we British use birds, pigeons, to take messages to each other. "The birds are well trained and they too risk their lives to fight in this war".

He looks at me carefully to see if I am joking but then shakes his head in admiration.

"The bird must be very brave, Captain Armstrong".

This is something I would never even contemplate and I'm trying to think of an appropriate answer when the Padre chips in. He too must have been reflecting on the time that has passed since we left Qingdao.

"Just think how our lives have changed", he muses. "It took an age to get here but we were fortunate. I was talking to one of the doctors at the Chinese hospital who told me that early last year a German submarine attacked and sank a French transport ship called the 'S.S. Athos'. That was off the coast of Malta in the Mediterranean. It went down with the loss of over five hundred Chinese lives. The ship took what they thought would be a safer route. The authorities believed that German sympathisers who remained in Qingdao after the Japanese takeover could be supplying intelligence on shipping schedules to Huns back in Germany. Many of those who perished had been recruited without the direct knowledge of the Chinese government and so they were unidentifiable, as official records of their brief service did not exist. Something of a disgrace, I think."

I'm puzzled why the Padre is talking like this and I look at Li Cheng-fang who is listening intently.

"Li Cheng-fang and a few others in the camp have been talking to me about the future for China after the war. It spices up our English classes quite a bit".

He finishes his story with a look of embarrassment and I agree that if the story is true then it certainly is a disgrace and I wonder if the families of those drowned received any compensation.

"I think this story very true and is important reason China declare war on Germany after this happen".

Li Cheng-fang has joined in to my increasing surprise. We're talking politics, for goodness sake. And, moreover, Li Cheng-fang seems to be much more knowledgeable than I imagined. I feel a surge of shame. Why shouldn't he be? Am I as prejudiced as so many others thinking that the men are all uneducated coolies?

I'm listening closely now as Li Cheng-fang continues with increased pride and authority in his voice.

"China will join in peace process when war ends and will be given honour it deserves as a sovereign state. Now Germans stopped, maybe war stop and British win. We then go home to China. What you think, Captain Armstrong?"

"Well", I fluster, "Ludendorff's offensive has certainly been brought to a halt. With the arrival of the Americans I believe this could very well be the end to the war. It's perfectly reasonable that you should begin thinking of going home if that's what you want".

I'm still rather confused as to why he is talking this way and I'm totally unprepared for his next question.

"When war finish, Chinamen go home to China, Mr Padre say he too go home to China, we want you go home to China also".

Chapter Nineteen
A new vision

I spent the night with my mind in turmoil and not, for a pleasant change, because of dreaming about Billy Bissel.

Li Cheng-fang's words are resonating. Could I really go back 'home' to China when all this is over? The death of my grandparents means that the only close family I have now, back 'home' in England, is my elder brother, Norman. The thought of going back to work with him in the Kibblesworth colliery does not appeal to me at all but what else am I suited for in the village? This war has left me totally disenchanted with the Army and so I need to look elsewhere to find a new life that will have some meaning for me. Nana always encouraged me to think in a broad sense about my future but even she would never have contemplated a life living in China. Why not? The Padre has done it. Hastings grew up in China, obviously loves the place and is keen to return. The Jew I met in the YMCA, Henri, obviously lived there contentedly and he only came back to Europe in the hope that it was less prejudiced, which of course it isn't. Goodness knows I've had to contend with heaps of prejudice myself from snotty-nosed Englishmen from the South, especially those with pretentions of being 'upper-class'. Snobs, the lot of them. Perhaps I should use this spell of 'excused-duties' to explore the possibilities?

After breakfast, I find a quiet spot in the mess and, armed with a field notebook and a strong cup of coffee, I settle in to make some plans. I asked Lieutenant Hastings to come and find me when he had a break in his duties and this obviously intrigued him. He arrives within twenty minutes.

"You wanted to see me, Sir?"

"Yes, I do and you can relax, you are not in any strife and what I want to talk to you about has nothing to do with Army. Grab a coffee and sit down, please".

The lad does as he is told, but my use of the word 'please' raises his eyebrows a bit.

"I'm thinking about what I will do after the war. I know that it is unhealthy to think this way during the sort of heavy conflict that is still going on all around us ... tempting fate and all that ... but it has been suggested to me that I should think about going back to China. What do you think?"

Hastings looks at me in amazement, then his face creases into a huge smile.

"Excellent idea, Sir. You're just the sort of person China needs right now. The men think the world of you and will follow you anywhere. That is not something I can say about many of the officers I have come across here. Most of them regard the Chinese with little to no respect. There are Chinamen here who have ancestries that would put many of our pretentious officers to shame. Li Cheng-fang sings your praises for all to hear and his ancestry could be classed as nobility in English terms. His family goes back generations and he is only working with the Corps because the family fell on hard times, having been trapped by a greedy landlord and crippling debt due to the famine at the end of last century. Many noble families are in this position. Landlords are parasites and should be flogged".

"That's all well and good but how would I fit in to this?"

Hastings sits back and becomes thoughtful.

"Well, for a start, Sir, I would suggest that you return to one of the larger cities in China. Shanghai would be an obvious choice as there are many Westerners there and the opportunities for you would be quite extensive. As I've already told you, Sir, my father works for a subsidiary of the Jardine-Matheson Group in Shanghai. I would be happy to write to him and tell him about you and about your interest in working in China. Your Mandarin is not that extensive but with effort you could improve it enormously. You have an excellent chance to do that here, almost as good as living in China. I'd be happy to help and the men love it when you speak to them in their own tongue. It's only natural. Plus the respect you are gaining will follow you over there".

Hastings is sitting up straight as an arrow, looking at me with bright, excited eyes. His enthusiasm is catching and I beam back at him.

"Write to your father, by all means. It is very kind of you to offer. Meanwhile I'll take your advice and redouble my efforts with the language. Erm … thank you very much".

The young man, impervious to my embarrassment, stands and says, "My apologies, Sir, but I'm expected in the Q store. I have to go, if you'll excuse me".

I nod my assent and he grabs his cap and rushes out with a final smile and a very non-military wave.

So much for any doubt I may have as to my suitability.

I decide to find the Padre and talk about this new idea of mine but he is focused on other issues.

"Have you heard the stories about the state of the German prisoners we took. Poor blighters are starving. They talk openly about conditions back in Germany, which are apparently pretty appalling too. Some of them told stories of men who have been sent to join in at the front after being charged with insurrection back in Germany. They relate stories of terrible deprivation within the civilian population and talk of widespread strikes throughout their homeland. The leaders of these strikes and other radicals and what have you have been brought to trial and then sent to the front. Instead of going to prison they have been sent to serve with fighting units! How silly is that? They are spreading their discontent among the troops first hand. It's incredibly stupid!"

The Padre pauses to light a cigarette and then continues incredulously, "They are even sending pacifists to the front. Not surprisingly, all they are doing is preaching disruptive doctrines and, so it seems, to a very receptive audience. The negative effect on German morale has apparently been immense."

"Good".

This was not the reaction the Padre expected, but I continued, "The lower their morale the better, Padre. The lower it gets, the more chance there will be for us to end this madness. Feeling sorry for the enemy may be the Christian way of looking at things but really, Padre, really! Get a grip! We are at war with these so-called 'poor Germans', for goodness sake".

The Padre's rushed off on some other mission of mercy or whatever and I wander over to the YMCA hut. Being 'excused duties' is all very well but I'm used to my life being run in an orderly way, according to routines. When I enter the hut, I'm greeted by a few familiar faces, those of my men who are on rest days, the shy face of Mr Bertram and then the welcoming smile of Henri, the rather odd French Jew of Spanish origin who understands the Chinese language and way of life. We sit at a table and Henri orders a pot of tea.

"How very English", I think, but the tea arrives with cups that have no handles and without the English accompaniments of milk and sugar. Tea as it was meant to be drunk?

"You look very pensive, mon ami".

Henri is relaxed and friendly but he too is taken aback when I blurt out, "I'm thinking of going back to China after this is all over. What do you think?"

The Frenchman's advice mirrors that of young Hastings. Go to Shanghai. Use the time here to improve my Mandarin. When I mention Jardine Matheson, Henri spits and mumbles something about capitalists, which I do not understand, but he quickly adds, "Yes, they would be an excellent starting point for you. But if you join them, we must keep in touch. I too will return to Shanghai. There is much work to be done there".

I'm at a loss to understand what sort of work he is talking about, but for the moment my idea gets another vote of approval from someone I trust so I drink my tea and enjoy his company. When it is time to have lunch, I say farewell to the occupants of the canteen and meet with the Padre in the Officer's Mess. The missionary has mellowed his tone and tells me that he is going to pay another visit the Chinese hospital where our men are recovering. I readily accept his offer to go along with him. It'll help fill the day in a productive way.

When we arrive at the Chinese hospital in Noyelles, I have to agree with the Padre about the way it has been set up. Nearly everyone there is either Chinese or a Chinese speaker. I'm told that even the ward staff who do basic duties have been taught enough of the language to be able to communicate with the patients on simple matters. I'll wager to say they would not get treatment like this back in China. It's a good news story for a change and why on Earth not. Why shouldn't the Chinese get decent treatment? I notice that every ward has a caged canary. The Chinese love their birds and Gray, the hospital CO, has catered for this brilliantly. He has also had a wooden pagoda built beside the main entrance and it has been painted in bright colours. Gaudy to our eyes but I bet the Chinese love it. It serves as a fire tower and has a clock with a gong that strikes the hour on the hour. There's a ward dedicated to mental cases and an isolation ward for sixteen or so lepers! How they got through all of our medical checks I have no idea. They certainly didn't get leprosy here in France, however bad things are.

We visit our two wounded men who are recovering well and are quite happy with the treatment they are getting. While the Padre goes off to talk to one of the doctors I spot an English language magazine lying on a table near the entrance to the hospital. It's a copy of *The London Illustrated News* and I grab it quickly and read more about the role of the newly appointed Minister of Propaganda. I'm not sure how I feel about that. Telling lies on a grand scale could be counter-productive. If we are lying so much to the enemy, perhaps we are being lied to as well … by our own government. When I went to the airstrip we worked on when we first arrived, I met one of the Royal Flying Corps people there, a chap called Gregory. He told me that we are now flying over the enemy and dropping thousands of leaflets. These messages are telling the German troops that we are feeding POWs as well as we feed ourselves. The leaflets offer safe passage to good conditions to any German soldier who surrenders. This is bloody underhand, if you ask me. There are some very nasty things coming out of this war. We're actually spying on each other like thieves in the night. My grandad always told me a decent man did not read another man's letters but I hear we are doing much worse.

Getting intelligence about the enemy is one thing but we are going too far. The whole of Society is changing and not for the better. Britain will be a very different place after the war than it was before and once more I think about the idea of going to China.

The padre re-joins me and we drive back to camp.

"Well, our men seem in good shape and their morale is high, don't you think?"

"Their morale may be high, Padre, but Sergeant Major Peters is not very happy about Asmiroff and his miserable attitude. It takes a lot for an NCO to bad mouth an officer to another officer. It borders on mutiny really, but our good sergeant major is not a happy man. At least we have Li Cheng-fang in number one section. He's turned out to be a rock. Keep an eye out for me if you would, Padre. The men deserve better than Asmiroff."

The Padre nods but replies, "Talking of Li Cheng-fang, I took our friend to a service in the local Catholic church last Sunday. He was appalled when I told the meaning of the Catholic Eucharist. He saw it as an act of cannibalism, for goodness sake. There are stories floating around China in which we missionaries, and Catholic nuns in particular, are accused of taking body parts from orphans for medicinal purposes. The stories focus on us removing hearts and eyes but how can I explain autopsies to someone like Li Cheng-fang? He's convinced now, after seeing the Eucharist, that the stories must be true. It's maddening."

My friend seems to be all over the place. Happy one minute, depressed the next.

"Cheer up, Malcolm. You're supposed to cheer us all up. The lads depend on you to be positive, eh?"

"The 'lads', as you call them, tell me story after story that 'lads' should not be faced with. I went to a clearing station for the wounded last week after a recent big push and talked to a young chap about seventeen years old from Falkirk in Scotland. He told me with pride that he 'kept the line' as he advanced with his regiment into enemy fire. They were line abreast, fixed bayonets, bagpipes playing and his friends falling like flies all around him. He was carried back with shocking wounds, but he lay there smiling. 'I didn't break the line, Padre', he told me, as if that was what really mattered. He should be home playing football or courting girls. Another young man told me that, while he was lying injured in a shell hole half filled with water, his mother came to him and sat with him. He swears blind that his mother was there, and a shell landed two feet away. It didn't go off and he is convinced it was because of his mother. Other men have told me stories of dead companions who have come back to save their lives by telling them to change positions or turn right instead of left or whatever. These men actually believe these ghost stories and others listen. God is taking a back seat. You yourself have said to me that there are no atheists in the trenches, but what kind of faith is taking hold in the minds of so many, I wonder?"

I'm at a complete loss to answer and try changing the subject.

"Did you hear the German pilot, Baron von Richthofen, the ace they call the Red Barron, got his comeuppance yesterday? We're not sure who brought him down but what matters is that he is no longer a threat."

The Padre stares back at me dully.

"Another life lost and you are happy?"

I decide to leave telling him of my plans for the future to another time.

Chapter Twenty
The Tide is Slowly Turning

Lieutenant Bertram and Mr Flaxton walk in to the Mess mid-morning, wearing rather smug, self-important smiles on their faces.

"Good morning, Sir. I hope we are not disturbing you. It's St Georges Day and we thought it a good day to visit".

Bertram has gained in confidence since his move to the YMCA role but what an odd way to start a conversation. The American, Flaxton, as officious as ever, interrupts him.

"Yes, yes, yes Colin. All in good time. We are here to help Li Cheng-fang get some recompense for his injuries. Under the terms of his contract, he is entitled to compensation for his injuries. We have submitted claims on behalf of the families of those who were killed, but he should also receive financial recompense."

He pulls some papers from the bag he is carrying and shows them to me.

"As you are so close to Li Cheng-fang, we thought that you may like to approach him yourself, rather than have us do it. This is just one of the many services we're providing to our Chinese brethren while they're here in France."

I'm not sure how to react as the pair are irritating me.

"Sergeant Elliott handles all pay matters. This for him to handle. I'm sure your help is appreciated but let us do our duties first before you interfere".

My words are like water off a duck's back as Flaxton replies, "Yes, yes, yes but surely you will want to help the man after all he did for you".

It is part statement and part question but, whichever way, I feel my anger rise.

"The YMCA is doing a good job but do not overstep the mark. Help but do not interfere when it is not necessary. I'll talk to Elliott and leave the matter with him".

The hardness in my voice sets Bertram back on his heels but the American is oblivious.

"Just think of the good we are doing, Captain Armstrong. Our staff are helping more and more labourers to write letters and to read any replies. In some cases we are writing more or less standard letters for them; letters that express a positive attitude, in order to comply with the strict rules of your military censorship. These are being printed out and used by our staff who add a labourer's name and the family address, getting them ready for posting. The Association is also providing stationary that is printed in English and Chinese and all of this is free of charge."

He pauses waiting for me to give a sign of approval and when I say nothing he continues.

"The men are also being given return envelopes printed in French and Chinese to ensure that return mail will be correctly and speedily delivered back here to this camp! This service is not only good for the men's morale, it is prompting many of our brethren to try to learn how to read and write themselves."

He pauses once more, looking very pleased with himself, before launching forth again.

"Are you aware that a graduate of Yale University, a man called Yan Yang-chu, asked for volunteers among the YMCA staff, those who would be willing to be taught one thousand basic Chinese characters that he himself had invented. Just think, Captain, he has invented a new way of writing for the Chinese language. Isn't that fantastic?"

They both look at me expectantly and this time I show reluctant interest. It sounds to me to be an excellent idea but I'm still irritated by their attitudes. Any move towards helping these Chinamen raise their levels of knowledge, however, will be most welcome.

"The first group proved to be so successful he asked the Commander of the Chinese Labour Corps to send a number of Chinese YMCA student volunteers to Boulogne for one week, to observe his teaching method so that they could also start classes of their own. Three of our Chinese colleagues who work in Amiens have gone. This revolutionary new teaching method could prove to be the foundation of widespread literacy programs in China. Yan Yang-chu has vowed to devote the rest of his life offering what he calls the release of the pent-up, God-given powers in the people."

Flaxton obviously regards the success of Yan Yang-chu's program as evidence of the power of his Christian faith but I can see the benefits this man's work could bring to our men. I wonder if the Padre is aware of this program?

Next morning the CO hands me a copy of a communiqué that has been written in uncharacteristically detailed terms about recent activity in our immediate vicinity.

"It's been written by the French but it's probably a damn sight more accurate than some of the so-called intelligence we've been getting".

It reads: "At dawn on the 24th of April 1918 German troops tried yet again to break through the Allied lines. This time they captured Villers-Bretonneux using tanks and infantry. They led their attack with thirteen tanks at two points, at Villers-Bretonneux and a kilometre further south. Wherever they attacked, they broke through immediately. Troops defending the area were driven back. The majority of these troops were boys merely eighteen and nineteen who had yet to fire a shot in anger. Unlike the Australians stationed nearby, they had received no preparation in the "nursery area" and were far from ready for battle. The enemy took over two thousand prisoners during the engagement. Before the sector commanders have even heard of the attack, Villers-Bretonneux and Abbey Wood beyond it had been captured, along with Hangard village".

I look at the CO with concern but he tells me to read on.

"The job of retaking Villers-Bretonneux was assigned to two Australian brigades. The plan of attack devised by the Australian General, Sir John Monash, was to encircle and trap the Germans. There was to be no preliminary bombardment. Instead, the Australians launched a surprise attack at night. Two battalions began the assault from the south towards the east of Villers-Bretonneux while three battalions attacked from the north at the same time. The assault began on the evening of the 24th April. The Australians silenced the German machine guns, then fought the enemy in a ferocious house-to-house confrontation. A German POW, an officer, is said to have remarked that the Australians, "were magnificent. Nothing seemed to stop them. When our fire was heaviest, they just disappeared in shell holes and came up as soon as it slackened." By dawn on the 25th of April, the Australians had broken through the German positions and the French and Australian flags were raised over Villers-Bretonneux. It took the rest of the day and into the next to secure the town but secure it they did and the Australians established a new front line, marking the end of the German offensive on the Somme. British Brigadier General Grogan VC called the attack, 'perhaps the greatest individual feat of the war and the Allied Supreme Commander, Marshal Foch, referred to the "altogether astonishing valiance" of the Australians".

The CO smiled and said, "That last bit. Foch probably meant to use the word 'valour'".

Major Roberts is in a cautious but cheerful mood when he holds his CO's 'O' Group on Saturday 28th April.

"I truly believe we have the Germans on the run this time. I know I said that last time, but reports are coming in from all over that the Hun is finished. They are falling back everywhere. There's still plenty for us to do, more in fact, as we have been asked to assist with burial parties. This task is a bad one. Losses have again been horrendous and we must be wary of how the Chinese will react to this work. They must also be warned that there is a lot of unexploded ordnance around where they will be working. It'll be a horrible job and extremely dangerous too. Brief your men accordingly. Charlie, you are to resume full duties with Number One Section. Captain Asmiroff, you will continue with Section Two. Remember the reports we got from further north where some of the Chinese took reprisals against German prisoners. We want none of that here, so talk to your men. Sound them out and allay their fears. I'm sure that it was fear that made them kill up north. I could be wrong, of course, but stay close with them."

"I'm planning to visit our men in the Chinese hospital again. Why don't you come with me and this time bring a *p'aitou* from each section? Li Cheng-fang, of course, and I'll ask Asmiroff to release one of his men too".

The next day was a Sunday and we set out early. Asmiroff sent the gangster, Zhou Xiao-bing, to represent Number Two Section, a choice that I could sense troubled Li Cheng-fang. However, this may be an opportunity for me to learn more about the gangster's level of influence within our Company.

When we are back in camp, I take Li Cheng-fang to one side and give him a grilling.

"If I am going to return with you to China and continue to work with you, I must be able to trust you completely. Your English is good enough for you to understand me so tell me, what is it that makes you so unhappy when you are with Zhou Xiao-bing? Out with it, now".

The young Chinaman looks shocked at my tone and I think that he is going to clamp up and walk away but he suddenly bursts out, "He is very danger man".

I don't say anything and then, after a long silence, Li Cheng-fang continues.

"Zhou Xiao-bing is very important man in Honourable Society of Qing Bang, what you English call Green Gang. He and his brother are bad men but we all fear them and try to live without them being part of our lives. In China, family is most important. Is more important than anything. Li Zhang is *p'aitou* in Number One Section like me. He is a son of my uncle. He have trouble in China army when Republic start and he hide from army. If army know where he is, he will be killed by China army so he hide in Chinese Labour Corps. Zhao Da-hai is interpreter in camp in Shandong. He learn about Li Zhang problem and he take money from Li Zhang. If Li Zhang not pay, Zhao Da-hai tell China army where he is. When we on ship, Li Zhang tell gangster Zhou Xiao-bing problem with Zhao Da-hai. Qing Bang not like this thing and Zhao Da-hai get push over side of boat into sea. Now my family owe debt to Honourable Qing Bang Society".

Well, I did ask. I'm flabbergasted and do not know what to say. Li Cheng-fang stays silent for a moment or two then quietly leaves me with my thoughts. We have a murderer in our ranks. As the reality of Li Cheng-fang's news sinks in to my consciousness, I suddenly remember that this murderer we have in our ranks has a brother who has just been arrested. How much more do I need to know about my men?

The Padre is surprised when I tackle him about Zhou Xiao-jin's arrest.

"According to him, he took up with a French woman, a widow. Her brother objected and accused him of rape. He denies the charge but he has been arrested. There is nothing we can do at the moment. He will be brought to trial and will have to face the consequences".

"What are they likely to be?"

"For the crime he's charged with and being a Chinaman and the victim a French woman, it will be the death penalty for sure".

When I pass on the Padre's words to Li Cheng-fang, he looks anxious.

"It is important that you go see Zhou Xiao-jin. Take letter from his brother. Can this be done please?"

"I'm sure that I can deliver a letter to him if that will help"

The young *p'aitou* looks miserable but replies, "Please just you take letter".

He is pleading and I have no idea why.

As things turned out, my duties take me into Amiens two days later and I'm able to visit the prison. The prison guards are disinterested and, if anything, rather bored looking, though one guard in particular shows an interest when I mention Zhou Xiao-jin's name. I'm taken through foul-smelling corridors to his cell to be greeted by our man with an unpleasant sneer on his face.

"*Ni hao*, Captain".

He really is an unpleasant character and when I hand him the letter I'm carrying from his brother, he snatches it from my hand and hides it in his shirt. This is all done in the presence of the guard who looks at me as if I am a fool.

"These pigs have me emptying buckets of shit each day. I need to get out of here".

As Zhou Xiao-jin is speaking, he turns his back on me and ignores me and I find myself being led back to the prison entrance by the same guard and given a perfunctory farewell as the gate is closed in my face. I'm bemused but I have done as I was asked, so I return to camp.

"That was one of the most bizarre experiences of my life. The man is facing a firing squad or the hangman or having his head chopped off, whatever they do here, and yet he complained about emptying buckets of filth. Am I missing something?"

The padre looks quite shocked.

"I think that you may have been used in some way, Charlie. What was in that letter you took?"

"I have no idea and now I don't want to know".

As April gives way to May, Mr Flaxton huffs and puffs his way back into my office. Li Cheng-fang's claim for compensation has been rejected, which comes as no surprise. So many men are dying or being maimed and his injury is trivial by comparison. Flaxton is making a big issue over the matter but I do not respond to his posturing. The men are content with the money they are earning. The system is fair. Monthly remittances from the Corps will be mounting up at home and they live frugally here in France. In addition, I understand that most are able to accumulate a nice amount of the locally-paid French francs. The British authorities have set up a Savings Bank and each man can watch the balance on his account grow each month. Even so, when I talk to the men, I can tell that they miss their families and there is a deep sense of longing to return home.

Chapter Twenty-one
Workers of the World

"Goodness me, Malcolm, you look terrible!"

We're sitting in a café on the outskirts of Amiens. The building has a low roof, an open iron stove and wooden benches and tables. It's a complete contrast to the Officer's Mess, and I've brought my friend here because I am increasingly worried about both his physical and his mental health. We sit down to quizzical looks from other patrons, most of whom are rank and file soldiers. Officers don't appear to be the norm as customers but the proprietress is cheerful, as is her greeting. We're offered wine, cognac or beer and I break my self-imposed pledge, choosing a red vintage that pleases both our unsophisticated palates. The speciality of the house is fried eggs and chips with fresh bread, cheese and fresh fruit to follow. It's hardly the fare of a flash hotel but a delightful change from army rations. The Padre is exhausted, both physically and spiritually, after spending long hours over many days tending to the sick and injured in hospitals that are filled to overflowing and the strain is telling.

"They call this sort of place an 'estaminet', don't you know".

I try to cheer the Padre up with some small talk.

He responds in a rather detached way, "Yes, I know. I'm told that it's a Belgian word for a café. It makes me ponder on how so many foreign words are used in a bastardised way with our soldiers? Mind you, they do quite well misusing our own words. They refer to me as a 'devil dodger' and to a buried soldier as having 'real estate' in a 'rest camp'. That's their way of talking about a cemetery".

This is not what I had in mind, and I counter with, "Yes, Malcolm, but it's a way of coping with unpleasantness. Pilots talk about 'dodging Archie', which is avoiding exploding shells from ack-ack guns, and even that is slang. Ack-ack is phonetic speech for A-A or anti-aircraft guns. I do like the phrase 'gunfire' though, which is what they call a rum ration added to morning tea before 'going over the top'. We talk in jargon as a form of bonding. Only those who endure the hardship of war understand the language. The one I find really interesting for us is a 'Chinese attack'. This is when we launch a fake attack. The preliminary bombardment stops and the enemy defences come out of their shelters and man the trenches. The bombardment starts again, catching them vulnerable to air-bursting shells. It's sneaky, but why call it Chinese, I wonder?"

The Padre begins to relax as we continue to chat in this inconsequential way. The sky is clear and the evening warm. Suddenly he sneezes and says, "I'm getting a cold, Charlie. A good night's sleep will work wonders and to that end I'm going to have a large cognac. That should help, don't you agree?"

Next morning my friend is admitted to hospital with a dose of this dreaded Spanish 'flu.

The Padre is being kept in an isolation ward. If he survives the first three days, he will be moved into a general ward and given a strong chance of survival, but I fear that for many of us it will be a long three days. I concentrate on my duties, which now tend to be routine in nature, but I spend my spare time practising my Mandarin with the men. As Hastings predicted, the men are delighted and I get involved in a wide range of discussions. One of the men I met all those months ago in the YMCA in Qingdao, a skilled mechanic called Hu Chu-xing, comes into camp to visit his former comrades. He impresses me with his excellent command of English, which he speaks with an American accent. He apparently worked for some time on an American freighter and learned much of his trade there. His mechanical skills are being well used here in France, and I sit with him as he tells about the adventures he has had since he arrived and was seconded to work in a factory building and repairing tanks.

"They're a mixed bunch, the French."

He smiles shyly at me as he says this but when I nod both my understanding of what he is saying and my agreement with his words, he beams.

"As I say, they're a mixed bunch. They're sick of this war too. I've heard there have been massive mutinies in the French army in the past. Whole regiments have rebelled against the stupidity of their generals. You will find this hard to believe but one regiment was sent into an impossible attack. The attack failed and the generals accused the men of cowardice. They picked one man in every ten and shot them as an example to the rest. How can they sleep at night, these generals? Their losses are in the millions, which is why they want skilled workers like me. I work in a factory where they repair tanks and motor vehicles and motor bicycles. There're a few Frenchmen working there too, mainly older men or men who can no longer fight, but mainly the workers are women. Once we show we can be of use, they're all over us. The men appreciate the help and the women appreciate our youth. Many are widowed and there has been a lot of what the bosses call fraternisation. Because of our skills, we have much more freedom than what I hear your guys have. I have a very nice arrangement with a young widow of nineteen."

He grins smugly like a naughty boy, the horror of his tale of executions lost in his tale of lust for his woman.

"Why you here?" one of the men listening in asks.

He lifts up his shirt to show us a dressing on his side.

"I was burned by a piece of hot metal when welding during a repair job. Not as heroic as Li Cheng-fang's injury or anywhere near as bad. Everybody's heard of the hero Li Cheng-fang who walked into heavy machine-gun fire and rescued several wounded Englishmen. I'm only here for the day."

His grin is infectious and, despite his outlandish exaggeration, there is a lot of happy murmuring around me. I'm impressed with the men's attitudes. They are worked hard and restricted in so many ways and yet, despite their natural feelings of homesickness, they maintain a happy acceptance of their lot in life. I reflect again on the idea of moving to China when the opportunity arises.

Our visitor begins telling his stories again as others gather round to listen.

"Working on tanks is interesting but I would hate to go into battle in one. The latest models are much better but the early ones were terrible and that was just in the way they were made. They got as hot as Hell inside and the fumes were shocking. The soldiers who travelled in them were as much at risk from gas inside as out. I much prefer working on the motorbikes as this will lead to work after this war is over. I am thinking of staying here and setting up my own business."

I look at him in surprise but he continues enthusiastically.

"My girl is really nice and will make me a good wife. I am saving my money and making heaps more on the side. There are empty shells and metal waste all over. In my spare time, I'm making souvenirs, which the troops are buying in droves. I make them and my girl and her brother sell them. I can't make them quick enough. I tell you, it's a little gold mine."

He continues to chatter and I feel really happy for him. It is ironic that he, as a Chinaman, wants to stay here and I, as an Englishman, want to go back to China, but it is pleasing to see one of our men with such a positive attitude towards foreigners. I can see how he could be happy staying here and I silently wish him well. This war must finish sometime.

"How's the Padre today, Charlie?"

The CO's morning 'O' group is coming to a close and Major Roberts looks at me with concern.

"I called in at the hospital early this morning, Sir. His temperature is down and he's breathing easier but his blasted smoking habit hasn't helped. It's been nearly a week now and the medics think he may be over the worst. Not everyone dies and he is a tough old nut under the surface. He's survived hardship in the past and could beat this now. I'm seeing him again this evening, Sir. I'll pass on your concerns."

I leave the CO's office and head for the lines with Sergeant Major Peters to brief the men on their duties for the day. Emphasis is once again on the work in the railway marshalling yards. Li Cheng-fang is back at work but is limited to light duties. Su Ting-fu has stepped up to take his place as acting foreman for his group and is handling the extra responsibility well. Despite his extra duties, he still finds time to run a gambling game called 'pak-a-pu'. Eighty characters are written on a board and gamblers select ten of them, which are written on a 'white pigeon ticket'. Twenty numbers are then drawn from a closed bag and prizes given for five or more correct guesses. It is a very profitable venture.

Li Cheng-fang has conceded defeat where his friend's gambling activities are concerned. He reckons that gambling is in the Chinese soul. The young *p'aitou* is spending most of his time in the YMCA helping maintain morale and sorting out any personal, non-gambling problems the Chinese in Company 21 may be having. He is well suited to the role. It's now the 11th of May and I have a surprise in store for my young friend.

"How's your side, Chen-fang?"

He beams with pleasure as I use his given name and not his full formal name or worse his number as some other Englishmen do. The Padre briefed me on this facet of Chinese culture and I have been waiting my chance to impress. We're sitting on a bench in the camp enjoying a beautiful evening. The sky is alight with fire, a brilliant vista of red, wispy clouds as the sun sets, the sky set aflame by nature and not by man for a change.

"I'm good," Li Cheng-fang replies with a happy smile, "I'm moving good now and I like my job you have given me here in camp. What about you and Mr. Padre?"

"I'm fine, old chap, and the good news is that the Padre is well on the mend. He could be out of hospital soon. It's been a scare for us all. He's in good spirits again and has stopped smoking."

We both laugh at this and, despite the obvious barriers imposed by our military situation, we bond tighter than ever.

"Chen-fang, I have something for you."

I suddenly feel rather embarrassed but I press on.

"Mr Flaxton came to see me. He told me that your claim for compensation has been turned down and he also told me that you accepted this well. I would have expected nothing less but I told the CO, and he told people in the mess to collect money for you. Sergeant Major Peters did the same in the sergeant's mess and Corporal Anderson talked to the squaddies. Cutting it short, we collected a few bob to acknowledge what you did. Not much but we would like you to put this towards the savings you are making. I know you are trying to do the best for your family and this could help."

I'm sure that the young Chinaman didn't understand a lot of what I said but he certainly understood the result as I handed him a cigar box. The money inside is far more than he could have expected as 'compensation' and will be a huge boost to his savings account. He bows his gratitude, unable to find any words.

My time in the YMCA hut has brought me in greater contact with Henri Isakson. We have become friends and he shares with me his radical thoughts, although I'm conscious that his views border on the mutinous.

"This war is nothing but a struggle for power by rich bastards who want more and more wealth than they could ever do anything useful with. The greedy swine are using ordinary people like you and I to further their ends. Millions are dying and millions more suffering and for what? Everyone is losing in the end. The Russians had the right idea. They've got rid of their royalty and have quit this stupid war, yet we fight on. The French troops are sick to the point of mutiny, the German people are starving to death, the British are running out of men they can send to the slaughter, and the Americans are joining in to get a share of any spoils as the war runs out of steam. A curse on the lot of them."

My grandad brought us up to respect what he called the 'dignity of labour' and he was never one to praise the royalty or bow down to the gentry, but Henri's words go much further. Even so, I'm drawn towards his arguments. What has been the point of this war? Who will gain from it? The Americans will for sure but the mighty empires of Europe have spent their last penny on this stupid waste. And here we have the Chinese involved too. What benefit will they gain, I wonder?

We are sitting in the YMCA hut late at night. Henri has brought a stranger along and has introduced him as 'Comrade Qingxi'. It's a form of address Henri seems to favour now when he speaks of anyone for whom he has respect. He has joined Henri and me and we sit talking alone, apart from Agnes. She's a young French girl, another widow in a land of many. She works here in the YMCA and has taken a shine to Henri, staying near to him at every opportunity. We are speaking in English as we finish our day but she says nothing. She just sits near to Henri and smiles sleepily.

Henri tells me his friend is a student from Paris and the serious young man says, "Our government has accepted an offer from the French government to send many young men like me to study in France. The Chinese Minister for education has been pushing our government to not only send students to study in France, but to send teachers to educate labourers like your men. I'm studying in Paris and have been directed, as part of my studies, to visit Labour units and YMCA support elements to promote the Chinese government's views. It gives me a great opportunity to meet bright young men like many in your employment and to share our thoughts for the future. That future lies with the Chinese Communist Party. We communists are worldwide. Henri and I are both Comrades and Henri tells me you want to go back to China after the war ends. You could be a good friend to us and we could be very helpful to you".

'Comrade' Qingxi then quotes a man called Karl Marx, telling me about his dream of a society where everyone is equal and wealth is shared.

"All these labourers want is the chance to earn good money, fair money, and to reclaim their land from the parasite landlords who are sucking their families dry. In truth, the land belongs to everyone and so does the means of production. We must all work to the best of our ability and share to the limit of our needs."

"The Russian people now live better lives," Henri chips in.

"The German people are starving because of your naval blockade. They tried to respond by dropping bombs on British civilians in retaliation, sending their Zeppelins over to England and dropped bombs on innocent civilians. They call this 'total war'. They want everyone to be involved, not just soldiers and sailors. The kings and emperors and factory owners and landlords who sanction this should be destroyed and the people put in power. Those in charge are telling us lies about everything. The world is going mad and we must fight back together. Together!"

I'm feeling very uncomfortable with this talk, but I also feel the need to listen. If we are being subjected to disruptive political agitators, I should gather whatever information I can and report it to our Intelligence people. I need to take them a bit further and I tell them that the Chinese Labour Corps could be a way in which China would raise itself in the eyes of the world powers.

"China's joined in the struggle against Germany and surely the Allies will recognise this when the spoils of war are shared among the victors? For example, Shandong has been a German concession, so the Allies should return the province to the new Chinese Republic when the war is over in recognition for her efforts".

Henri and 'Comrade' Qingxi both laugh and dismiss this idea as naïve.

"The Japanese took a strong hold of many parts of China when they defeated the Qing Emperor in '95," says 'Comrade' Qingxi, who is well into his stride on yet another monologue.

"As a result of their success in that war, the island of Formosa was also ceded to the Land of the Rising Sun".

His face twists in a sign of sheer hatred as he speaks. This man is certainly one to be wary of.

"You mark my words. These will be just the first steps in Japanese imperial expansion. Their ambition has already grown as we have seen in their actions in Shandong. Do you know that in January 1915 they sent a secret ultimatum called the Twenty-One Demands to our government in Peking? They wanted our government to extend more of our land to them and to sell them any of our businesses that owed them money. They also demanded a formal turning over of Qingdao to Japan as a concession!"

'Comrade' Qingxi had become strident again, his features radiant with rage and indignation.

"There were anti-Japanese demonstrations nation-wide and there was a national boycott of Japanese goods. Our President, Yuan Shiki, made a decision to agree to nearly all of the demands just before he died. He said that many of the requests, as he called them, were mere extensions of treaties agreed to by the old Qing dynasty. The old Qing dynasty! We got rid of those parasites and here we had our own President acting as if our republic had never happened. I never trusted that man. He pushed out Sun Yat-sen, the true father of our republic, and then he tried to take power into his own hands like the emperors of old. You mark my words, his successors will all be the same!"

Henri can see that his guest is going a bit too far in his rhetoric and tries to change the subject, but I decide to finish for the night and take to my bed. The rest of the student's audience agree with me with obvious relief.

The Padre is released from hospital in the middle of May.

"I feel there's now some purpose in life for me again, Charlie".

We sit drinking tea together in a quiet corner of the Officer's mess.

"This illness was God's way of testing me and I feel I have renewed my faith as a result. I promised Him that if I survived and returned to duty, things would be much different. I've experienced near death as so many of the people around me are doing every day. Faith, Charlie, is what brought me through. I must share this Faith with others as they too face death. This is what I am meant to do and I can't wait to get back into it".

I smile at my friend and remark, "I see you have stopped smoking, which is a good thing *and* you ordered tea. I hope that does not mean you have abandoned your love of a gin and tonic. I'm back onto a life without alcohol. That wine we drank just before you became ill did not impress or seduce me. I'm much happier without the grog and I enjoy the mornings after".

Unlike our rejuvenated Padre, my erstwhile companions, Henri and 'Comrade' Qingxi, are not Christian. It is clear that they both despise and denigrate religion, but to what end. Henri is a Jew and his religion believes in a supreme being, one God who sees everything. He agreed with me when I mentioned this as we engaged in heavy conversation one night shortly after the student 'comrade's' visit but he argues that religion is a way to maintain those in power where they are at the expense of common people. I was not brought up with any religious ideas but I know that the Jewish God is the same God the Christians worship, so why do the Christians persecute the Jews I wonder?

'Comrade' Qingxi seems to have a more logical approach as he denounces all religion and puts his faith in what he calls 'the ordinary man'. He argues that it is for this 'ordinary man' to rise up and take over so that all men can be equal. But just as I tell my men what to do, if we were all equal who would know what to do, who should do it and when?

I need to learn more about 'Comrade' Qingxi's communism. Given what he has told me, it seems to be a fairer system of living than we have at present but there must be something beyond being born, existing and then just dying. There must be a better way and it must be for everyone.

I'm spending another evening idling away in the YMCA hut with the men. 'Comrade' Qingxi comes in and makes a beeline for Henri and I as we sit talking to a small group of labourers. At his request, we excuse ourselves from the group and move to a quiet table.

"I want to tell you how much you can learn from the revolution that took place in Imperial Russia last year," the student says without any sign of a precursory pleasant greeting.

"Captain, you are obviously interested in what we spoke about last time I was here so I have brought you some reading matter, which will tell you more. It will help you to understand our ideas if you read the works of men such as Marx, Engels and Lenin. Try these books as a start but be careful though. Your government is worried English people will follow Russia's lead. The French and Germans are also shit scared".

His foul language surprises me but I take the books he has brought and agree to read them. I'm still conflicted about his presence and the support he is getting here in the YMCA and from Henri in particular.

Henri is focused on his own problems and in his own country.

"The French people are war weary," he tells us yet again.

"They're appalled at the way our government has handled this war. If Russia can rebel and throw out its privileged classes, why not the same in France?"

This is a step too far for me and I exclaim quietly, "Steady on Henri. What you are saying now is treasonable. You could end up facing a firing squad, civilian or not".

"One day, perhaps I will," he replies defiantly.

"I know that many of our troops are close to mutiny again."

I can feel myself getting angry but I want to learn more.

"What has this got to do with China?" I ask. "Your friend indicated that these ideas are strong over there. How do you see it?"

"China's enemies are foreigners and a corrupt elite. It's up to the people to get rid of them first and then look at a more progressive form of government after that. China's great leader, Sun Yat-sen, espoused three principles, those of Nationalism, Democracy and Social Welfare. I've been studying his work and I feel he's on to something worthwhile."

Back in my room I make a perfunctory glance inside the books Qingxi brought. They seem to focus on what is described as the proletariat and the workers of the world and there are pages and pages of statistics. More boring than inflammatory. I've been giving his argument a lot of thought but. from the little I've read, I think that the Russian revolution was one of workers rising up against the owners of factories. The cry that came out of Bolshevism was 'Workers of the World Unite'. In China's case, the problems look to be quite different. China is a nation of peasant farmers where rich landlords own the land. All they need is the chance to get back their land to work it for their own benefit and not that of a landlord.

Next evening as I visit the YMCA hut once again and sit with Henri. The fog of conjecture my mood has settled in, however, takes an unexpected turn. When Henri goes to relieve his bladder, Agnes comes over to sit beside me and puts her hand on my thigh in a very disturbing way. All thoughts of politics evaporate.

Chapter Twenty-two
The End of the War is near

"This man Monash is a bit of fresh air, don't you agree? An Australian Jew, so I understand, but his tactics are just what the doctor ordered. Here we have a general who actually takes care to protect his troops from unnecessary slaughter. He has his men advance with maximum use of artillery, machine guns, mortars, tanks and aeroplanes, all coordinated to provide the men with cover as they move forward. He uses aeroplanes to mask the sound of his advancing tanks, for goodness sake. Brilliant! Largely due to him, we have the Hun on the run."

Major Roberts is in a happy mood and the members of his 'O' group smile happily with him. The Padre has been invited to attend the 'O' group today and the CO acknowledges his presence by saying, "You could see the end of the war any time now, Padre. Your prayers are to be answered at last."

I'm just as happy at the prospect for peace but more of our men have succumbed to the 'flu epidemic as the war has dragged on into August. The men accept this stoically and work continues without interruption. More supplies and ordnance arrive at the Amiens marshalling yards and more injured are moved away from the continual carnage at the Front. This carriage of men and materiel is now routine and works smoothly, however recent battles have once again seen men killed or injured in the thousands, often in just a day or two of fighting. Many of these men have ended their lives in an unidentifiable mix of flesh, cloth and mud. Humanity shredded into an horrific sludge. Friend and foe alike, often with identity tags as the only means of telling who was who. The vast list of men marked 'missing in action' is an indication of the totally destructive nature of this bloody war. Men simply disappear. The CLC is deeply involved in the task of cleaning up battlefields as the conflict has moved forward. The men have been tasked with collecting, identifying and burying the dead of both sides.

The 'flu epidemic intensifies as more and more people around us fall ill. It apparently began in earnest earlier this year and has resulted in the death of millions of people worldwide. Doc Hammond reckons it could be one of the deadliest natural disasters in human history.

"In most of Europe, government censors, both military and on the home front, are playing down reports of both the numbers infected and the level to which the disease is ending in death", he tells me as morose as ever.

"Once again, the people in charge are lying to us. They are hiding the truth to hide their incompetence. Most European nations are suppressing media reports on the size of the problem but the Spanish media is under no such restrain. The public in most countries have falsely concluded that the disease comes from Spain. This has led to many media reports referring to the strain as the 'Spanish Flu'. It just goes to show how powerful the media is and how much our governments are using the newspapers to mislead us. What else are they lying about, I wonder?"

What he says may be true and it looks like our good doctor has lost none of his bitterness.

Henri has brought me a copy of a magazine called *Xin Qingnian*.

"It's a powerful publication, which is also known as *La Jeunesse* in French and *New Youth* in English", he tells me, as intense as ever.

"This magazine's causing a bit of a stir both in China and here in Europe. It's the journal of an organization called the New Culture Movement. A lot of important people are unhappy with how the new Chinese Republic has been betrayed by President Yuan Shikai and his successors, and they have formed this movement. These people blame what they call 'the failure of traditional Chinese culture' and they've banded together to try to address China's problems. Many of them are scholars. You should be aware of this".

What I'm more aware of is the memory of his girlfriend's touch on my leg. It was not accidental.

Henri continues to chatter as I reflect on his girl's actions. What on earth should I do? The Frenchman's words hardly sink in.

"These scholars are beginning to lead a revolt against Confucianism. The old ways are dead. They have studied much and are calling for the creation of a new Chinese culture based on global and western standards, especially democracy and science."

I try to focus on what Henri is saying. The magazine is written in part in English and in part in Chinese but I am still totally confused by Chinese characters, no matter how hard I have tried to study them. Hopefully the English content may be of interest.

There's an essay in English called 'Chastity'. I read that, in the traditional Chinese context, this refers not only to virginity of women before marriage, but also to their remaining chaste after the husband's death. The author writes that this is an unequal and illogical view of life, that there is no natural or moral law upholding such a practice, that chastity is a mutual value for both men and women, and that he vigorously opposes any legislation favouring traditional practices on chastity. The article is interesting to an extent, but it leads me to think of Henri and the French widow, Agnes. They are obviously on intimate terms but she makes no secret of the fact that she is attracted to me. What really annoys me is that Henri is aware of this and seems to find it amusing. The woman has no shame and the only mention Henri has made of her lust is an oblique comment about sexual freedom as a principle of his communist ideology. To Hell with that idea! I want to respond to her advances but her actions concern me, especially her involvement with Henri.

As these thoughts enter my mind, I realise that I am ready to embark on my first foray into the realm of sexual relationships. I ask myself if this is love or just carnal lust. The response I get is that I don't really care. I'm ready for female companionship.

"I've been chatting with a number of people now about the end of the war and what it may mean to all of us. Have you made any progress with your plans, Malcolm?"

The Padre smiles. He's much more at peace with himself since his brush with his own death at the hands of the deadly virus. It still rages on taking lives everywhere, matching the destruction of the carnage that man imposes on himself, but the preacher goes about his business calmly.

"I'm going back to China as I told you, Charlie. That is my calling and my time here in Europe has just been a selfish interlude on my part. I remain hopeful Margaret may join me but it's a vain hope, I know. I've been in touch with my superiors in Belfast and there's a place for me in Shanghai when the war ends. Not long now by all reports."

"Goodness my friend, that really is good to hear. Lieutenant Hastings has written to his father at the merchant firm Jardine, Matheson about my chances of getting a post there so I too could be joining you in Shanghai. He hasn't heard back yet but hopefully they'll give me a chance. I may return home to Tyneside and seek my discharge from the Army and say my farewells. Then I'm off! This war has changed me in so many ways. Do you know that when I was lying in bed in hospital, the twit in the next bed referred to me as 'this oik with the cushy number'? He obviously thought I was sleeping but, really, Padre, calling me an 'oik'. An inferior person, ill-educated, ignorant and above all, lower-class! I borrowed a dictionary and looked it up. I do have it easy at the moment, 'a cushy number' as he called it, but I've done my bit. A year or so ago, this comment would have upset me greatly. Now I just see him for what he is, an upper-class snob, one of the users and abusers who are losing their power. England has broken itself with this war and will never be the same. Europe's a mess. The future lies with two giant nations in my view, America and China. The Yanks have the money but China has the potential in the long term. My Mandarin is becoming quite good and I like the way the Chinese operate. They're underestimated, Malcolm. I think you see that too."

The Padre pauses and then asks me, "What about Russia?"

"Possibly, but they are basing their future on violence and division. An 'us against them' approach but who decides who is 'us' and who is 'them'? It's all about 'oiks' in reverse, really. This may be simplistic on my part however I'm going to give China a shot. We will see each other again over there, old chap. You mark my words".

There are fewer casualties coming through and the emphasis on trench work is much less than it was last month. The men are in better spirits, especially the clown, Su Ting-fu, who is spending more and more time gambling. I despair at times but his infectious good nature continues to keep everyone's spirits up. The war drags on and the Germans fall back everywhere.

It's been a while since Billy Bissel invaded my sleep and I've become quite used to drinking tea rather than whiskey. I have no need of an alcoholic crutch, especially now as I focus on Agnes and my quest for her companionship.

I'm deliberately spending more and more of my free time in the YMCA hut where I practice my Mandarin, listen to Henri's political chatter and engage Agnes in fleeting snippets of conversation. Henri is conscious of my growing feelings towards the young, French widow and now treats the matter with more seriousness. He actually encourages my contact with his girlfriend and I decide to tackle him outright.

"What are your intentions as far as Agnes is concerned?"

Henri looks at me in amazement and then bursts out laughing.

"How very English you sound, mon ami. You sound like the woman's father. Will you now ask me what my fortune is?"

As he chuckles, I feel myself going red in the face. My embarrassment turns to anger but before I can reply to his retort, he continues quickly," Mon ami, mon ami. I have no 'intentions' as you put it. She is a friend and I give her comfort in her loss. She is attracted to you and if you wish I will send her your way but you must do your part and make her feel wanted, eh?"

Henri brings yet another visitor to the YMCA hut one evening in late August. His name is Morris Abraham Cohen, but I have to smile when he refers to himself as 'Two-gun Cohen'. He tells us he originally comes from Stepney in London's East End. Like Henri, he's Jewish, having been born to an immigrant Jewish couple from Poland. He says he was sent to Canada at the age of 16, after having come into conflict with the authorities, and, while living there, learnt to ride, shoot and gamble. It was in Canada that he first had dealings with Chinese people and he tells me that he came to like and respect them. He goes on to tell me has been elected into the Tsing Chung-hui tong, a secret society who pledged to overthrow the Manchu dynasty and liberate the Chinese people. Another tale about another Chinese secret society! How little I know of this other world.

I'm interested as he relates how he joined the Canadian infantry and landed in England in 1917 where he was then sent on to France. Like many foreigners who speak Mandarin, he has been seconded to the Chinese Labour Corps. He is another source of learning for me and I listen intently to the plans that he has to go back to China and support the return to authority of the founder of the Chinese Republic, Dr Sun Yat-sen.

He's another distraction as the war staggers towards a bitter end. What he distracts me from however, is not the war but the French widow who now occupies my thoughts on a continual basis. I decide to ask her to have dinner with me far from the confines of the camp if my nerves will let me.

Chapter Twenty-three
The War comes to an End

I'm sitting in a corner of the mess listening intently to the words of a visiting staff officer from Brigade Head Quarters. He has launched into a cheerful monologue, fuelled in large part by a heavy intake of alcohol over lunch.

"Germany is in political turmoil both at home and on the front line", he announces grandly to a captivated audience of fellow officers that surrounds him.

"There are riots on the streets of most towns and cities and the whole of the country hate their Kaiser and what he stands for. The German high command knows full well that, in order to preserve some semblance of order in Germany, troops will need to return home in great numbers and we understand they have advised their government that their position at the front is becoming hopeless. The German government has decided to sue for peace. I was there, watching in amazement I can tell you, as several civilian cars bearing large white flags came into view as they approached our front line. The cars contained a civilian delegation from the German government who were told to engage in talks to end the fighting. They're throwing in the towel, chaps! Calling it off, don't you know!"

An excited cheer went up and I gripped my mug of tea tightly telling myself, "This chap's from HQ. He's not likely to be talking rot."

The staff officer continued.

"The Jerry civilians were taken to a forest in Compiegne and to a railway carriage that is part of the private train allocated to Marshal Foch, the supreme Commander of the Allied forces. Marshal Foch and members of the French and British military forces met the Germans who were apparently led by a politician called Matthias Erzberger. They tried to negotiate on the basis of proposals that the American president, Woodrow Wilson, has put forward, but Old Foch took a hard line demanding that Germany take responsibility for the war and agree to punitive reparations. They responded by requesting time to contact their government to get further instructions but agreed in principal to an armistice and suggested an immediate cease-fire. Foch refused! The bloody slaughter is going to continue but we are almost there. It'll soon be over and then it's home to Blighty, lads. God save the King!"

With that the mess erupted into a scrum of cheering, laughing backslapping men and for once, I joined in without reservation.

"If Germany wants to stop the war, why are we still killing each other?"

The Padre has a good point but I don't have an answer for him. I agree totally. Why not call a truce? We are sitting on the edge of the camp looking out through the wire at troops who continue to go about their duties with exhausted faces and stooped bodies.

"Malcolm, I have no idea. The French have a deep-seated hatred now for the Germans. They have them at their mercy and they will be as harsh as they can. France has lost so many men and suffered so much destruction. Mercy is no longer a word they understand. They don't want a negotiated end, they want a victory that comes with unconditional surrender."

"Talking of mercy, Charlie, I'd be interested to know what was in the letter you took to Zhou Xiao-jin. He's to be released from jail and deported back to China. All charges against him have been dropped".

Henri is despondent and as confused as my missionary friend when I relate the news to him later in the day. He tells me that there are reports that in some areas, the rate of fire from the guns is actually increasing.

"I've been told that some of the allied artillery are firing for the sake of it. No clear targets, just a frantic desire to continue killing before the end is called. Your High Command has gone mad."

There is a flurry of chatter in the mess as rumour chases fact, which then chases rumour in turn. Solid news arrives, however, that sailors in Germany mutinied on the night of 29-30th October, sparking a rebellion that spread across the nation. This forced the Kaiser to abdicate during the following week and a desperate German government sent a message to its representatives authorising them to negotiate peace terms on any basis. The message was not sent in code and was read by the allied Commanders before they passed it on to the hapless German delegation. Marshal Foch gets his punitive terms accepted in full with an armistice that is agreed to on the eighth of November 1918.

I join others in celebrating the joy that the news of an armistice brings, but I also join in the confusion, anger and despair when I learn that the armistice is not to come into force for another three days. The armistice document does not get signed until 5 a.m. on the eleventh day of November and even then the ceasefire is not to come into effect until precisely 11 o'clock on that day. Surely common sense will prevail and commanders at the Front will cancel any orders to attack an enemy who has given up the fight. Surely?

For three days I watch in disbelief, hearing that allied troops are continuing to carry out assaults on German positions. Everyone knows there is to be an armistice but they continue to fight to take ground that they will be able to walk on peacefully in such a short time in the future. This is happening along the entire front line and the Americans are no exception. If anything, they seem to be keener than anyone to stay involved. Officers, desperate to continue the fighting in the hope they will gain promotion, give orders that men from junior officer down to the newest enlistee can see are a pointless waste of life and limb.

In the evening, I write sadly in my diary: 'At 0500 hours, as dawn broke on the very last day of the War to End All Wars, the armistice was at last signed. The document called for an end to the war at the dramatic time of eleven o'clock on this day, the eleventh day of the eleventh month. This was taken literally by many however, and the American Expeditionary Forces are said to have suffered more than thirty-five hundred casualties in assaults that began *after* 5 a.m.! Infantry soldiers were ordered to assault German positions in the face of the same withering and murderous machine gun fire that has killed millions in the preceding four years of conflict. I'm told that none of the dead or dismembered troops that day were field rank officers.'

The war has ended. All I feel at the moment is shame. How must the Chinese I command and work see us? The Western powers have been shown to be totally lacking in either compassion for the ordinary man or in honour itself. We have surely earned the insulting word they use to describe us, '*yangguizi*' - foreign devils. How can they expect decency from us when we treat our own people as we do? Over one million British and Commonwealth soldiers have died in the four years of the war. Over eight hundred died needlessly in the last hour! The French have suffered a staggering six million casualties during the war and yet they too fought on until the very last minute. The American Commander, General Pershing, has been openly critical of the armistice, wanting to continue fighting until we have driven the Germans back to Berlin and achieved an unconditional surrender. He argues that the armistice will leave the situation unresolved in many German minds and says the time will soon come when the war will need to be repeated all over again. For those of us who have managed to live through four years of conflict however, the end of the fighting is a blessed relief, even if it has come too late for so many.

I've been drinking heavily. The Padre is watching over me as I break my habit and return to the whiskey. We're in my room, far from prying eyes, not that anyone would begrudge me or anyone else for getting drunk today, not even the CO.

"Listen to me my friend. This war has brought an end to the German, Austro-Hungarian, Russian and Ottoman Empires," I burble. "It has plunged the British, French, Belgian and Dutch Empires into massive debt. America will emerge effectively as the driving force from now on. They are talking about a New World Order with themselves at the helm. But my money's on the Chinese in the long term. Empires depend on trade and taking advantage of others, using force where it is needed, whereas the Chinese have existed for hundreds ... thousands of years on their own. It all worked well until we imperialists came along and it will work well again when we've gone. I'm sure one day it will, and I'm going to hook my future onto their wagon, old chap."

I take another swig from the rapidly emptying bottle and continue burbling.

"They need to watch out for Japan though. They want to have an empire too, just like the Europeans, but in their part of the world. There's going to be a peace conference. I've read it will be held in Versailles and that the Chinese will participate. So they bloody well should! They're part of the victorious group of nations to partake in the sharing of spoils and restitution for losses incurred, aren't they? The men in the Labour Corps will be recognised for their efforts and we should all feel an immense sense of pride. The Chinese Labour Corps has made a huge contribution. What do you think, my friend?""

The Padre is smiling indulgently.

"I think it's time to clean up, Charlie. Time to bury this mess and move on."

Chapter Twenty-four
Cleaning up the Mess

Su Ting-fu is singing softly as he strikes an unexploded shell with his spade and has the lower half of his body blown into small pieces. Su Ting-fu, the clown who trained in China, sailed across the world and worked solidly here in war-torn France. The man who refused to be cowed by bullies, acted the fool to keep everyone amused, gambled constantly, fought when others fled, now ends his life in a horrible, pointless way.

The war is over but the horror continues as we start to 'clean up the mess' here on the battlefields in front of Villers-Bretonneux. We fill in the trenches, those we recently maintained so carefully, and we try to restore the landscape to normality. There is wire to roll up and massive amounts of debris to collect and remove. The weather is harsh, the work is hard and dangerous, but the most depressing task we have is clearing the dead. So many of them and more continue to be found every day. The task of recovering dead bodies often gives way to uncovering parts of the dead or just digging through an appalling sludge, all that remains of those who fell and were mangled without human form into the mire of battle. Su Ting-fu now joins those who have fallen before him. The war that ended four days ago continues to take a cruel toll.

Many of the men in Company 21 who survived the shelling, fatal accidents and the Spanish 'flu are now considered to be surplus to requirements and are being sent home. I've been told that there are over eight hundred graves in and around Noyelles-sur-Mer for those in the Labour Corps who did not survive, and that there could be many more for those who are buried all over this foreign land. But it seems the British High Command can't wait to begin shipping men back to China. Their haste is obscene and lacks any semblance of dignity. They begin by repatriating the sick.

Lieutenant Bertram has been discharged from the Army is now working full time for the YMCA. He tells me this morning that he is going back to China. I'm surprised to hear that, as his reputation as a coward when he arrived in Qingdao will not be overlooked. He tells me of his decision happily adding, "Three hundred and fifty of the patients at the hospital in Noyelles-sur-Mer are being sent home this week and I'll be going with them. We sail on the 5th of December."

"Three hundred and fifty sick people? That's terrible. Why are we sending the sick back while they are in poor condition? Why not let them recover first? This is just another example of our lack of concern for the Chinese. They are not animals. Where is our respect for the job they have done, and are still doing?"

Bertram look startled at my reaction, but before I can go further, the Padre joins us.

"Bertram's just told me that we are shipping three hundred and fifty sick labourers back to China. It's appalling".

My missionary friend agrees with me, but adds," That's not all Charlie. We are also sending men who have been diagnosed with mental conditions. A large number of the men have succumbed to the pressure of working close to the front lines where they have seen people killed or maimed and have cracked under the strain. The High Command no longer wants to care for them. The argument is that we need doctors and nurses back in Britain to staff the hospitals there. We have so many sick and wounded of our own and they are getting priority over everyone else. It's not just the Chinese sick and wounded who are being sent back, it's everyone who can be got rid of".

"I'll be interested to see how many of our sick comrades return to China safely. The journey out here was long and exhausting but we were all fit and healthy then and we still had men die on the way. I fear these men will suffer greatly. I'm going to take this up with the CO".

"I agree. It's a bit of a shambles, Charlie".

The CO is as unhappy as I am, but with more cause.

"I've been asked to identify what the Brass are calling 'slackers'. These men are to be the first to go along with the sick. The guidelines call for me to pick those who have transgressed during their time here or who have been marked out as being less useful than others. Some of our people are taking the opportunity to pay out personal debts and grievances, however slight. I heard some of them bragging about this. Several good men are bound to be targeted for early repatriation. There is no proper system in place, just a process dominated by haste and spite. Mind you, it's not just the Chinese in the gun, so to speak. Captain Asmiroff has nowhere to go. Russia is closed to him and rumour has it we don't want him either. Any of the Russians with money or real friends amongst our aristocracy will be looked after but, as for the rest, they are now regarded as stateless. I cannot personally imagine a worse situation to be in, however, he's another trying to settle old scores while he still has the chance. He gave me a list of names he regards as slackers. Li Cheng-fang's name was on it, for God's sake. One of the best men we have. Asmiroff reckons that Li Cheng-fang has communist friends here in camp and to him, that is cause enough to have him shipped out".

I immediately think of Henri and his friends who come to talk to us and think to myself, "I've got communist friends too. I'll keep this to myself though. I'm making good progress in courting Agnes with Henri's aid and I do not want to put that in jeopardy".

As our numbers shrink, Chinese Labour Corps Companies 21, 22 and 23 are being reformed into a combined unit, deemed CLC Company 8, with Major Roberts in command. Sergeant Major Peters and Corporal Anderson from Company 21 are two familiar faces who will also stay with the revamped unit, but many of the other British officers and men who have worked alongside the Chinese are being discharged. On December 15th I say farewell to Lieutenant Hastings. He's returning to China but not before handing me a letter of introduction to his father. Hastings tells me that his father wants to ask him face to face about my desire to go to China to work.

"My father seems to be open-minded about the idea, Sir and I'll put in a very good word for you when I get back. Meanwhile this letter should get you in to see him, should I not be there to greet you when you arrive in Shanghai".

He is grinning at me and his good humour and optimism is refreshing. I wonder how Agnes will like Shanghai, I ask myself, but time for that later. For the moment it's unsettling and, for the Corps, it's made worse by the changing attitude of the civilian population around us.

French soldiers are being demobilised in the tens of thousands and they are returning to their homes as bitter and angry men. The social structure has been badly damaged and work is not readily available for them. Seeing Chinese employed while they are not has built a savage resentment towards my men. Some in the Corps have taken French women as their mistresses, some even marrying, and this adds fuel to the French hatred. The Chinese are blamed unfairly for any crime or disturbance that may occur in their area and this blame is often followed by summary 'justice'. It's a difficult time for us all.

Exceptions are rare. Hu Chu-xing, the cocky mechanic who came to visit us, has married his girl and has left the CLC to set up a motor repair shop in Vignacourt. He is doing well and providing a good service, which is accepted by his neighbours, but when another of our men sets up a small café near to camp, his business is targeted and destroyed. He has moved to Paris with his French wife and has opened a restaurant there. Mechanics are wanted but any Frenchman can run a café. He may do better in a large city.

The French government has been asked to intervene but they have not helped at all. A notice from the Interior Ministry has been posted around town, in the newspapers and on the notice board at the YMCA. It discourages French women from marrying any Chinese men. They are described in poor terms and women are warned that Chinamen who want to marry a French woman may already be married with wives back in China. Chinese government officials have responded by offering to check if this is true but I see this as just another example of universal prejudice against the Chinese. Some members of the Corps who have married or become engaged are deliberately singled out for early repatriation along with the 'slackers'. Despite protests from their wives or sweethearts, they are being sent back to China and yet, at the same time, thousands of others remain behind to do unpleasant and dangerous work for the Allies. Often this is work that they do not want their own people to do. There is no dignity or respect shown to the Chinese whatsoever.

Some of the men in the old Company Number 21 who are to return home begin to gather their things ready for departure. Most are wearing the uniforms we issued them ages ago and in many cases these clothes are now in poor condition. I feel they should at least be issued with fresh clothing for the return journey. They've performed well and are a credit to China and they should return home with pride. They'll be arriving back in China with money saved, more money than many will have ever had. More to the point, they will be going back with more worldly attitudes. The naivety most had when they arrived in France has gone, replaced by political and social experiences they would never have come across before. Their worlds are now different. It's in our interests that they are seen in a good light. As matters stand, many of the men look like refugees.

Sergeant Major Peters tells me that he has had no success in getting any new gear from the system so I approach the Quartermaster myself. He is not helpful.

"The men have been well paid and are returning with pockets full of money," he growls. "If they cannot look after the clothing they were provided with, then they can buy their own replacements. How dare you suggest they be dressed like gentlemen, they are nothing but serfs for goodness sake".

Time to take the matter higher.

Having made my mind up to return to China, I'm keen to get any news I can find of conditions back there. Sadly, I read a report in The Times that 'this winter has been harsh in

Shandong province as a government in disarray struggles to govern the fledgling Republic of China. Warlords have taken effective control of more and more of the country. Secret societies are flourishing and farmers now focus on survival as another drought hits Shandong and neighbouring provinces. To the horror of the British who are trying to gain influence in the country, returning members of the Chinese Labour Corps do little to boost our prestige. Of the sick who have been sent back so inhumanely, over twenty died on the way while there are reports that two more who were suffering 'shell-shock' committed suicide during the voyage home. The haste with which the repatriation is taking place and the meanness in sending men home in rags has prompted the British War Office representative in Qingdao to write a letter of protest to the government. He bemoans the fact the men are not returning in a contented frame of mind given the great expense the British have incurred in the CLC enterprise'.

Armed with this report I approach the CO who takes the matter higher and we at last get a degree of success. Each of our men returning to China will be issued one new set of clothing.

Meanwhile, for those remaining, we have issued large wooden boxes into which the men are to place any identification tags they come across as they carry out their disgusting work. These discs, which we call 'dog-tags', have been issued in sets of two to all British and Imperial forces. Each disc bears the name, serial number, blood group and religion of the owner. In the event the wearer is wounded and unable to communicate, the discs provide essential information that could provide life-saving information to medical staff. In the event the wearer is killed, one of the discs is removed and passed on to his unit while the other remains with the body until burial. In this manner, a humane record can be maintained of the troops who enter the field of conflict. This is the reasoning behind their use. The reality, however, is that many battles have been fought in this war, resulting in wholesale butchery. Huge numbers of mangled, dehumanised bodies have to be buried in graves marked as 'the unknown soldier'. In places where we now work, the mud and mire is yielding identification discs from remains that lack any form of further identification, friend or foe, human or animal, all minced together. I've ordered the men to put any discs they find into the wooden boxes, including any discs of 'enemy' troops who are identified by similar means.

As well as the dog-tags, the men are finding many other interesting things that they uncover as they work, some of which they keep as souvenirs. One of them shows me a belt buckle he dug up. It's quite heavy and shows a bird with wide-spread wings, head to one side and the words 'Gott mit uns' inscribed in a circle around the outside. The wearer received no protection from this talisman, as there was nothing else left of him in the shell hole where it was found.

Added to the arduous and unpleasant work is an increase in restriction of movement outside the camp for the men unless they are on work details. We take them to work and then return them each day and place them back in what they are now calling their 'cages'. Morale plummets. The humour that has been so common a feature during their time here deserts them completely.

The men are not alone in losing their sense of humour. My courtship of Agnes ends abruptly when I discover that she is pregnant. As I have not yet plucked up the courage to take our relationship to the point where I could even remotely be accused of being the father, I leave her sitting at the table in the YMCA hut where she confessed to her condition. Henri sees me leaving and rushes out after me.

"Wait, mon ami. What is wrong? Please, why are you so angry? What has happened?"

His flood of questions stops me in my tracks and I spin round to face him.

"Agnes is with child!" I yell at him, feeling confused and out of control.

"With child, you say. How very English".

He is smiling at me in a way that I find insulting and I suddenly realise who the father of her child must be.

"Is the child yours?" I growl at him.

He doesn't reply, he just smirks and I have my answer.

I only hit him once but it's some time before he's released from hospital.

Chapter Twenty-five
A new life

It's the 12th January 1919 and my thirtieth birthday. The Padre and I decide to celebrate and to take my rescuer and friend Li Cheng-fang with us. We head for a small café in Amiens which the Padre recommends. The Chinese are being treated as virtual prisoners now that the war is over, and so many of them are to be shipped back to China. It's as if the High Command expect them all to abscond and stay here in this terrible place. In order to escort our Chinese friend out of the camp on a non-work detail, I have had to get him a special pass for 'good conduct'. Li Cheng-fang is not impressed and he tells me that he wants to discuss the new rules that have been introduced.

We enjoy a pleasant meal together, despite a number of hostile stares from other patrons. Our Chinese guest remarks that his stomach has been educated during his time here as well as his mind.

"I still look Chinese in their foreign eyes but I wonder how my family will react when I get home. My eating habits have changed; I speak reasonable English and some French; I can read and write, both in English as well as Chinese; my queue has gone; hair has grown over my forehead and it is cut in a European way. Even my clothing now has a European style to it with my peaked cap, smart jacket and shirt, as well as European trousers reaching down to the top of my Army boots. I know that my brothers will find humour in my appearance but what else about me has changed, I wonder?

The Padre smiles and says, "Chen-fang, my friend, we have some news to share with you. Wallace and I will be leaving you soon and we will have to say goodbye but we have some good news as well".

The Chinaman sits expressionless waiting for the Padre to continue. I've heard the word 'inscrutable' used to describe our Oriental colleagues and, looking at Li Cheng-fang now, I understand why. He would make a great poker player.

"I'm returning to China to spread the Word of the Lord and will start my missionary work again. This time I'll be working in Shanghai and I leave next week. My journey home will take a while but I want to keep in touch. If I can be of help to you when you return home, please let me know. Anything at all, Chen-fang. This friendship of ours is too valuable to end, don't you agree?"

His reply catches us both by surprise.

"You've been a good friend and teacher to me. I too would like to continue our friendship back in China, but I'm no longer the young farmer you first met in Shandong and this is due, in many ways, to your teaching. You are a missionary. I wish you well in your future life and thank you for all your kindness but I do not see that China needs to embrace your religion. I honour you as a man, a good man, but you offer *me* your help when we return to my country. My country! It is I who should be offering to help you!"

The Padre sits back as if he had been slapped in the face. I cautiously break the silence that had descended.

"Chen-fang, I'm also planning to return to China. I'll seek my discharge from the Army and head for China as soon as I can but for the moment I still have work to do here. I'm hoping to get a position in Shanghai too so, here's to 'hope'".

I raise my teacup and my two friends raise theirs in response, smiling together as we do so.

The Padre is still smarting from the Chinese giant's words but he reacts by asking, "looking back on our time together, what stands out for you, Chen-fang?"

Our friend takes a deep breath and looks at us with a serious expression now lining his features.

"What I have found to be of greatest interest is the superior way we have been treated by so many of you foreigners. You must know we refer to you as 'yangguizi', as foreign devils, and yet, despite that, many of my companions have managed to form friendships similar to ours. But we all start with the need to counter your bias towards us and this is something I cannot understand. We're a civilised people and we were civilised many centuries before you were. I've read much while I've been here, both in the English books you have both given me and in Chinese books and papers I found in the YMCA. In my opinion, we have no need to bow before you. Why do we have to prove our worth before friendship can happen? I have a copy of the new rules that have been published. My men are very unhappy and have asked me to tell you this."

He places a document on the table before us, which the Padre picks up and reads aloud.

1.   Passes should take the form of an entry on the back of the work ticket, dated, stamped and signed. The *p'aitou* (foreman) who is in charge of the party should have a pass giving the regimental number of his party, which should be checked on return. Members of the Chinese Labour Corps are not allowed to leave their camps in the evenings.

2.   Surprise roll calls should be frequently held, during which the camp should be searched for possible refugees.

3.   Camp police should be held responsible for immediately reporting the arrival of any Chinese labourers visiting the camp.

4.   More responsibility should be placed on foremen who are directly responsible for the presence and behaviour of all coolies under them, both at work and in the camp. Any culpable delay in reporting the absence of any coolies should be severely dealt with.

5.   Foremen and coolies should be forbidden to be in possession of civilian clothing (other than headgear) as such has been frequently used for the purpose of disguise.

6.   Gambling has become one of the chief causes of discipline problems. The proclamation forbidding this crime is being reissued from the Chinese Labour Corps Headquarters and should be maintained prominently posted in each camp.

When he finishes, Li Cheng-fang asks, "What crimes have we committed to make you treat us in this way? Have we not served you well during your war? Are we now to be treated as a problem even though we are still working for you, doing work that is both dangerous and disgusting? You sadden me greatly!"

The Padre and I are both flabbergasted. It is the first time I have heard the huge Chinaman or any of the other Chinese speak in such blunt terms and he is not finished.

"If you are to return to China as you say, you must do so with respect for the Chinese as a people, as a nation.

Many foreigners express surprise when they actually work closely with us. We work hard, we work well and we complain little. We do not get drunk like the British soldiers do. I hear of houses nearby where women offer their bodies for money and there are lines of soldiers every day waiting their turn to enter. I see this as demeaning for both the men and the women. We came here to work and to earn money. Most of us will return home with large savings and the money we have sent to our families has been of great benefit. But many of my companions will have seen little of the land you live in. We have been kept behind wire fences and locked gates. We saw a little of your country, England, as we travelled here and will no doubt see little more when we travel home but most of us know nothing about you. I have been fortunate in my friendship with you two gentlemen and have told my men stories about our time together but believe me when I say that as a people you have not earned our respect. You have missed a great opportunity."

As he pauses for breath, I sit back amazed both at what he has said and the excellent use he has made of his knowledge of English. Just as I will not be returning to my coal mining home, I cannot see him returning to a life scraping a living on a family farm in Shandong. I decide to draw him out a bit further.

"Chen-fang, you have every right to think this way. We are not perfect and we have our own divisions in our own society. It's because of this I plan to leave my home and seek a new life in your country. But you must admit you and your people have superior attitudes too. As you say, you refer to us as yangguizi, as foreign devils, and even when you are being polite, we are 'Barbarians'! However, I have heard your men laugh when they see black men and call them '*hei gui*', which is black devil and I know you call the Japanese '*Riben guizi*', Japanese devils. When we were working alongside an Indian regiment, I heard the word '*san*', I think. You call them 'red heads' and laugh. I've no idea what this term means but you seem to be every bit as racist as us."

The Padre butts in saying, "Really, my friends, this is not what I expected when we planned this outing. Let's not talk any further about such unpleasantries, please. Let me order more tea and please let us change the subject."

Chapter Twenty-six
Into the Future

Following the horrible death of Su Ting-fu, I have made attempts to provide my men with better training so that they can carry out the clearance work with greater safety. There are disturbing stories about incidents in other camps, news of which quickly spreads via the YMCA people. I'm told of men who are dying or being horribly injured in growing numbers as a result of preventable accidents. Incidents are reported in which Chinamen have been seen shaking live shells or tapping them to empty the explosives they contain. These are not the empty shells that were in abundance during the fighting, they are live shells carelessly discarded by war-weary troops heading home who have lost interest. Some of our men have been killed instantly and a number of Labour Corps units have gone on strike in protest. The *p'aitou*, Sun Jun, tackles me angrily one morning.

"My father taught me that 'the superior man cherishes subordinates'. We are not being trained effectively by an uncaring British command who would do well to study Confucianism!"

One story sickens me. A British soldier in a camp to the north saw men of the local CLC unit clearing rubbish from the area. He placed a Mills bomb into one of the dustbins with the pin removed and when the bin was emptied, the bomb exploded. One of the Chinamen was killed and two other seriously injured. The soldier was arrested after bragging about what he had done but this story and others like it have done much to undo any of the respect that we may have earned from the Chinese in our care.

The Padre has departed and I find myself patronising the YMCA hut in our camp more and more. Neither Henri nor Agnes are to be seen. Henri has been moved to a civilian hospital and Agnes has moved to take up a position teaching English somewhere away from here. News of my dealings with them both has also circulated and the respect I personally have enjoyed and still enjoy is tinged now with caution. I'm obviously seen as someone not to be trifled with.

As a semblance of normality returns to the French countryside, I notice that the attitudes of both the military and civilian populations continue to be hostile towards the Chinese. Assisting the war effort was one thing but now the war-weary populations of Europe want to get on with a return to peaceful conditions and my men become an object of increased prejudice. Many returning French soldiers still see them as being a threat to their prospects for employment even though, in reality, there is a severe shortage of labour everywhere. Many regard them as being no more than cheap labour and a weapon that can be used by what they are calling the 'capitalist classes' to keep down wage levels.

Communism is becoming a major force in French politics but the slogan 'Workers of the World Unite' is underwritten with the caveat that Chinese workers are exempt from any such 'unity'.

In the absence of the Padre and, to a lesser extent, Lieutenant Hastings, I find myself seeking out the company of Li Cheng-fang to try to understand the issues that are influencing all our lives here. I'm aware that Henri's friend from Paris, the student Quan Qingxi, visits the YMCA in our compound regularly now. He is often in deep discussions with a number of my men and I notice that this sometimes leads to angry exchanges. I'm concerned that this subversive man could be a source of trouble and I ask Li Cheng-fang to be my eyes and ears when he is around. He agrees to do this but tells me that Captain Asmiroff is also becoming a problem. He is increasingly suspicious of my Chinese friendship and is agitating even more to having Li Cheng-fang sent back to China as an undesirable.

"Some of the things these communists are saying make sense but they really want to change China completely and I fear that this will cause too many problems".

Li Cheng-fang is telling me about the latest visit by the student from Paris.

"He brought one of his colleagues yesterday evening when you were not here. This man is proposing changes that are fundamental to our way of living. For example, he told me they want all of our literature to be written in the vernacular. When I asked what that meant he said that we must have things written in ways that everyone can understand. In common language, dialect and so on. We must bring an end to high, academic language that confuses the ordinary person. This makes a lot of sense to me but he then said that we must bring an end to the custom of a patriarchal family. He believes that the practice of reverence to the father as the head of the family and giving him absolute power over his children and grandchildren is holding us back. He argues that we must encourage individual freedom especially for women. I honour and respect my father who works hard for our family. How can this be a problem? Captain Armstrong, my father has given me the freedom to come here to France to help the family. It was my idea not his instruction, and as for freedom for women, my mother is respected by us all as is my sister and my grandmother. They all have our respect".

I pour more tea for us both. I've taken to drinking it as my friend does without adding the milk and sugar I was brought up to do.

"This man then started talking about China itself. He says that we must look at China as being a nation among nations and not as a uniquely Confucian society. I told him that my father brought me up to respect Confucian ideas and, when I look at other ideas like Christianity or Communism, I feel that my father's principles are good enough for me to follow. Also, I did not understand what he meant by saying China should be a nation among nations. I understand that Britain and France are 'nations' but they have subjugated millions and treat these subjects as slaves. Germany is a 'nation' and has been prepared to go to war to share in the spoils of Empire. Look at how many millions have been killed as these so called 'nations' fight each other. China should not follow their example. We are not a nation among nations; we are above them all. We are truly the Middle Kingdom between heaven above and the Barbarian tribes who scrap around beneath us".

This is fascinating talk but I hold my tongue and keep listening.

"As for Communism, it seems to be a selfish, inward looking idea with no clear end. Christians promises a life of peace after death but only if their faith is followed during our time on Earth. Communism seems to promise a never-ending struggle to have a better life now, just by taking from those who have more than us. I believe China must be better than all of this. We must work with respect and reverence for our fathers and their fathers and work the land or practice our trades for the benefit of us all. It's landlords and corrupt officials and foreigners who are the problem. If we can get rid of them, things would improve".

Li Cheng-fang seems oblivious to the fact that he is talking to a foreigner who wants to go and work in his country for other foreigners. He is in full flow however and again I do not interrupt.

"He told me that we must re-examine Confucian texts and all the ancient classics. They have formed an organisation called the Doubting Antiquity School of Thought but this is far too complicated for me, Captain Armstrong. I'm a simple man who honours his father, his family and his country. All that I am looking for is a better way for us to live. I fear that these communists are tearing down what we have believed in for thousands of years, without a clear idea of what they want to put in its place. I told him that their ideas are of little interest to me but he does not listen. He just kept on telling me that change is always difficult to accept. He says they believe in democratic values where all of us have a say in what happens, where every man is equal before the law. He argues that rich men or poor men, they are all the same. I told him that it seems to me powerful men say one thing but do something far different when they get more power. All they ever want is power. We need a system where everyone has a say and no one has power over everyone else. I have no time for such talk but I worry that there are many amongst us who are starting to believe his way of thinking. To me this could become dangerous".

"You are becoming quite a scholar", I tell my friend, "but I think that you may just be scratching the surface. Tell me something more about yourself. Tell me about your days as a child so that I can learn more about Chinese customs".

He sits opposite from me for quite a while and then surprises me with quite a monologue.

"I'm the eldest son of Li Qiang and I am grown up with my two younger brothers. We work together on land that we used to own but now have to rent from man called Landlord Zhal Yao-xing. When I was in hospital they say landlords like leech that suck blood from Chinese people. We work hard and well. Our rice harvest can be good one and our cabbage, pumpkin, melons and beans grow well. This all should provide ample food for our family but the landlord takes rent. This rent takes half of what we grow. Half! And then we have pay taxes to the regional authorities on top of that. I feel sad when I think we work so hard to produce such a little left for our family that includes our mother, sister and our two grandparents. If only we did not have to pay rent!"

His face hardens as he speaks.

"There must be a better way! There is a rich few who live in comfort in China while a family such as ours lives among hundreds of others who work just as hard as we do yet only just live. I have grown up knowing of the big load our father carries. I have a huge respect for him. When I young child, my father not many times beat me in the way that other fathers do with their sons, only his cutting words built knowledge in me, and whenever I do wrong his look in his eyes fill me with a plan to do better next time".

The young man talks softly and easily.

"My family live in the village of Xihan, near from Qingdao. We all together one thousand persons living together, being happy, not rich in money, but we live happy in harmony. When word arrived in the village of huge war among the *yangguizi* far, far away other side of the world, my father told me China had entered into this war. We declared war on Germany but at the time I not know what this meant. But I feel much excitement when I hear this news. My father just spits onto ground with anger when he tells me. He says that China has joined the war against Germany but that our army sit doing nothing, not used by the foreign powers. He says we were being treated with little respect again as always. My Grandmother Jinghua knows so much about so many things and so I asked for her advice. She tell me that Qing dynasty has ended and that our young

Emperor, Pu Yi, has given up his Empire. She tell me that we now have Republic, and that this make life so much better for us all. She spoke always about her hero, a man called Sun Yat-sen. Many in the village very happy when he was President of new Chinese Republic. This is man who speaks of great things, but life for my family did not change. Then a powerful general called Yuan Shikai replace Sun Yat-sen as President. He die soon after and my father say he want to make himself as Emperor and that his death was suspicious. We get another President but then he go too. It seems to me, now we do not have an emperor, China is having trouble everywhere".

Li Cheng-fang stops to take a drink of his tea and I sit fascinated by his words and the openness of them. Having refreshed himself, he continues.

"My father's father, Li Jian, and his wife live with us as grandparents should, but he has left the family with a debt that shames him greatly. He married a high lady and brought to the village a wife, my Grandmother Jinghua, who wanted much of life. She demanded better things than our grandfather could pay for and they had much debt. When we have the famine years, their debts grew and grandfather had to sell our land that had been with our ancestors for many generations. He sold to a rich merchant called Zhal Yao-xing who rent it back to us and now we work to feed him as well as ourselves".

His eyes glisten with tears of anger but his voice is steady as he goes on.

"Grandfather Li Jian is now old and no help to our family. Grandmother Jinghua is now cripple and has always pain. Her feet were tied up when she was a child. It was the custom and over the years she has crushed bone and flesh for feet that should hold up her old body in old age, but they only give her much pain. My mother's only one brother start smoking opium like many others. He think it protect him from harm. One day he working in the mine his thinking is bad and this make accident and his death underground".

Li Cheng-fang looks at me angrily and says, "Why so many of my people drug themselves with this opium of yours? Why is life so hard and miserable they take opium as the only way to better life? Landlord Zhal Yao-xing try to force us to planting 'black rice'. This is how we call this opium. There are some in village who grow these crops and they are prosperous indeed, but my father refuse to do the same. We know there a much higher price this 'black rice' crop can produce, but my father says opium causes men to become sick and useless and to die in poverty and misery. He will have none of it. He's a truly good man and I spent much of my time thinking of ways to be a good son and help him and our family from the bad life we have been given. Grandmother always telling me have big thoughts, even when I small child, and when news come to village of good money to be paid working for the *yangguizi* they excited me greatly. This why I joined the Labour Corps".

I thought of my own Nanna and felt the bond between us grow stronger but the Chinaman continues talking.

"She spend much time on me as eldest grandchild and she want many good things for me. When I was five years old, when we still had our own land and no debt, she make sure I be given private teacher in reading and writing. I was taught how to read and to write from at a child's age despite my father unhappy, but at a cost to the family wealth. I have some lessons in your language. While my father saw me as his number one heir on the farm, my grandmother wanted better things for me as I grew. She argued with my father, telling him that learning is only way to go past the bad class system in this country. The annual imperial exams allow even the poorest subject to step outside his poverty to become an official. She said that I would be very good candidate. Father would keep an angry but respecting silence when she said things like this, but I had many lessons with big cost".

So, he has been hiding his early knowledge of English all this time. It explains the way in which he progressed so much. I chuckle to myself and think I must write and tell the Padre that he was not such a brilliant teacher after all.

Chapter Twenty-seven
Reports from China

As the catastrophe of war comes to an end in Europe, I'm reading many reports in the newspapers that the Chinese Republic that Sun Yat-sen dreamed of is not yet a nation, but rather a loose collection of provinces ruled by powerful warlords. The Padre writes in letters to me that there have been triumphal processions in Peking where anticipation of restored sovereignty of former German possessions runs high. He tells me there is a high level of expectation that Shandong province will be returned to Chinese control. This contrasts with news sent to Li Cheng-fang from his family that in Shandong province, the power of the Peking administration is extremely weak. Japan apparently still has a tight grip on the province, as the former Chinese Premier, Duan Qirui, granted Japan huge concessions in return for huge loans. As Li Cheng-fang and I compare contrasting news, I show him an article in The Times, which reports that back in October 1918, Duan Qirui resigned from office after making a number of secret deals with the Japanese. He used the money the Japanese 'loaned' to China to enhance his own independent military power, thus further weakening the central power of his successor in Peking. We agree sadly that it looks as if Shandong is to become a political battlefield.

July 1919 approaches and I receive another letter from Hastings.

EWO Cotton Spinning and Weaving Company
Yangshupu
Shanghai

My dear Captain Armstrong,
   I trust that you are well and that the great work you are doing is nearing a point where you can consider taking your discharge from the Army and take the next step in life.
   I am now working with my father at the EWO Cotton Spinning and Weaving Company, which is another subsidiary of Jardine Matheson and I am delighted to tell you that my father has proposed to senior management here that you be offered a position as a line manager. I hope that you will be getting a formal offer from the Company in the near future.
   You may be interested to know that the Padre, who as you know is working in a mission here in Shanghai, came to visit me last month. He is in good health and good spirits

and he sends his regards and joins me in the hope that we will soon all be reunited.

I'm sure you will also be interested to know that Captain Asmiroff is also here. He has joined the ever-growing diaspora of Russian émigrés who are living here, most on the edge of destitution and almost all living off one another. It is a very tragic situation for them. The Count is working as a waiter at the Astor House Hotel. He must feel totally humiliated as my father and I regularly dine there with our family and friends and, on occasions, he has waited on us. So far he has not deemed to acknowledge me and I would never cause him embarrassment by doing so myself, but it is a 'rum' situation, don't you agree?

Captain Armstrong, until the next time, I remain your friend,

Brian Hastings,

12th April 1919.

The news in Hastings' letter regarding Asmiroff leaves me flabbergasted. He disappeared from our camp three months ago. While Li Cheng-fang and I were celebrating his absence and the CO raged about the arrogance of 'bloody aristocrats' it seems that the Russian had made his way to Shanghai, of all places. Am I never to be rid of the man?

The Spring has brought kinder weather and the work becomes less dangerous. We start to repair and restore the normal infrastructure of roads, buildings, railways and communications. Corporal Anderson returns home at the end of the month, leaving Sergeant Major Peters and me the only members of the staff of Chinese Labour Corps Company Number 21, apart from the CO, still involved in France.

My mind is still set on going to China but, from what Li Cheng-fang and I continue to read of the situation, there is chaos and confusion everywhere. Warlords are gaining more and more power as the central government is losing influence. Here in Amiens, the Officer's Mess is virtually deserted. Billie Bissel doesn't haunt me nearly as often and my mind is focussing on a new future. I now spend much of my spare hours in the camp discussing the situation in China with Li Cheng-fang and the others, with continual visits from the student, Quan Qingxi. He arrives from Paris one evening with an article written by Cai Yuanpei, the first Minister of Education in the new Republic. The minister is a prominent member of a Chinese Francophile group who regard the recruitment of labourers as a heaven-sent opportunity to challenge what they say are character deficiencies in the Chinese people. Cai Yuanpei and his group believe that, since they consider the French to be both diligent and proficient at accumulating money, they can serve as suitable role models for what they describe as the 'irresponsible and spendthrift' Chinese labourer. As Quan Qingxi translates this for me, I look around at my companions and agree that some of the gamblers will return home with little to show for their efforts. The majority, however, are saving up a lot of money and I do not think that Minister Cai and his elite friends are taking into account the money they have been sending direct to their families back in China each month. I'm confident that the Labour Corps is something China can be proud of.

Quan Qingxi tells me that the minister has compiled a series of lectures, which he is presenting at the Peking University to promote Western values and social conduct. The Minister to France has picked up on this approach and has quite rightly expressed his concern with protecting China's reputation. He insists that Chinese workers in France are to be seen as being frugal and industrious in order to avoid ridicule and scorn from our hosts. This may just be diplomacy on his part but as far as I can see, most of my men *are* being frugal.

These evenings with the men are now a part of my daily routine. I'm accepted, they talk freely, and I have the approval of the CO but the time is drawing near for me to make plans for a move.

Chapter Twenty-eight
Betrayal at Versailles

A report in the English language edition of the Chinese magazine *New Youth*, July 1919 reads, 'The political manoeuvring that has taken place among the Allies at the end of this Great War has resulted in more than one treaty to officially end hostilities. The Treaty of Versailles, which brings an end to the actual state of war, is signed on the 28th of June 1919 after six months of negotiations at the Paris Peace Conference. Separate treaties are signed with Austria and Hungary but the Treaty of Versailles, the treaty signed by the Allies with the Germans, is impossible for China to accept'.

It goes on to say that, 'the victorious Allies require Germany to accept full responsibility for causing the war as well as to disarm, make substantial territorial concessions and pay heavy reparations. But the Allies squabble amongst themselves, with compromises made by all, leaving no one satisfied with the outcome. Germany is not pacified or internally reconciled nor is it permanently weakened. A rising nationalism in the devastated Weimar Republic has emerged in Germany after the fall of the Kaiser, a nationalism that competes with a strong communist movement. The country is left in chaos but for the Chinese delegation entering into the negotiations in Versailles with high hopes, the outcome is disastrous'.

I read that a sixty-two strong delegation of Chinese officials attended the negotiations at Versailles. They were devastated to learn of secret deals made earlier in the war between the Allies and the Japanese. In 1917, in return for Japan's naval assistance against the Germans, it seems that Britain, France and Italy signed a secret treaty ensuring their support of Japan's claims in regard to the disposal of German concessions in Shandong when war ended. When the American President, Woodrow Wilson, got involved, he had initially been sympathetic to China's claim for a return of German concessions to China but on 30th April 1919, he agreed with David Lloyd George of Britain and Georges Clemenceau of France to transfer all of Germany's Shandong rights to Japan.

When this news becomes public knowledge in China, even as negotiations continue, a large gathering of students from several Peking universities assembles in Tiananmen Square in protest. There's a report in The Times that these students met on the fourth of May and drafted five resolutions.

1.   *To oppose the granting of Shandong to the Japanese under former German concessions,*

2.   *To draw awareness of China's precarious position to the masses in China,*

3.   *To recommend a large-scale gathering in Beijing,*

4.   *To promote the creation of a Beijing student union, and,*

5.   *To hold demonstrations that afternoon in protest to the terms of the Treaty of Versailles.*

The demonstrators distribute fliers declaring the Chinese people will not accept the concession of Chinese territory to Japan. The group then marches to the legation quarter, the location of foreign embassies in Peking. Student protestors present letters to foreign ministers and in the afternoon, the group confronts the three Chinese cabinet officials who were responsible for the secret treaties with the Allies that had encouraged Japan to enter the war. The Chinese Minister to Japan is beaten and a pro-Japanese cabinet minister's house is set on fire, following which the police attack the protestors and arrest thirty-two students.

In Amiens, we read news of the students' demonstration and arrest with great interest. The press begins demanding the release of the students even as more demonstrations are springing up in many parts of China. In June, shops close their doors, exacerbating the situation and this is followed by a boycott of Japanese goods all over

China, as well as clashes with Japanese residents. Recently-formed Chinese labour unions stage strikes. The protests, shop closings and strikes continue until the Chinese government agrees to release the students and fire the three cabinet officials. The demonstrations also lead to a full resignation by the cabinet ... but the Japanese remain in Shandong.

The May Fourth Movement, as *New Youth* calls it, quickly becomes a symbol of China's rising nationalism. The Chinese government refuses to sign the Versailles treaty and seeks a separate end to its war with Germany. Meanwhile Japan's imperial ambitions in China continue to cause despair to our group of radicals here in Amiens. Li Cheng-fang and I debate these matters intensely and I try to follow matters in China and on the international front through *New Youth* and Yan Yang-chu's *Chinese Labourers Weekly*. Following his success at teaching so many of the Labour Corps to read and write, Yan Yang-chu has started this newspaper and has it printed in Paris. It is written in the one thousand basic characters he invented to simplify the Chinese written script after one of the Labour Corps labourers contributed his savings to help finance the paper. The results that Yan Yang-chu has achieved in less than a year, teaching the labourers have so moved him, he has resolved to dedicate his life to the education and development of fellow Chinese who have no opportunity for schooling. It's a great achievement.

"So, what do you think of all this, Chen-fang?"

"We have been betrayed by the British and the French. We have taken part in your war and should be rewarded, but you are favouring the Japanese. We are exchanging one imperial master for another. How can you justify this?"

I had meant to get his reaction to the work of Yan Yang-chu but he is obviously focussed on his anger about the situation in Shandong. I feel as angry and as betrayed as my Chinese friend and tell him, "According to this English newspaper, when the students protested, they were arrested. What were the Chinese authorities thinking about?"

Li Cheng-fang snorts in disgust.

"We do not have any Chinese 'authorities'. We have a country divided into small groups, each of which is its own 'authority'. I will go back soon and join with Sun Yet Sen in Nanking. He is the only one who can bring sense to all of this. Others are talking about going to Shanghai and joining the communists there but I fear that this will only make things worse. You will arrange for me to be released from my contract now please. I can no longer serve with the English. I have decided not to return to my family's farm, Captain Armstrong. I will go instead to meet with people who are working to free China from foreign interests".

The young giant looks sombre. This is obviously a huge decision on his part. The choice is between family and his country, and he is putting his country's interests first.

Mr Flaxton visits our YMCA hut one evening in June with the news that the one thousand basic characters Yan Yang-chu devised here in France are now arranged in a set of four books selling in China and in France for very little money. Each set contains 24 lessons and presents 10 characters per lesson, each with exercises in reading and composition. By learning one lesson a day, the basic vocabulary can be mastered in less than four months. Hundreds of booklets are being produced in this basic Chinese on such topics as the lives of great men and women of Chinese history, translations of Confucian classics, folk tales and songs, simple and practical modern farming methods, rural hygiene, cooperatives and democratic citizenship and many others. Despite the Christian verve that motivates Yan Yang-chu, I encourage the CO to promote his system among our men as much as possible. Literacy among those still remaining in France with the CLC improves significantly and I even try my hand at some of the basics myself with some moderate success.

Overall, I think the YMCA has done a magnificent job in France for the Chinese Labour Corps. They now employ a staff of over one thousand men and over seven hundred women. Flaxton tells me this represents a significant increase over the position in early 1917 when the total was only around six hundred staff of both sexes. The number of non-Chinese staff who can speak Mandarin, however, has become limited and I find myself engaged more and more as a de facto member of the YMCA, assisting in many different ways to minister to the needs of the men.

August is a delightful time of year in France. Li Cheng-fang and Zhou Xiao-bing request permission to visit the grave of their friends who are buried in Noyelles-sur-Mer. The CO suggests that Sergeant Major Peters and I go with them, so I tell Peters to commandeer a vehicle. Su Ting-fu lies buried near a grave marked '35768 Bai Tao'. It's the boy that the gangster Zhou Xiao-bing was so strangely attached to. He fell victim to the influenza epidemic, not that Zhou Xiao-bing has shown any sadness over his loss. He really is a hard man. Another grave we come across is inscribed with the name Li Yufeng with the low 'regimental' number 53. He came from Rongcheng in Shandong as a member of the first batch of volunteers in 1916 and he too died of influenza in June 1918. It is a sad end so far from home. The overwhelming majority of those buried here came from Shandong and Zhili provinces, the area the Allies took from the defeated Germans and have now handed over to the Japanese. I'm disgusted to think these Chinese citizens have paid the ultimate sacrifice for such an ungrateful employer. The majority of the graves are the result of the Spanish flu, which continues to be the new enemy. People are still dying of this disease by the tens of thousands.

When we get back to camp, I say good night to Peters but ask Li Cheng-fang to join me for an evening mug of tea. Zhou Xiao-bing grunts cynically and wanders off, leaving us alone, and I take my young friend into my office. Once we are settled and the tea brewed, I ask him to tell me more about his family.

Li Cheng-fang sits quietly looking at me in a quizzical way as if not sure what to say next. When he does speak, I'm drawn even more into a world that disturbs me.

"When I was in my seventh year, I heard my Grandmother argue with my father about people called *Qing Bang*. Then I not understand what they talking about but I remember my father was very angry and told Grandmother Jinghua never to tell about these people to me. I remember her saying, "It would make him strong and powerful man and it would bring back the family fortune. Please think, Li Qiang. You know I right. The matter was never spoken with me and I think it is being no importance, but her wanting things for me all those years ago and the private teacher costs for me added to the debts we have during the years of famine. I now live with the shameful thought that I am the reason for our present situation and this just adds to my determination to free my family from this heavy load of shame and return us to the life we had when I was very, very young. This is why I am travelling to Nanking to seek a more productive life than I would have back in my village. I will join with friends of Zhou Xiao-bing".

I suddenly realised what he was saying.

"Do you mean that you have joined this secret society, this *Qing Bang*?"

I have been member for six months, Captain. Zhou Xiao-bing has taken me into his group".

Li Cheng-fang is still looking at me in a questioning way so I decide to tackle him about a couple of things I would like answers to.

"Right, my friend. If you are so pally now with Zhou Xiao-bing, perhaps you can explain a few things to me. When his brother was in jail and facing very serious consequences, you asked me to take a letter from him to his brother. When I did that, he was released soon after and deported to China. We expected the worse, that he would be executed. What was in that letter?"

The big Chinaman has the grace to look sheepish as he replies, "*Qing Bang* have a good contact in the French police. This contact is working with one of the prison bosses. We want for his brother to be free from prison and sent back to China, but for this we have to pay the French *yangguizi* a large sum of money. The 'letter' you took was what we call a 'marker' from our people in Qingdao. It is a promise to pay much money to whoever holds it. It was change to money in Noyelles-sur-Mere. We knew that you not be asked many questions to closely so you were the best person to deliver the package".

"You used me?"

I feel both angry and mortified.

"That was not the act of a friend".

"The needs of the *Qing Bang* rise above friendship, even at times above family. The *Qing Bang* is supreme."

The Chinaman now sits with a defiant expression on his usually expressionless face.

"And does this code apply to your political idols?" I ask.

The inscrutable expression returns and my friend sits in silence, leaving my question unanswered.

"Right. Let me ask you about something else. Zhou Xiao-bing seems to have had a strange, almost unnatural relationship with that young boy, Bai Tao. We visited his grave today but he seemed unmoved, yet for a long time he was treating the boy almost like a pet animal. What is that all about?"

Once again Li Cheng-fang looks defiant.

"In China, some men have relationship with other men. We call this *fentaozhihao*, 'the love of sharing a peach'. He was sleeping with Bai Tao, and not sleeping like you think. They go to bed as a man and a woman would. Captain Armstrong, Zhou Xiao-bing was shagging, I think you call it, Bai Tao."

I feel my face burn with embarrassment. I've never heard of such a thing before.

"Goodness me, Chen-fang, is there anything else you think I need to know?"

He sits before me once again in a silent state, obviously thinking deeply and struggling with something that is troubling him. What more is there to tell, I wonder?

"Yes, Captain, I think that now you should know this. The interpreter from the camp in China, Zhao Da-hai, was very bad man. Zhou Xiao-bing threw him into sea."

Chapter Twenty-nine

Going Home

Three days later, Sergeant Major Peters comes into my office just as I am leaving for breakfast.

"I just wanted to call in and see you before I leave, Sir," he tells me and my stomach falls.

"I've just received my orders to report to the CLC Headquarters to begin my posting back to Blighty".

His use of the slang word for England sounds strange, given the extent to which we have both been involved with China and the Chinese for so long.

"I understand that you may be heading back to China, Sir, and I wanted to wish you well for the future".

We stand looking at each other in an awkward way, not quite knowing what to say until I tell him to have a seat.

"Please sit down, CSM. I'd offer you a scotch but I haven't touched the stuff for months now".

We both laugh at this and he replies, "Bit early in the day anyway, Sir. Can I ask, Sir, with respect, when are you finishing up?"

There! The big question. I've received a formal offer from EWO Cotton for a job as an under-manager in one of their mills. Three months' probation. Cost of getting to

Shanghai to be reimbursed if probation is completed satisfactorily. I'm to cable my response by the end of September, at which point further details will be made available. This gives me nearly a month to think things over. I'll accept, of course, but Billy Bissel has been visiting my sleep again, which is a sure sign that I'm stressing over the prospects of starting a completely new life. The shocking revelations from Li Cheng-fang have not helped. I'm tempted to talk to the CO about what he has revealed about the death of the Interpreter, but there has been so much death. I wonder what purpose it would serve digging up that now virtually forgotten issue. Justice, perhaps? In the world we now live in? I decide to keep silent.

"I'm taking my discharge from the Army here in France and heading for China as a civilian"

This obviously comes as no surprise to the CSM who grins at me and stands to offer his hand.

"Good stuff, Sir. You'll do them nicely and do us proud too".

We shake hands and part with respect. I'll miss the man.

My discharge has been processed swiftly and I'm booked to sail from Le Havre in three days' time. I'm travelling with Li Cheng-fang, Zhou Xiao-bing and fifteen other members of the old CLC Company Number 21. My contact with Li Cheng-fang has become much more reserved since our last conversation, and I now know that Zhou Xiao-bing is not only the gangster we long suspected, but he is also a murderer. He implicated me in the release of his brother in circumstances I would as soon forget and I need to treat him with extreme caution, especially as I no longer have any control over his actions. We are both civilians now and we are all travelling as normal passengers, but the last thing I want to do is to arrive at my new position linked with a Chinese secret society. I'll also make sure that I declare my connections with the fledgling communists to Hastings just in case. On the positive side of things, I have a position to go to and a first-class ticket befitting my rank. I reflect on how my life has changed. If my Nanna and Grandad could see me now!

We'll complete our journey to China in a reverse fashion, crossing Canada by rail and then by sea from Vancouver. I intend to continue to talk as much as possible with the men I served with, both to strengthen my knowledge of Mandarin but also to glean more about their thoughts and opinions of the past two years since we left China on the Big Adventure.

When I said farewell to Quan Qingxi during his last visit to our YMCA hut, he suggested that I make contact with a man called Zhang Guotao in Shanghai. This is the man he talked so much about during our meetings in France. He spoke passionately of this man's proposal to bring about real change in China, a change that would see an end to warlords and the introduction of the principles Sun Yat-sen promised to bring to the people. He also mentioned a great orator and patriot I should look out for, a young man who goes by the name Mao Zedong.

I'll be making contact with the Padre and Lieutenant Hastings when we reach China but I'm still keen to stay in contact with Li Cheng-fang, despite our last chat together. The gentle giant who is not so gentle any more has been so prominent in my life these past two years. Putting the shock of our previous conversation to one side, I seek his company again as we sit waiting for the transport to take us to the docks and I ask him to think back again over our time together. Once again his words surprised me.

"I return home a richer and better-educated man but I need to improve the lives of my fellow countrymen. I can understand, read and speak much English. I've studied Christian teachings and seen two faces in them when I watch Christian Kings and Emperors of Europe slaughter each other's peoples in the millions. I have learned some communist thinking of Marx and Engels and I read speeches of Lenin but I cannot see this as giving answers to China's problems. Russian communism is an attack on the people who have factories and make things. What I want is fair system for farmers to own and operate their own land. As in many, many other things, we need a political system for China, not system that is good for foreign lands".

He didn't need much prompting to continue.

"I've seen my friends take part in many bad things in what you say was a War to End All Wars. Some of my friends died while others still live like me with no bad injury and no disease. One hundred and forty thousand Chinaman have their lives changed, most for good but my question is how to get better lives each day for all Chinaman and it is not answered. There must be a better way, a Chinese way, and I must to help find it".

Feeling just as determined to find a better life for myself, I put the memory of Kibblesworth colliery, the horror that is France and, hopefully the haunting of Billy Bissel, behind me as we climb together on board the S.S. Melita bound for Newfoundland, the first stage in our journey back across the world, each of us looking to a new adventure.

I feel a surge of excitement. What, I wonder, lies ahead?